I0772328

Taylor Zane
COUNTER PUNCH
MARYL MORGAN MARKS: BOOK 1
Taylor Zane
COUNTER PUNCH
MARYL MORGAN MARKS: BOOK 1
Taylor Zane
COUNTER PUNCH
MORGAN MARKS: BOOK 1

COUNTERPUNCH

MARYL MORGAN MARKS: BOOK 1

TAYLOR ZANE

Canterwood Press LLC

To Roy, who was my first real mentor.

To my dead mother, who didn't know any better.

And to my biggest fan, the most awesome son on this planet, who knows the power of words.

Cover Design by Taylor Zane

Names: Zane, Taylor, author

Title: COUNTERPUNCH: A Novel / Taylor Zane

Subtitle: Maryl Morgan Marks: Book 1

Description: First edition 2024

Identifiers: ISBN 9798991621144 (print) | ISBN 9798991621106 (ebook)

ISBN 9798991621137 (hardcover) | ISBN 9798991621120 (audio)

Library of Congress Control Number: 2024920802

Subjects: Literature & Fiction > Genre Fiction >Psychological Manipulation

Literature & Fiction > Genre Women's Fiction > PowerStruggles

Thriller & Suspense > Psychological Suspense

Literature & Fiction > Women's Fiction > Revenge /Justice vs. Revenge

Mystery, Thriller & Suspense > Thrillers >Corporate Drama

Literature & Fiction > Genre Fiction > Coming of Age

Literature & Fiction > Genre Women's Fiction > Contemporary Women's Fiction

Contents

ONE

Her eight-year-old hands were taped into an old pair of her father's boxing gloves. It was 1965.

She and her brothers settled all their grievances in the makeshift boxing ring in the musty basement under the strict eye of their tall, take-no-prisoners, ex-military father.

"Ouch! Not fair," she yelled as Steven took another jab at her face, leaving a red mark under her eye.

"Well, hold your damn left glove up, Maryl," her father said.

"I'm trying."

"Well, try harder. And try a counterpunch."

"These gloves are too big." She pivoted on her left foot, covered her face with her left glove, and did a quick uppercut into Steven's jaw with her right. She could taste metal—that sharp piquancy of rebellion.

"That's more like it," boomed Dad.

"Ow," yelled Steven. "She's cheating."

"No, she's doing it right. You just let your guard down. Didn't think your little sister could get you, did you? Remember. Light on your feet. Be brave. May the best man win."

"May the best *girl* win," she muttered. "And I won, right, Daddy? I hurt him more."

George stared hard at his daughter as she dutifully stretched one arm toward him. He ripped the tape off quickly, scanning her face for the pain reaction. She made sure that she showed nothing.

"Good girl." He swatted her on the butt. "Now hang these up where they belong and go help your mother with dinner."

Two

Twelve years later.

It hadn't been an act of defiance. She had just wanted to explore.

Instead of jumping into corporate America with a briefcase and pinstriped suit as her father wished for her after college, Maryl had jumped out of airplanes and cultivated a portfolio of parental heart attacks, one unauthorized thrill at a time. For a year and a half, she lived just outside of Sun Valley in a tiny dome in the middle of the woods. By night she riveted ski boots and waited tables. By day she worked in a small art gallery. She liked it there.

It was a cathartic time back in the late 70s. The air there smelled green, the days began soft yellow and turned bright white, the lakes crystal clear surrounded by hiking trails that led to camping alcoves with layers of pine needles that had collected in that same spot for fifty years. It was an amber-filtered world. The local art supply store had let her use their empty craft room in the back during the evenings to spread out her cotton fabric, waxes, and vegetable dyes. No one locked their doors or drove anywhere, and the men were young, tan, and friendly. The perfect life. Until she was publicly accused—

Back then, Maryl clung to a fragile hope—a belief that somewhere beneath her mother's cold exterior lay a flicker of maternal love. Devastated about the accusation, she had called home for some solace about the whole affair.

"Mom, all these people believe that woman. Why would she do that to me? I don't even know her." Sitting in jeans and a t-shirt on the wooden stool at the window of the tiny mountain apartment she shared with a roommate, Jackie, her eyes took in the deep green of the pines, across the gravel parking lot that bordered Warm Springs Road, and on up to Bald Mountain, all blending through her tears like a beautiful watercolor painting. It was warm in Ketchum that time of year, just outside of Sun Valley, and she could hear the Big Wood River rushing past as a slight breeze rattled the screen door that they never locked.

"You've always been a sexpot." Her mother's voice grated over the phone, like tires on gravel. "Your father thinks you're a slut."

"Wh-what?" Maryl had swallowed hard and sniffed louder, feeling the burn of instant rage. "No. No, he doesn't! That's a lie. And goddammit, Mom, I didn't. I didn't have an affair with my boss. That's a lie, too! His wife was just assuming. And you're—you're just jealous that I have a life!" She slammed down the black receiver.

Maryl yanked at her unruly red curls, her fingers trembling with fury as she huddled into herself on the kitchen stool. Her mind raced, a whirlwind of confusion and anger. Why was her mother so obsessed with sex—especially Maryl's sex life? It's not like she knew anything about it. Hell, Maryl barely had a sex life to speak of, let alone the sordid affairs her mother seemed to imagine.

She groaned, pressing her forehead against her knees. What was her mother's deal? Did she think sex was evil? Some kind of moral failing? Maryl's thoughts darted to her siblings—five children—all two years apart. Clearly, her parents had done the deed at least that many times. So why the puritanical attitude?

A nauseating thought wormed its way into her mind. Was her father's affair—the one nobody talked about but everyone knew happened—a result of her mother's repression? Had her mother always been this way, treating sex as a necessary evil, a distasteful duty she owed her husband? A duty she owed God in exchange for a child?

Maryl's stomach churned. Was Regina secretly okay with George getting it somewhere else? Talk about double standards—her mother's judgmental attitude, her father's infidelity—and here she was, being branded a slut for something she hadn't even done.

A few months later, her very platonic and very wealthy friend Leonard, who enjoyed her quick wit and humor, had pleaded with her to join them.

"Come on, Mare, it'll be fun, an all-expenses-paid wedding present for Jen and Jerry. Come on, please? Say yes." He stuck out his bottom lip, mimicking Elmer Fudd, she thought. She could almost hear "Be vewy vewy quiet."

Jen was a Spanish beauty, the editor of the local paper, and Jerry, owner of the bookstore brandished a wicked wit and a penchant for Winstons. The four of them hung out at their favorite pub on Thursdays and skied cross-country every other Wednesday.

Maryl rolled her eyes and shook her head with a laugh.

Leonard was not deterred. "Mare, you know you want to, and after everything that's happened, a change of scenery could be just what you need. And there're no strings attached. You'd just be going as my guest. My friend."

She sighed, and he took it as a sign to press on. "It's only for a week or so. Why not just enjoy the perks of being friends with a rich man, like Jen and Jerry are doing?"

"You don't like the word no, do you?"

"Why, no ma'am. No. I don't allow nos," Leonard said with a smirk.

So, of course, she said yes to a free sailing adventure in Key West with three of her Sun Valley friends.

They all flew from Seattle to Miami and rented a limo van for the trip down the Keys, where Leonard had reserved a Santa Cruz fifty-foot luxury sailboat with five double bunks, one for Leonard, one for Jen and Jerry, one for Maryl and the other space for the captain. As soon as they arrived at the Key West marina, the guys leapt into action, readying the boat, as apparently these sailboats were the divas of the sea. Overpriced ones at that, she thought.

Maryl and Jen explored the marina, a chaotic symphony of nautical life—weathered wooden docks stretched into the turquoise waters, and a forest of masts from sleek racing yachts to sea-worn fishing trawlers surrounded them.

"Wow," Jen said as she breathed in. "Salt, diesel, and sunscreen."

"Yep, I smell it too," said Maryl, "and I haven't seen pelicans this close ever. Check em out up on those pilings."

"Looking for an easy meal," laughed Jen.

A tan, blond hunk of a sailor strode by and smiled at Maryl. "My type!" she half-whispered to Jen, who giggled.

"I can see why," Jen said, and then, "Oh! Keep it together. He's coming back this way."

"Um, hi," he said as he fell in step along the waterfront. "Do you ladies want to come to our dock party?"

Jen and Maryl stopped walking. "Dock party?" they asked in unison.

"Yes. We have one every Friday afternoon. It's right down here. You should come. It just started, and we're looking for—well, we're inviting—"

"Women?" Jen giggled. "Sure! We'll come. I'm on vacation with my new husband, so what the heck." She pulled the twisty from her wrist and began piling her gorgeous Spanish-black hair into a bun.

"Okay, great. See you down there. Oh, and by the way, my name is Rick." He waved and was off.

His eyes were blue and stunning like her grandma's silver that she had to polish before every Christmas.

"Maryl, I've seen that look on you before."

"Oh my god, is he dreamy or what?"

"But what about Lenny?"

"Leonard?" She stared at Jen. Their wealthy, rather pudgy friend, with a crown of messy red hair around a noticeable bald patch? I mean, he's brilliant and can be hilarious when he chooses but definitely not a romantic interest...

Maryl shook her head. "No, no. Leonard and I are just friends. Did he tell you otherwise?"

"Well, no. Jerry and I just assumed—sorry." An awkward silence hung between them before she added, "Yeah, I can't really see you with him, anyway."

They both snickered and headed down the dock to the party. It would be a few more hours until the guys stopped working on the boat, so why not? Maryl wondered why there was so much prep work to do on such an overpriced floating playground, feeling about as nautically savvy as a camel in a swim meet.

Besides, twenty minutes later, with a margarita in hand, Maryl spied Rick again. He strode over immediately.

"So, you rented the Santa Cruz 50?"

"The what-what?" Her mind whizzed back to a particularly potent smoothie made with Mad Dog.

"The boat?"

"Oh right. Yep, that's us."

"You're not a sailing person?"

"Oh, I love being out on the water with the wind and the sun. But I'm pretty clueless about boats.

"Ah," a slight smile crossed Rick's face. "Well, that's a fast boat you rented. Are you in some sort of race down here?"

"I hope not. The trip is a wedding present for Jen and Jerry. I was just invited along for the comic relief, I think."

"Got it. You're a comic. Well, Miss Funnybone, I'm more into cosmic relief. Want to see my Zen den?"

"Sure," said Maryl, moving to follow after him, only to snag her flip-flop on a raised board and trip into him with her outstretched hands. "Oops. Sorry." She tried to recover. "So, your Zen den?"

"Yes, Janine."

"Janine?"

"My little briny beauty. A bunch of us live here on our boats and keep busy by taking people on sunset tours."

"Sounds fun. So, what do you do during the day?" She was admiring his strong shoulders and tight glutes, all signs of a hard worker out in the weather inspecting rigging, checking lines, cranking winches, and pumping bilges—terms she had read in novels about hunky sailors.

She thought his day job might be inside a gym, as she imagined him climbing the mast with those toned arms and legs.

"I teach underprivileged kids in the Keys."

Maryl blinked. "Oh. Kids. That's commendable. Teach them what?"

"Mostly how not to be ruffians, but technically, it's a math class."

Maryl loved math nerds—something about how their brains worked on two different levels at a time—math and music, math and puzzles, math and astronomy. Her first crush in fourth grade walked with his toes pointing outward, but he could recite his timetables backward from the fifteens. Fifteen times seven was one hundred five. She always remembered that.

"I get it now. Your affinity for math helps you with all the calculations you make on the boat—for navigation and stuff."

Rick smiled. "Yes. That stuff. Latitude. Longitude. Wind drift. Speed. Distance. Currents. Tidal flows. All that stuff."

"I'm liking your wind drift." She wrinkled her nose at him.

"The coolest part is night navigation by the stars—it can be very romantic." He winked.

"So, do you use sailing examples to teach these kids about math?"

"You guessed it. I plan on making enough money here to go to Haiti and start teaching for real. My friend runs a mission there," Rick continued. "It's all I want to do."

"Besides sailing." Maryl smiled, accidentally tipping her drink onto her sky-blue capris. "Oh! Crap!"

"Well, yes, and no worries. I got you." He grabbed a towel and dabbed at her pants.

She blushed. He pretended not to notice.

"In fact, I'm about to board some people for a harbor tour. Why don't you come? Free margaritas. In deeper cups than that." He grinned. "You might want to forgo the trousers, though. I mean, not saying you can't wear any. I mean, you could change them…"

Maryl laughed. "Let me run back and tell Jen and meet you here in a few minutes."

"Better idea. I'll swing Janine around and pick you up on the dock where we met."

Maryl saluted, felt stupid, said Aye Aye Captain, and felt stupid again.

She walked with deliberate poise back up top and onto the dock, but the second her rubber sandals slapped against the wide wood planks, she ran to find Jen and tell her the plan.

Jen clapped her hands, wished her luck, and said she would meet her later back at the boat.

The sunset tour was everything a twenty-something dreamed of—cruising slowly on a boat with this sailor-man paying close attention to her every need in the perfect warmth of the evening. Here was a stand-up guy, intending to make the world a better place, one young student at a time.

An hour into the trip, Rick sat down by her, resting his arm on her shoulder, and instructed the crew that it was time to return the guests to the dock. Shoot. It was like being told the all-you-can-eat buffet was closing just as you got there.

He deposited her onto the dock closest to her friends' boat and draped his tan arms around her. "You made my evening," he whispered into her messy mass of frizz. "We are definitely two ships passing in the night."

She smelled the ocean on him, drinking it in, knowing the odds of seeing him again were approximately zero. This gorgeous, confident man liked her with no caveats. She swayed, a little tipsy, over to her friends' rental boat.

The next day, as colorful flags flapped on the masts, the horizon blurred into a hazy mirage where sea met sky, promising adventure to those brave enough to sail beyond the shelter of the harbor, especially with the wind picking up. Leonard's friend, the captain, or Captain Ahab as Maryl was soon inclined to call him, insisted on setting sail, despite the looming storm clouds. Maryl thought that a bit odd, but she was no sailor. As they pushed out into open waters, the wind intensified, whipping her hair across her face as her sweatshirt lifted daintily off her shoulders and dive-bombed into the sea.

"Oh, a lovely evening sail. This will be exciting." Jen hugged her new husband, savoring the adventure. "Isn't this fun?"

"Yeah. Fun." Maryl tried to sound calm as her arms crossed and her hands worked to shelter herself from the cold gusts because nothing says nautical adventure like impending terror.

The storm prowled after them, forcing Leonard and Jerry to jump up and help with the winches, which they seemed to enjoy—the manhood thing and all. Maryl was thinking they were lucky to have a vast ocean to practice on, as the sails slapped from side to side, but they were not alone in those choppy waters.

Out on the rolling blue waves, another vessel materialized like a ghost ship, drawing their boat too close, and boarding quickly. *Boarding!* Leonard was shaking the hand of the largest man. Maryl's instinct was to scurry down below because what the hell—*pirates*. The men were a rogues' gallery of hardened faces and suspicious glares, their furtive movements setting her nerves on edge. One of them climbed down into the galley near her and grabbed the shapeless white packages, one by one, from the men above, and stashed them in empty cupboards. He stunk of cigarettes and booze. It was swift, wordless, and left her with a gnawing in the pit of her stomach. Not pirates—pirates *took* stuff, they didn't *give* stuff.

After the men's hasty retreat, and now with the sails stowed and the engines on, the Santa Cruz 50 transformed into a nautical washing machine, tumbling its human laundry from port to starboard. Leonard called down to Maryl to come out of the galley where things might crash into her, so she climbed back up the ladder and gripped the lines like a frightened cat with abandonment issues. "Lovely evening sail, my ass," she spit some saltwater over the edge.

Suddenly, she remembered Rick's comment. It's a racing boat.

Maryl thought it was odd that Leonard was so calm. Jen and Jerry were simply having an adventure of a lifetime, but Maryl knew something wasn't right. Were they running drugs?? Did everyone know except her?

When they finally reached the harbor, she was relieved, but it was short-lived.

As she moved to disembark, last in line, Jen and Jerry were already down the dock describing their thrilling adventure to some new friends. Leonard extended his hand.

A warm meal and a damn explanation would be good right about now.

She gave him a forced smile, placing her hand in his. Their eyes met, and her smile faltered as his face hardened into a nasty stare.

His hand clamped around hers as he pushed her back into the boat. "I saw the way you were flirting with that sailor. You bitch. As long as this is my dime, you are mine." He dragged her down into his berth and pinned her beneath his weight.

"What the hell, Leonard. What are you doing? Stop! No! Leonard, No!"

"Not in my vocabulary, remember?"

Remembering her boxing lessons, she tried to punch him in the face, but he pinned her hands over her head with one hand and ripped her shorts down with the other. Her knee drove upwards to block his hand, but his one hundred ninety pounds came down on her legs. She screamed. No one came. He rammed into her, and she screamed again, paralyzed under his weight. His free hand slapped her hard and clamped down on her open mouth. She bit down on his palm, and he slapped her again. "Oh, you feisty bitch! I see you like it rough." Ramming and ramming. She thought her neck would break from the force of his hand on her face. Her tensed body finally went limp. She couldn't breathe and slowly spiraled into a deep pool of dark denial, rocking and rocking with the pain of his ongoing attack.

She lurched awake to the sound of Leonard snoring beside her, his shorts crumpled around his ankles, exposing his fleshy bum, and his mouth open, drooling slightly. With fresh panic, she dragged her legs off the bed and pulled on her shorts gingerly. There was blood on the sheet and searing pain in her groin. What had he done to her? Scrambling clumsily up the ladder, she barely made it to the railing before retching over the side. Kneeling, she screamed inside her head.

A hint of movement behind her caused her eyes to jerk and her body to freeze up, but it was Jen. "Hey, we didn't see you in your berth when we came back from dinner. Are you OK? Did you go out drinking with Rick or something?"

Maryl grabbed Jen's hand and led her off the boat to the dock, sobbing and spitting out words.

Minutes later, they stood next to each other, Maryl with her elbows locked and hands crammed in her pockets, Jen wringing her own as she fidgeted.

"Maryl, I'm so sorry," Jen said and then hugged her.

Maryl patted the woman's back once and awkwardly, before slipping her hands back into her pockets. They began to walk farther from the boat.

"I'm sorry. Jerry and I came back from dinner and thought you were both out."

"Look, Jen, could I borrow some money to get out of here? I didn't bring much, and I need to get away from him. I'll pay you back."

Jen blinked. "You mean you want to leave? Now? We're loading up the van tomorrow, you know. Why don't you stay for the rest of the trip? I'm sure this will all blow over."

"What?" Maryl's nausea returned. "Are you serious, Jen? Leonard raped me. That's not something that just blows over." Her crotch was throbbing as she bent over to rest her hands on her knees to try to ease the pain.

"You know what they say, Maryl." Jen took a long look at Maryl. "It's not rape if it's not the first date."

"What? Who says that? Nobody says that!" Maryl straightened. "Unbelievable, Jen."

Jen sighed. "I'm sorry, Mel. It's called assumed consent. I'm just in a difficult position. You are my friend. Lenny is our friend. You know you hurt his feelings when you went off with Rick." Jen tucked a stray wisp of black hair behind her ear. "This is our wedding present from Lenny, remember? Can we just," she shrugged, "I dunno, let this pass for now?"

"Hurt his feelings? A good screaming match would have been warranted, but rape? You're saying I caused this? Well, I would like to go home now, Jen. But the closest bus station is forty-four miles away."

She had thirty dollars left of her already-limited resources, three thousand miles from home, and she definitely couldn't call her parents.

"Okay. Okay. Look. I'll give you a hundred for the bus. You don't have to pay it back. Just please don't make this any worse."

Maryl gaped at her so-called friend who was acting like she would buy her an ice cream if she would only stop her tantrum. Shaking her head, she turned back toward the boat to collect her things. Luckily, the men were up at the showers. She searched the docks for Rick, but he and Janine were gone. A woman on the adjacent boat gave her a wave.

"Hi." Maryl walked over to her. "Do you know how I can get to the bus station from here? I don't have a car and there's an emergency back home," she lied.

"Oh, sure. Just walk up to the harbormaster's shack. They'll hook you up with someone driving up there today."

Across the parking lot, she could see Jen and Jerry helping to stuff the mystery packages into the walls of the luxury limo van, the powder within promising more wealth for Leonard. Why would Jen and Jerry want any part of that? Jerry held a beer and a Winston, and Jen a Harvey Wallbanger from the marina bar, their joy a stark contrast to the hollow ache inside her. In another world—one where last night's horror hadn't shattered her reality—perhaps she'd be joining them, her laughter mingling with theirs. But now, she felt like a stranger in her own skin, as if the violent invasion had turned her inside out.

She moved through the day in a coffin with the lid closed, suffocating, feeling the movement around her but seeing only darkness. She had left the pier quickly, forgoing a shower in her haste, stuffing tissues in her underwear to catch the bleeding. Each step was a jarring reminder of the rawness below, a searing pain that went beyond the physical.

I must stink like hell. She mumbled something to the driver by way of an apology.

The weather-beaten pickup dropped her at the bus station.

Was this her fault? Had she somehow brought this on herself? Did she owe him? Why was everyone acting like it was normal?

She was a wounded insect with one tattered wing, drawn to the flickering fluorescent lights of the station. Freedom. She stopped and counted out sixty-eight dollars for the fare. As she opened the grimy doors and made her way to the counter, she knew she had to shut down her emotions completely or risk a public meltdown she might not come back from.

The four-day bus ride was grueling but allowed Maryl some processing time. Trapped in a rolling box of stale breath and dirty socks, she took full advantage of the solitude and slept on and off for 20 hours. Existing in a half-sleep state, she tried to apply logic to what had happened. She couldn't. It must have been her fault, of course. Regina would say that. She wondered if her father would hunt Leonard down and punch his face to a pulp. She wouldn't tell either of them. Ever.

She went back to her waitressing job but spent most of her time in her bed staring at the ceiling or standing in a hot shower for the next three days. She ached all over. She felt dirty, guilty, embarrassed, and responsible. She didn't sleep. She visited her doctor, who, of course, knew Leonard, and so did the rest of the town. Dr. Perkins examined her, gave her some sleeping pills, and a shot of penicillin "just in case."

"Ms. Marks, I've completed the examination. There is notable trauma to your genital area, consistent with the assault you reported. You'll likely experience discomfort and some bleeding for a few days. However, I want to assure you that the vaginal tissues are among the fastest healing in the body. With proper care, you should see significant improvement within a week to ten days. I'm prescribing an antibiotic ointment to prevent infection and recommending over-the-counter pain relievers for your comfort."

"Fine."

"You're not really going to accuse Leonard of rape, are you? We see you two skiing every Wednesday. He's an integral part of the community, Maryl."

She stared at him and then down at the ugly hospital gown. "Well, Doc. Where do you think that vaginal trauma came from?" She slid off the exam pad and turned her back.

Are you frikken kidding me? A primal scream of rage erupted in her mind, a torrent of obscenities threatening to burst forth and drown every man, every doctor, every complicit participant in this monstrous system. The violent assault she'd endured pulsed through her body, a phantom pain that society seemed all too eager to ignore. She seethed at the injustice: if this had been a man attacking another man—with a shovel, with fists, with anything—it would have made headlines. Sirens would have wailed, cameras would have flashed, and justice would have been demanded. But this? This trauma was being swept away, filed under 'regrettable incident', and left to fester in silence. How many times, she wondered, her thoughts a maelstrom of fury and despair, how many times a year, a month, a day, was this horror normalized, minimized, forgotten? As if we are lying.

She retreated to the mountain village apartment, suddenly hating it and everyone in the town. She raged in her sleep. Pregnancy couldn't be determined for another few weeks. When the test came back neg-ative, she slept better and began brushing her hair and teeth again. She would recover. She needed to make plans to get out of that town. Jackie was eager to move on as well, so they rented a musty cabin in Leavenworth and waited tables in the charming Bavarian village nestled in the Cascade Mountains of Washington. Jackie made friends quickly, but Maryl was content to simply walk the mountain trails in her spare time. She wasn't ready to re-engage with society yet.

THREE

I n the summer of '78, still deaf to the siren song of the corporate ladder and partly to spite her overbearing father, she embarked on her next adventure. This time, it was alongside a man she trusted.

"Come out." Her little brother, Billy, had said, trying to coax her into the god-forsaken desert in the middle of Wyoming. "You can make a ton of money out here. And you just have to dress like you're, well, sort of doing anyway these days. Like a guy. You know. Stuff your hair up inside your hard hat, wear some foggy safety glasses and baggy T-shirts, and they won't know until after you're hired. I'll get you in."

At least it wasn't near an ocean. A sad sliver of solace that was.

The scars from her sea voyage had faded a bit, but definitely hadn't vanished, nor would they ever. Although they no longer screamed their presence, they still whispered reminders, and promises of fun and adventure, once siren songs of excitement, now rang hollow. Men, once viewed as potential co-adventurers, could be fraught with danger.

But she would be with her protective little brother, so off she went in her faithful Fiat 128, driving up to a makeshift road in the middle of nowhere where the temperature soared to 105° F. Fifteen times seven.

She stood in a dust cloud and looked at the grim dirt yard that housed a dozen lookalike one-room adobes. *Well, isn't this a charming little inferno?*

The glaring whitewash of the buildings attacked her eyeballs making her brain hurt, and the heat waves wiggled and danced on the road. It was hot. The kind of sweltering heat that forced your body to go horizontal. She felt like a snake looking for a crack to wriggle into before she shriveled up.

The compound housed oil rig workers, motorcycle gang members, her brother Billy, and families who crammed eight people into the tiny plain structures. Each unit consisted of a bed, a toilet, a sink, a small shower, and an overhead fan. A grungy fan that flung dirt around the room when it spun.

She and Billy were picked up every morning out on the road by a truck that hauled a dozen filthy fellows; some with no teeth and missing fingers that were still somewhere down in the mud under the rig. Stinky men who didn't bother bathing since each day was hotter than the last. If misery loves company, it must be throwing a block party here, she thought. Billy had bought her a Smith and Wesson M457 and taught her how to shoot it. Just in case.

With the intense summer sun reflecting off the metal buildings and platforms, the rig was even hotter. Buckets of diesel and brooms to scrub the buildings free of mud and oil were everywhere.

Her job title was "worm." For three long months, she worked up on the metal platform where the huge diamond-bit drills were screwed into five-inch steel pipe sections and lowered into the ground. Miles of pipe were manually screwed together and sent down the hole every day, and miles of pipe were brought back up and manually unscrewed to change that one bit every shift. She would hold a firehose, brace herself against metal railings, and point the surging water at the floor around the hole when the pipes were coming back out of the ground, spewing dirt and mud. The worm's job was to keep the platform clear so the deckhands could see what they were doing.

She did that job until two weeks ago. She didn't plan on going back, nor was she welcome.

The pusher (man in charge) had made too many rude advances and, one day on the platform, had shoved his fat paw down her diesel-soaked Carhart coveralls, saying in a thick voice, "You know you want it."

That was it. She turned the firehose on full force and knocked him off his feet. Billy had watched in horror. Or maybe pride. Before the pusher had time to lunge at her, she let go of the hose and, while it corkscrewed and spewed water, she scrambled down the ladder to the ground and ran for her car as fast as her steel-toed boots would allow.

Not in your wildest dreams.

Her days of roughnecking ended there, along with any doubt about her resilience.

Christmastime 1979

Now, at twenty-two, Maryl Morgan Marks stood in her parents' living room in middle-class Seattle suburbia that had no similarities to the suffocating town where she was raised in southeastern Washington—in the house with the musty basement and the boxing ring—unless one counted a critical father with a stinging belt and an overbearing mother with a rosary and a wooden spoon. Their location had been upgraded, but they hadn't, still trapped inside the strict system of guilt and fear meant to mold Maryl into a nice Catholic girl.

It hadn't, and she wasn't.

After a year and a half of her post-college adventures, and fresh from the Wyoming dustbowl, she was just home for a visit this Christmas and was regretting it already.

"Why does it matter so much that I jump into corporate America right now, Dad?" Maryl crossed her arms, standing near her father's favorite chair. "I have plenty of time for that if I choose it."

George let out a long breath, carrying the telltale aroma of his forbidden cigars. He stared at the talking head on the TV and responded as if he'd said it a thousand times.

"Because you need to get out there and start making money instead of playing around in Sun Valley and jetting off to sailing trips in the Keys. You young kids think you deserve a break after four short years of university, but college is a gift. You were given a gift, and it should have instilled an urgency in you to get out there and use your education."

"I know, Dad. I know. But I am making some money, just not a lot. And I'm OK with that. Waiting tables and building ski boots and jumping out of planes teaches a lot too, you know. It's real-world stuff. I'm just not ready to subject myself to the world you live in."

"And what would that world be?" George set his jaw.

"The one where you must do whatever your Board tells you to do. Sit at a desk nine to five. Drink your lunch. Make the numbers lie. The world where you're only rewarded for profit. And greed. And power grabs."

"Power and greed. I see. So why the business degree then? Why didn't you follow your original path of painting and poetry?" George turned in his chair to face her.

"You know why, Dad. The professors kept demanding six charcoal sketches by Monday and three poems by Tuesday, and I sort of lost my passion. Besides, I'm going to start my own business someday, so I need to know what's involved." Maryl remembered a day when she and her father were close. He had been her hero, and many childhood wounds had been healed by just sitting in his lap, enveloped by the smoky fragrance of safety.

"Yeah. Right. Someday." He turned back to the TV. Maryl felt tears gathering but held them back, knowing that somehow, she had lost her daddy, her champion, her referee.

Maryl's mother, Regina, marched into the room clutching the dishtowel.

"Yes, when is someday, Miss Marks? It seems to me that your issue is with authority, not greed. You're plenty greedy. You just fail to notice it. And why don't you look in the mirror at that messy mop of hair and baggy sweatshirts? That's not the way I raised you, young lady."

Her mother came from a respectable lineage, the daughter of the town pharmacist, the president of her high school class, and a true believer in Jesus. Once a beautiful woman, she had descended into a bitter one, always angry—largely at Maryl. But coifed. Always coifed.

Maryl ignored her and stomped around the couch to block the TV hypnotizing her father. Please hear me.

"Dad! Someday is whenever I figure out what I can contribute to make the world a better place. And why is it any of your business which job I take next? I'm out of your house now. I pay my own bills. I work hard. I play hard. Isn't that what you taught me to do?"

George turned his icy blue eyes to her, his six-foot-three frame twisting in the oversized brown chair at the center of the room. "Listen, young lady. It's my business because you're my daughter. You don't know the first thing about running a business or what awaits you in the real world. Now get out of the way."

The familiar sting of disagreement ignited the air as she clashed with her parents these days over an endless parade of issues—from the merits of marijuana legalization to the corridors of corporate power to the Vatican's doctrine. Each confrontation was a fresh wound, and she longed to stop the downward spiral of their communication, but she didn't know how.

It had all started with God.

She had enough of the Catholic religion as she began seeing the hypocrisy when she was just a child back in Walla Walla: Mr. Riley singing hymns of love and acceptance in the pew in front of her, then using the N-word when he shouted at the street cleaner outside his shop; Miss Lorena doing the handshake of peace in Mass, then badmouthing her neighbor to Maryl's mother the next day. In fact, this last Monday, Maryl watched as Miss Lorena stopped her mother in the driveway to dish. "I swear that woman drinks every penny he brings home," Miss Lorena had said. "Can you believe the rickety old car she drives? It's a nuisance to the neighborhood, and the old sweater she wears?"

Her mother never replied, pursing her lips in that way that she did. But she also never admonished Miss Lorena for gossiping, because, after all, Lorena was going to hell and Regina was not because, well, she said her rosary each night before she lay in bed with her adulterous husband.

Yes, her father, the light of her life as a child, had started an affair with one of her mother's best friends, and because of the meek and sniveling way that Regina suffered through it to this day, Maryl had lost respect for her. *Why does she put up with it?*

Maryl was no angel, nor was she a virgin, but the mere thought of all the hypocrisy of the church made her want to race around the boxing ring like a Ring Girl with a sign that said "Stop! Stop it now!" instead of "Round 3."

"I prefer good-hearted sinners to so-called good people who are intolerant," was a quote from her favorite spiritual leader, Paramahansa Yogananda, whose life story she had read, and whose words made more sense to her than any catechism. His theory was that all religions had their own paths, and they were just different paths up the same mountain. From him she learned to breathe. In-two-three-four-hold-two-three-out-two-three-four-five-six—and she was doing that silently right now.

Her parents believed that everyone went to hell if they weren't Catholic. But Maryl knew plenty of people of strong moral fiber who weren't Catholic. Some were even atheists, and she was absolutely sure they weren't going to burst into flames. She refused to attend church at all, except maybe Christmas night when all the spirits danced against the ceiling in the candlelight and the incense made her woozy and horny for the high school altar boys in their starched collars and black robes.

POP!

The quick snap of a dish-towel-turned-whip brought Maryl's thoughts back to the present.

Her mother stood in the living room, not far from Maryl, hands on her still-slim hips, her golf-tanned legs slightly apart in her usual bossy stance. Gravity and stress had melted her face into the sag of too many children in too few years. Regina picked up Joey, her beloved dachshund, and cradled him. "Maryl, are you listening to me?" she demanded. "Your father and I work very hard to give you kids a good life…"

"No, Mom. I'm not listening to you…"

Maryl exited the living room and headed out the front door.

She heard her father's weight shift out of the chair, his limbs snap and pop, his strides lengthen, his voice rise. "You come back here and help your mother with—"

She slammed the door behind her, jumped into her Fiat, jammed her foot on the clutch, and eased into first gear. "I need a drink," she said, speeding out of the manicured neighborhood, and immediately into the busy suburb.

Every lamp post had a red plastic ribbon and shoppers in thick wool scarves scurried past, their faces twisted masks of stress and barely concealed panic. It was cold—a wet cold—not the dry crisp cold of Sun Valley where your nose hairs would freeze on your first breath outside.

The only bar she could find was a swinging-fern bar near the mall—each window had a fern swinging above the table—packed with holiday shoppers and business suits escaping their jobs. She ordered a gin and tonic and nursed it at the bar, knowing she was out of place in her worn jeans and Sun Valley T-shirt that read "Ski Bald" on the front and "Ride Big Wood" on the back. She had done both.

Back in Sun Valley, the town would be blanketed in white, and teeming with tourists right now. Tourists who looked like these people, but in fashionable ski jumpers. Tourists who would demand service right now and never suspect the bar staff would spit in their drink if they were obnoxious. So much power behind the counter.

She smiled and was glad she had watched the bartender pour her own drink.

"Here you go!" he said, sliding a paper coaster under her glass. "Nice T-shirt."

"Thanks. So, what's with the chess board up here on the bar?" she asked as she eyed the game board.

"Oh, that's for customers to borrow. Usually during the evenings."

"That's cool. Do you play?

"Sure. It's a brain game, right? How about you?"

A slight smile crossed her face as she thought back to the chess/checkers tournaments they had in the basement when she was young. "Some." She lifted a knight from the chessboard, turning it in her fingers. The memory surfaced clearly: her father's voice, low and serious, saying "The knight teaches you how to jump over the other pieces on the board. He's the only one who can. Remember that."

"So, why this bar?" she asked the bartender, placing it back on the square.

"What?" He spun dirty glasses on the scrubber and refilled the olive tray.

"Why did you choose this place to work?" Her eyes took a long drink of him. Strong arms and a tight butt.

"Money." He grinned. "You give these folks a strong pour and they tip appropriately." He was speaking to her as if she were not a customer. "So, what brings you in?"

"I'm visiting my folks for Christmas and had to get out of the house. Do they need any help here?" She chewed on a stir stick.

"You would love working with me but hate working with them." He tossed his head in the direction of the three waitresses out on the floor.

"Got it." Maryl nodded. She realized the king was in jeopardy of checkmate, so she reached over and laid the piece on its side in defeat.

Max looked down at the board. "However." He came closer. "My cousin is looking for holiday help in her shop across the street. I could introduce you."

"What kind of shop?" Maryl was interested.

"Cheesy." He grinned. "And my name is Max by the way."

FIVE

——◆◇◆——

$\mathbf{M}$aryl clicked the Fiat key off in her parents' steep driveway, thankful that this suburb didn't get much snow.

She sighed. It was never any different, but never the same.

She reached for something in the glove compartment. The rain was pounding the roof as she looked up through the windshield and took a deep breath. Two, in fact. *What was she doing here? Her parents didn't even like her.*

The faded photo she held in her hand showed nine of her college friends sprawled on a lawn near Lake Washington during the summer of '73, where they had gathered to watch the hydroplane races and the Blue Angels jets that flew over every year on that day. More like *screamed* over. Together, sitting on wet blankets, some wearing plastic garbage bags over their shoulders, every face had a grin despite the Seattle rain. She traced her finger over the empty Rainier Beer cans, her own red freak flag matted in the drizzle, Brad sticking out his tongue with his sunglasses pushed up on his head, Richard clutching a plastic bottle of discount vodka, Fletcher sitting under a plastic bag, and Cris with her eyes crossed and her mouth full of orange something—Cheetos, Maryl thought.

Six years ago they had started college; the years when the Vietnam War protests were the loudest, when Janis sang "Me and Bobby McGee" and Charles Manson's cult murdered seven women. It was the era of anything-goes with themes of violence and morality—Clockwork Orange and Dirty Harry, Roe v. Wade, Nixon and Watergate.

There, right in front of her face, on the pretty brick and ivy campus, the world had gotten bigger. Much bigger. Jolted out of her Walla Walla naivete, her eyes were wide open and her hair on fire as they smoked pot with Vietnam vets who were missing legs and brain cells, drank beer with Black Panthers who ranted about social inequality and police brutality and real poverty, and they partied in the twin Corvettes of the unruly offspring of the Dow Jones families who disclosed the real story of who ran Wall Street and the White House-*their* fathers and the lobbyists and wealthy businessmen who came to dinner at their parents' mansions on the Potomac.

She held the photo to her cheek for a moment. Two already dead, one from suicide and one from a car accident. She loved these people who had been there for her during those long twenty years that were, in reality, just four. Seemed impossible. But now they were all successful—Cris a veterinarian, Brad a neurosurgeon, Richard with his own construction business, Fletcher, in a wheelchair now from a rope swing accident, had amassed a real estate portfolio in the sketchy neighborhoods of south Seattle. Dear sweet Helen, her best pal, was happily married to her high school sweetheart, the other two women were mothers with master's degrees. All "on their way" as her father would say.

She wasn't on her way.

Although she adored her friends, she didn't aspire to be any of the things they had become. And she definitely didn't want to live in poshville, join a country club, play golf, or get married.

Helen used to say, "Maryl, how will you ever decide what you want to be when you grow up? You have so many choices."

Helen was one of the good Catholics who said what she meant and meant what she said. She had choices as well, but she made her final choice in sixth grade. She would marry, have children, be kind to all, and do artwork.

What Helen meant was that Maryl started so many things, did them fairly well, then got bored and moved on to something else.

"I'm just a curious person," Maryl would say. "If more people were curious, more problems would be fixed. It seems to me that bad things happen *really* fast, but people's minds are in slow motion, waiting for a god or a president or the Valkyrie to swoop in and save the day."

Helen would giggle. "Well, when you're president, we can expect everything to be fixed."

Damn straight.

"But I'll be the Valkyrie." And they shook on it.

Maryl stowed the photo, turned her collar up, and scooted back into the world of George and Regina for the holidays. After the bar, she had stopped at QFC to pick up a pie as a sort of peace offering, but of course, they were out of pumpkin, so she bought a cherry one. And a quart of vanilla ice cream. *That should make George happy for at least a minute.*

"No wonder you wear baggy clothes now," said Regina as Maryl put the rain-soaked pie box on the counter. "If that's what you've been eating—"

"Mom. Stop. It's for Dad. I thought he would like it," Maryl said as she put the ice cream in the freezer and washed her hands so she could help Regina with dinner. Joey was dancing now, certain that it was a party, so Regina grabbed the treat bag that she kept nearby at all times. Maryl didn't want to discuss her personal appearance, or why she had been hacking at her own hair instead of visiting a salon. And her nails? Well, that was another matter altogether, bitten down to the quick. When people stared at them, she told them that she liked to work outside.

Regina leaned down to give Joey a treat, but she wouldn't let it go. "Then why do you wear those awful baggy clothes now? Some leftover Wyoming trend?"

"No, Mom. They're just comfortable. It's not like I have a corporate job."

"Boy, is that true," said George as he entered the kitchen to refill his scotch.

Maryl didn't want to fight. "What movie do you guys want to watch tonight? I might run down to the rental place after dinner and get a new release."

Maryl and her siblings had given her parents a VCR for Christmas last year and they had been thrilled with that new technology, but George liked old Westerns and Regina preferred feel-good family movies with a box of Kleenex and Joey in her lap, so they had stopped using it. Now they just drank and watched Archie Bunker until bedtime.

"Your mom and I want to watch some TV tonight."

"Okay. How about a quick game of chess before that?" George had taught her how to play, and she thought it might bring back some camaraderie.

George opened his mouth, and then closed it and walked away into the dining room.

Maryl stared after him. "Okay. Well, I brought a book, so I'll just read in bed."

She was absolutely going to take the job at the cheese shop tomorrow.

The next day was Tuesday.

"So many cheeses to learn!" Maryl grinned at Jean, Max's cousin, who had rescued her from a holiday of chopping vegetables at her parents' house, hearing over and over what a disappointment she was compared to her older brother, Steven, the awesome strait-laced lawyer.

"And so many smells to learn," answered Jean as she shoved a slice of stinky goat cheese under Maryl's nose. "What's this one?" she demanded.

"Gross cheese."

The two chuckled, smoothed their denim aprons, and then turned on their professional smiles as two suited businessmen pushed the tinkling door handle, stamped the wet off their shoes, and entered for their weekly soup-and-sandwich lunch. Jean told her they came in often from the high-rise building next door—some sort of startup company. Once Jean introduced them to her newest employee, they began ribbing Maryl for not putting her freshly minted business degree to use making the big bucks.

Over the next few weeks, Raymond and Kyle would come in often, even visiting just for coffee mid-afternoon. One would say, "The pot we brewed this morning is cold and no one wants to make a new one."

"So, you're just going to let it sit there on the burner until someone else dumps the coffee grinds?" she asked them.

"Yes," they said in unison, chuckling a little at their own joke. "Because, you know, we're the bosses." The more outgoing Raymond winked at her. Except for when he held a sandwich or coffee cup, Kyle kept his hands in his pockets.

More rumpled as the day progressed, they both looked like they lived in their suits. She guessed they needed these frequent breaks for their sanity. She couldn't imagine having a desk job in a high rise unless it was her own company. But working for suits like her father? No.

Between building roast beef sandwiches, slicing cheese wedges, and pulling wine bottles down for uppity clients to examine, she would banter with Raymond and Kyle. She regaled them with stories of her post-college adventures, and they shook their heads at her mischief, as they called it. They were good guys. Safe guys. Funny. The daily interaction with them was refreshing, and she looked forward to their visits.

"Blimey, an Irish lass such as yourself must be a wee bit of trouble," Kyle would say in a fake brogue. And then his engineering nerd brain would conjure up jokes about all those recessive redhead genes. Raymond would chime in with controversial behaviors bestowed upon redheads that were not imbued in a standard-issue blonde or brunette: Cheekiness. Feistiness. Passion.

"Well, aren't you both fortunate to bask in my presence? After all, I'm practically a genetic jackpot—red hair and blue peepers." And they would all chuckle as Jean winked and nodded in agreement.

When they would chide her about not having a real job, Jean would frown at them and shoo them out of the shop, winking at Maryl. "Enough of that nonsense," she would say.

But there they were the next day, at it again.

"Look, guys, give me a break. I'm only here for the holidays while I'm figuring out my next great adventure."

On one of those days between Christmas and New Year's, Raymond handed her a sheet of paper.

"What's this? Are you ordering for your entire office party or something?"

"It's called a job description, young lady," he said. "Read it. You can do this. You should do this." He grinned. She'd grown up on a diet of shoulds.

The sheet described what a support representative for their software product would do—learn the software, help customers figure out how to use it, and how to fix problems as they arise.

Jean came around the counter and peered at the paper. She looked at Maryl after a few minutes. "He's not wrong," she said.

A stuffy corporate desk job in a high-rise, pin-striped all-male office?

"Nope. Can't sit inside at a desk all day. Won't..." Maryl started and then stopped as she saw him nod at his partner, Kyle, and slap down a $5 bill.

"Told you," said Kyle.

"What?" Maryl stared at them both, and the men laughed.

"Come on. You don't belong here, and you know it. It's time you got down to business, no pun intended." And Raymond smiled again. "Why don't you just put together a resume and we'll talk next time we're in here."

They paid for their carefully wrapped turkey and provolone sandwiches and left. Raymond turned his head as he held the door open. "And we just won't get you a desk, okay? You can stand up all day." He smirked as he headed back out into the cold gray day.

Helen was on the other end of the phone. "Well, you told them you needed to think about it, right? Why don't you come visit and we'll talk it through." Even though they shared the same wit and brainpower, Helen and Maryl were opposites; Helen was buoyant and blonde with rosy cheeks and a giggle that went up the scale and stopped. She was sweet to everyone, and Maryl was, well, the fiery dragon lady. They counted on each other to fill in their gaps.

Maryl sighed as she parked along Helen's sidewalk after the four-hour drive to Walla Walla. The snow tire nazis up at the Pass had let her go through since the roads were nearly clear and she slowed to the speed limit for the remaining eighty percent of the trip, which, for Maryl, was difficult. The winter trip was always boring, but in the spring, once she got to Wallula Junction and saw the golden wheat swaying and the deep green cabbage and pea fields, it became magical once again. From there until she reached the town, her windows were down as she breathed in the smells of onions, alfalfa, rich brown earth, and cows. Downtown the streets were wide and clean, with stately oaks and maples lining the sidewalks, sprinklers sending sparkly beams of water onto emerald lawns, and children playing kick-the-can in the cul-de-sac.

But right now, it was winter, the trees had ghost arms and the sad sidewalk cracks leered at Maryl as she surveyed her friend's house.

She and Helen had lived only a mile from each other in their childhood but now Helen and her husband had settled into a neat cottage farther out of town. Helen came bounding out of the house, and Maryl gaped. "You didn't tell me you were pregnant!"

"Well, I wanted it to be a surprise. Surprise!"

"Do you know what it is?" The words tumbled from Maryl's lips before she could think about them.

"Well, it's actually going to be a tiny little human that pops out."

"I deserved that."

"Come in. Come in. It's freezing out here." Helen led the way.

They settled into the living room with cups of warm spearmint tea, Helen's favorite, which Doug had brought to them as he said hello-goodbye and left for his bowling league.

"What's new in Walla Walla?" Maryl grinned, knowing full well that nothing new ever happened there. *Part of the charm*, she had told her college friends.

"They're building a new mall out past the Dairy Queen. AND it will have an all-day daycare."

"A daycare? By the penitentiary?"

"Well, not next to it but out that way, yes."

"Oh, and Gary got a job as a guard out there."

"At the daycare?"

"No. Funny girl. At the Pen."

It was so good to see Helen. She had known from her pigtail days that she wanted to marry Doug and have children and a cute little house, and now she had. Maryl couldn't fathom it. She would be bored within a year and want to poke out her eyes.

"So, tell me all about this job offer." Helen took a sip of the warm drink and regarded her friend. She knew Maryl so well and could tell she was having a hard time with this decision.

"Well, you know that I only got a business degree so I could start my own business someday, right? But then these random guys came into the cheese shop talking about their cool startup company, and you also know I'm kind of a geek, and I love technology, and this is brand new stuff, and it's a small office, so it would be like working with a couple of buddies on a new idea and…"

"Okay." Helen stopped her. "But what about your art and writing and your quest to save the world from itself? And you always vowed not to become your father."

"You mean an overbearing father, a cheating husband, or a businessman driven by greed and trickery?"

"I think you called it 'A stiff in a gray suit sitting in a gray box.'"

"Yes, I did. I do. But this seems different to me. Like something the universe dropped in my lap to really look at. Like something that might make a difference."

"It's not like you to hesitate when an opportunity jumps out at you, Mel." Helen had shortened her friend's name when they were kids, and Maryl called her 'Hel' in return.

"Well, I've just had so much rapid-fire growth in the last few years, I don't want to give it up." Maryl stared at her drink.

"You mean rapid-fire fun?"

"Haha. That too. But look at our folks. They drudged through college, then got married and started having kids. I seriously think my folks just went through the motions of marriage for the sake of the kids. And mom with five kids by the time she was our age. God, I don't want that to be the rest of my story. I don't want to settle for something that's not awesome."

Helen cleared her throat. "Ouch," she said.

"Oh. No, I didn't mean you, Hel."

"No offense taken, my friend. You and I have always seen the future differently and that's the beauty of choices and all that. I'm very content with my life. And we both always knew that you would be the one to get out, to launch a thousand ships, to save the planet. Mel, I have a few talents and I intend to use them. Both of them. But you. You have so many talents. Start using them to get you where you want to go. You could do anything. Be anyone."

"Not according to George and Regina."

"Now, Maryl." Helen moved closer and took Maryl's hand. "I know you want to make your dad proud. And he is. He just doesn't know how to show it. You need to start making decisions based on your own goals, not theirs."

"You're right. As always. But Jesus, your hands are freezing."

Maryl and Helen spent the next morning at Pioneer Park, dressed in wool layers and winter boots, watching the geese waddle around the pond and listening to the birds screech in the small zoo nearby. They reminisced about the Little League games their brothers played on the ball field there, and which pitchers had been the cutest.

"But don't you sometimes want to escape this place?" she asked her friend as they rounded the perimeter of the pond. "I mean, don't you want to go conquer something? Shake things up a little?"

Helen smiled. Her breath came out in white clouds. "You've always been the one with the arrows in your back, Maryl. I'm just happy to follow along with the bandages."

Before Maryl left the next day, Helen reached into her pocket and pulled out the pounded piece of metal she had made in art class at St. Francis after Maryl had snuck into the sanctuary to taste the wine. Helen hadn't understood what made her do it but had marveled at Maryl's bravery. Instead of remorse, Maryl had felt powerful and didn't mind the ten Hail Marys and six Our Fathers penance.

"Remember?" Helen said. "I made this one for you. Don't know why I didn't give it to you back then. I found it last week when I was cleaning the guest room. Lord knows how much junk I have boxed up in that closet."

It had a tiny hole in the top with a chain through it, and a one-word inscription: "BRAVE."

As Maryl drove away wearing the coin around her neck, she had tears in her eyes. She missed Helen. She missed innocence. She missed the cocoon of not knowing all the bad stuff.

She hummed along with Freddie Mercury on the radio about shaking the dust from her shoes and following the road ahead and she made her decision.

Six

Two weeks later, at the end of a meeting in the high-rise office building that overlooked downtown Bellevue and the Seattle skyline beyond it, Maryl, Raymond and Kyle stood to shake hands.

"See there." Raymond's eyes twinkled. "That wasn't so difficult. So, we'll get this application sent off to Wilton. If they accept it, which of course they will, you'll be back and forth to Connecticut for your training for the next six months."

Kyle chimed in. "And then you'll be an expert in relational database software and client-server stuff. How exciting is that?" He snickered and shook her hand.

"Gag me," she shot back. "I'm just in it for the power over the universe."

"Oh, you're a trekkie?" Kyle raised his eyebrows.

"A what?"

"You know, 'I'm a doctor, not an escalator'."

Maryl gave him a poker stare.

Kyle snorted. "Well, well. So, you don't have a nerd quotient. You would need it for this job."

"That's highly illogical." She jabbed her chin in the air and turned.

Kyle was grinning, knowing he had been outplayed.

"Lunch break!" Raymond announced.

Maryl suggested the swinging-fern bar, which was crowded and loud with the aroma of sauteed onions and grilled steaks and garlicky Alfredo sauce. An hour later they had consumed their chicken pastas and scotch rocks because apparently that's what you did in corporate

America. The patrons were all in suits, except for one table of three nip-and-tuck women with huge wedding diamonds on their freshly manicured fingers.

Max was bartending and came to the table. "Hey Maryl," he said, eyeing the businessmen. "Jean told me about your high dive into the murky swamp of corporate suits."

"Yes, beware the corporate crocodiles." Kyle laughed at his own joke.

"Gentlemen, meet my shrink, Max."

Both men nodded at Max.

"Well, come see me when things get too funky." Max wandered off to the table of ladies, exaggerating his sexy swagger for Maryl's benefit.

"See you tomorrow." She called after him. Raymond rolled his eyes.

Maryl wanted more details about the technology she was jumping into, so the next day she was back in their offices overlooking the black-wet streets below, and the snow-capped Cascades mountain range in the distance. *At least they have a view.*

Kyle explained that their firm, CSNN, had purchased an IBM 360, and was subletting space on it. They called it computer timesharing.

Maryl was still unclear about it. "So, you just let companies rent part of your machine and dump their data onto it? How many of those computers do you have? Does each customer get their own? How do you keep them all separate?"

Kyle had laughed at her burst of interest. "Whoa, tiger."

"For now, we just have the one big computer. We have software that's like a traffic cop that keeps everything separate in these par-titions. And there's a database system they can also rent in order to play around with their data."

"Play around?"

"Come look at this drawer," Kyle said. Maryl walked around his desk to an open drawer stuffed with receipts. "Everyone here has this kind of drawer. This is data. This, plus your salary, is what it costs CSNN to keep you employed."

He led Maryl to the bookkeeper's cubicle and pointed to the tall tan metal filing cabinet next to her desk. "Behold all the customer data, including which deal was sold by which team."

Maryl waited for the punchline.

"But when Mr. Ray yells down the hall to get him our monthly numbers to see if we made any profit, I have to scramble and put all these in a spreadsheet, give them to the bookkeeper who combines them with customer payments for the month. Only then can I give him the *information* he wanted."

Maryl's face scrunched in puzzlement.

"Maryl, it's the information about who is pulling their weight in this district." Raymond cut in. "Remember your debits and credits from school? Revenue minus costs, Maryl. That's your value to the company. In numbers."

"Okay, but that's what your database system is for? It just sounds like VisiCalc on steroids." She crossed her arms.

"I'll wager your college professors loved you in class..." Ray laughed at her interruptions and impatience.

"I'm just a curious person," Maryl began.

"So, do your customers come to your IBM 360 and work on their data?

"No. No, they access their partition on our machine from their own office terminals. Remote computing."

"Interesting," Maryl said. "Sounds like you could really hold companies hostage."

Kyle's eyes darted briefly towards Raymond. "And we're off."

At the end of the day, armed with this exciting new insight, Maryl arrived at her parents' house and burst through the front door, nearly tripping over Joey who was wagging his tail and dancing on the slate flooring. "Guess what I'm doing next with my life?"

Regina had her arms full of laundry. The lines from the edges of her mouth were grooved in two arcs down her jaw, giving her a sour countenance.

"You're taking this to the living room to start folding." She thrust the clean laundry into Maryl's not-yet-ready arms, causing socks and underwear to peel off and fall to the floor.

George was in the family room with the tube on and ice cubes tinkling in his glass. Joey was now in his lap. He paid no attention as Maryl entered the room, deflated, and dumped the pile onto the couch. She eyed her father, decided against any conversation, did an about-face, and headed back out to the shrink counter.

Sitting in her car in the parking lot of Max's bar, she leaned back against the headrest, fingered her medallion at her neck, and recalled all the other times her mother had shut down her enthusiasm.

When Maryl had missed a step in dance class, Regina had pulled the ballet mistress aside and said, "I think I'm wasting my money here," and dragged her out to the car in her pink slippers. That was the last time she danced. And at Maryl's piano recital when she lost her place in the sheet music and panicked, nearly peeing her pants, her mother had stomped up to the stage and hissed "Maryl, remember what you practiced!"

Max's eyebrows arched in pleasant surprise as she slid onto the barstool. "So soon?" He gave her one of his best smiles.

Maryl shook her head. "No, it's not the job. *Yet.*" She managed a smile. "I have one foot in a new world and one in an old one."

"Well, spill your guts, sister. First drink's on me, and here's to your new world." He grabbed a knight off the chess board and set it next to her drink with a wink.

SEVEN

Three weeks later she wound her way up Coal Creek Parkway to her tiny apartment in Newport Hills behind the grocery store with its smelly garbage bins and climbed the thirteen ratty carpeted stairs. It was adequate. It was brown. It was away from her parents. She had her own parking space.

"Dang it," Maryl complained as she shrugged out of her blouse and jacket and kicked her nicest shoes back into the tiniest of closets. "I'm going to have to wear this stuff all the time now…"

Corporate headquarters had put up some resistance to her application since her background of painting, roughnecking, and waitressing didn't meet their rigorous standards. In the end, Raymond won out, pushing her 3.8 college grades, and her successful response to challenges in her past as reasons to give her a chance.

And, for sure, this new experience would be a challenge on several fronts.

Her training in Wilton, Connecticut would start in March along with eleven other twenty-somethings, some straight out of a computer science master's program, and some legacy trainees, their wealthy parents contributing to the 'right' technology lobbyists.

She was neither.

Each day they would sit through classes in hard plastic desks with glaring overhead fluorescent tubes set in white cardboard ceiling tiles. Each evening, they would gather in one hotel room or another and drink vodka with ice cubes from the machine down the hall. Then back to their corners (home cities) for a week to study, and back to Wilton again.

In May of 1980, Maryl was going over her notes back in her apartment in Newport Hills, munching on Pringles sour cream & onion. It was Spring, and her windows were wide open. That was the extent of her "spring cleaning." *OK, so our offering isn't so much a product as it is a software environment on a machine we bought from IBM and we needed an operating system to make the machine run, so we bought one of those too. Check.*

She continued reading her notes from class... *We put COBOL and FORTRAN on top of that operating system and let customers build... stuff* ... paging back through her notebook.

Hmmm, what were they building... what were they building...oh, yes, the word is 'applications.' So the customers built these applications in COBOL and FORTRAN -- these programs that organized their data maybe, and then migrated them over to their own machines. Brilliant. Maryl mused. *But wait. Why would we let them do that? Aren't we encouraging customers to take their shiny new applications and go away once they built them on our machines?*

She dialed Kyle.

"Time-sharing, Maryl. Time-sharing," Kyle chuckled.

"Well, yes, they are sharing time on our machines, but that's just letting them rent space until they want to go play on their own machines, right?

"Hold up. Hold up." Kyle was obviously smiling. "Why don't I come over and help you study?"

"Over here?" She glanced at the mess of papers. "Um, sure."

An hour later, Kyle lugged his briefcase and a bottle of wine up the thirteen steps.

"Study?" Maryl grinned as he handed her the wine. She and Kyle worked well together. It was so easy to be around him and banter about work. But Maryl was reluctant to have their relationship go any further.

"Oh, this is the reward if you do well on the Kyle Quiz. And the first question on the quiz is 'Do you know how much one of those machines would cost if a client had to buy it on their own?'"

"A jillion dollars?"

Kyle hung his coat on a chair and sat at the small round table piled with papers and three-ring binders.

Kyle continued, "But yes, regarding your question on the phone earlier. You're right. We don't want clients to leave the party before the band starts playing. So, we stack other products onto our machine for them to use. Products they can't afford on their own. Software programs too big for their own machines, and probably overkill for some of their needs."

"Soooo, kind of like we're the laundromat providing the machines *and* the water *and* the electricity *and* the soap *and* the dryer sheets so customers don't have to buy their own, and their clothes can still be as clean as the wealthies."

"The wealthies?"

"Yeah. The rich folks who can afford those high-end washers and dryers in their homes, and all the hot water they want, and all the fancy detergents and stuff."

"Umm, so I take it you did laundry today?" Kyle looked around for a washing machine and saw none.

"Yeah. Down the stairs, out the door, over to Building H, back to my building, and up the stairs. Three times."

"So, thrice then?" He smirked. "Using your analogy, then... the washers are pretty useless without the water and soap, right?"

"Unless you're a kid and you need to hide from your mom who has a wooden spoon. Then they can be pretty useful. I mean, who looks in a washer for a kid?"

Kyle blinked. "Uh-huh." He paused for a minute. "So, back to the answer to your question, our customers won't leave us since they can't afford their own washer/dryer, and more to the point, they can't afford the hot water and soap we include for them. Like SIMDAR."

"They talked about SIMDAR in training. It's the holy grail, right? A DBMS and a 4GL."

"Well, it's a database management system. It manages all that data they dump onto our machines."

"And a 4GL."

"Yes, a fourth-generation language."

"You realize you're talking nerd again," Maryl said. Kyle ignored her interruption.

"Speaking of nerds... our nerds at corporate keep everything partitioned so data breaches don't happen. And they even help the customers write their applications, so it's a trusted relationship."

"Sort of like ours, right?" Maryl smiled at Kyle. She wanted him to know that she trusted him.

"OK, enough studying. Where's your corkscrew?" Kyle grinned.

Two weeks later, when Maryl was back in the Bellevue office between training sessions, she and Kyle were in the conference room going over the company history for the upcoming quiz.

"So, SIMDAR is a competitive product to ours, right?" Maryl steered the conversation. "But we use it on our machines, so we're sort of partners. Then why do we hate these FOCAL4 guys? They're just another competitor."

"One word."

"What?"

"Cohen."

"What's a cohen?"

"It's a 'he.' Milt Cohen's company owned SIMDAR when we rented it from them to put on our machines so our customers could use it. He's sort of the reason we built DAMON—he raised our rates so high that we barely broke even. So, we figured it was time to create our own product."

"That just sounds like normal dog-eat-dog business stuff."

"Oh, he was a dog alright. Turns out he was secretly coding a copycat version of SIMDAR all along. So, he quit and started his own company and surprise, surprise, magically introduced a product called FOCAL4."

"So, he won?"

"Not so much. A month later, we released DAMON, which was a much better product for our clients." Kyle winked at her. "And that, Miss Red, is your history lesson for the day."

During those training months, the lightbulb went on. Well, a few lightbulbs, actually. One was the truth about who holds the power in high tech—the investors—and to some extent, the corporate bosses who called the shots. They all seemed to have the same chessboard where the king can't capture the enemy king, a pawn can't retreat once he's made his move, and a knight can be as devious as he wants.

The other crystal-clear revelation for Maryl was the flip side of that power. None of her training was about learning to operate computers. And they weren't teaching her to code software. Instead, they were training her about the power they had as a tech company and the power that their products gave to their customers.

Essentially, Maryl thought, *they were power kings and were also peddling power.* Power over chaos. Power over doubt.

They had created a system that gave their clients more power than they had ever had—the ability to pull out highly useful information from their own data without waiting in the MIS queue for months or years. Customers could merge their own cargo shipment data with maritime traffic data to speed up deliveries. They could merge their own drug formulas with national databases to search for patents and avoid lawsuits. They could combine data about advertising costs with customer buying behaviors to target their audience more closely.

Maryl's job was to understand the product so well that she could sit down with any customer, find their biggest data problem, and give them the power to solve it.

The rules of engagement finally crystallized in her mind. As a lowly pawn on this corporate chessboard, she recognized her potential to ascend from expendable to indispensable, trading up to Queen status if she could only make it to the far side of the board.

Having no idea what that would involve, she decided she was up for the challenge.

Maryl was on her usual bar stool, buzzing with enthusiasm over these newfound insights about power and the powerful, and Max was kind enough to feign interest.

"You are one funny girl," Max said as he mixed her a G&T. "You go from oil rig to cheese shop to nerd techie in what, six months? Geez, girl, now you're going to be a corporate queen?"

"Well, if it pays enough," she smirked. "But seriously, Max, I'm kinda into this technology stuff now."

"Well, good for you. And good for me. I get to live vicariously. Now, tell me the juiciest office gossip, my queen."

Max dressed in the latest fashions, and owned, Maryl guessed, at least twelve pairs of shades which he wore at the bar. He said it was to keep the bright lights out, but she knew it was to keep the middle-aged nip-and-tuck ladies from flirting with him. He had gorgeous blue eyes and long lashes, and as she might have expected, it turned out he was gay, which made him a fast friend of Maryl's. Gay men were comfortable for Maryl. This bar was comfortable for Maryl. And she loved that every time she left, Max would yell "Love you!" after her to make the other women hate her.

EIGHT

———◆◇◆———

On a bright June Wednesday in Connecticut, Maryl returned to her hotel room and found a note from the front desk to call home. Her father told her that her mother had fallen on the golf course and broken her hip, but when the doctors opened her up, they had found cancer.

"Oh, Dad." Maryl was shocked. "What do you do now? Is she going to get treatment? Should I come home? What do you need me to do?" She surprised herself that she cared.

"No. No. It's all being taken care of. I just wanted to tell you kids." And he hung up, sounding more tired than she had ever heard. *Tired? Or annoyed?* She couldn't tell.

She flew back to Seattle for the week, missing the training sessions, and Ray insisted she take a day off as soon as she showed up at the Bellevue office.

"Well, it's not like she's on her deathbed." Maryl worked at sounding strong. "She's just pretty sick from the chemo right now."

It was almost summer in Seattle; the two months of the year when people visited and fell in love with the sunny climate, only to turn suicidal once they moved there. The locals tried to tell the tourists about the rain, but they just kept moving there.

She worked in the office every day and visited her mom at their Bellevue house three nights that week, making spaghetti for them once and bringing home Chinese food on another night. She didn't even visit Max.

The house had a half-basement—her father's cigar room—where he shined his shoes for the week, a carryover from his military days. Maryl set up a small easel there and started an oil painting to pass the time. The smoke of her father's Havana mixed with the pungent smell of linseed oil and shoe polish. They were both used to it, as they had claimed this as a safe space, a quiet space—other than Nat King Cole on her father's radio—their joint retreat following turmoil events upstairs.

Today the turmoil was internal for both of them.

"Dad, do you ever think about death?" Maryl sat on her stool with her back to George.

"Don't like to. Don't need to. I watched my father die slowly in that plastic tent in the back shed."

"Do you think we come back? I mean, to this planet? To do it over again and get it right? Or do you think our soul gets to choose where it goes next?

"I don't know, Mel. I think my dad has visited me in the past. Can't really say."

"Were you able to communicate with him?"

"Not really."

"Does mom talk about death with you?"

"She just talks about what I should do after she dies."

They both fell silent again.

Regina was weak from the chemo. She didn't eat much. She didn't say much. Joey was constantly under her arm on the bed. Once she reached out and put her hand on Maryl's and gave it a little pat. She looked so small and vulnerable.

Maryl sat in the living room, remembering a mother from a different day.

"Devil, get out of my child," Regina had pleaded during her nightly prayers on the floor with ten-year-old Maryl. The neighbor had tattled on Maryl for looking at naked statues in her coffee table art book when she babysat her twins the night before.

In a perfect world, Regina would have defended her with 'Why do you leave those books out around children?' or 'Are you saying you leave pornography on your coffee table?'

But Maryl was banished to her room for the rest of the evening. A band of red bruises had formed on her forearm where Regina had grabbed her to drag her down the hall.

And then there was the incident when she was in third grade, escaping the heat of the house, lying on the grass watching the clouds float by, still in her school uniform. A man walked up to her and said he was a friend of her mother's and pulled her to her feet, asking her how much she weighed.

"How much I weigh?" She was eight years old and had no idea how much she weighed or why he would ask.

"How about I guess," he said with a weird smile. "I'll bet you're light enough for me to pick you up with one finger. Should we try?"

Maryl had looked at him and started backing away.

"No no. This is fun. I'll give you a quarter if I can't do it." With that, he pulled her toward him with one hand, lifted her blue and black plaid skirt, slid his other hand into her panties, and planted his middle finger inside her. "Now, I'll lift you." His eyes were suddenly glassy, and he put his head back with his eyes closed as he drove his finger deep inside her.

"Ow!" Maryl had been stunned by what he was doing. She didn't understand at all, but he said he was Mom's friend. She backed away, loosening his grip, and started wobbling back toward the house, and then picked up speed and ran.

Exploding into the house, she yelled, "Mom!"

"What do you want?" Regina was irritated. "I'm loading laundry. Come in here to talk to me if you want me to hear you. And you still haven't cleaned the upstairs bathroom, Maryl. Where have you been?" Regina wore her trademark angry frown as she finally turned to face Maryl.

Maryl stood there, not finding the words to describe what just happened outside.

"Well, what?" her mother demanded.

"Mom, a man was outside…"

Regina stepped closer.

"What man?"

"He said he was your friend, and he… he…"

"What, Maryl? What did he do?"

"He put his hand right here." Maryl pointed between her legs where a spot of blood was growing on her underwear.

Regina flew to the door and ran out to the yard, straining to see who had done this. There was no man in sight. She stomped back inside, annoyed.

"Maryl. Why do you do this? Why do you pretend these things? You truly have the devil in you. Now go clean the bathroom."

And that had been that.

Maryl knew there should be some feeling in her heart for her mother right now, but searching, she found nothing.

Her father was quiet and spent his time shining shoes or in the spare room that he was using as an office. He had hired a nurse to take Regina to her appointments. No one said much, Regina and Joey were inseparable, and it was uncomfortable to be at the house for long.

One evening when Regina was resting, Maryl went to her dad's room. She wanted to hug him and tell him she was there for him, how she knew he was in pain.

He was deep in conversation with another woman on the phone. She sensed it was the woman he was having an affair with. Joyce and her husband had been her parents' best friends for several years, through little league and camping trips and Sunday picnics. When Regina found out, she sat in a chair sobbing for three days, speaking to no one but the parish priest. When Dad finally came home, he had promised never to see Joyce again, and 'never' lasted about three months.

My dad is a jerk, and she shut the office door and left.

A blinking light on her phone was insistent when she walked in the door to the brown apartment.

"Hi, sweetie. This is your old dad. It was... It was good to have you here. You know I love your mom... It's just hard..."

Since that might have been the closest thing to an apology she would ever get, she picked up the phone.

"Hi, Dad."

"Hey, Sweetie."

"How bad is it?"

"You mean your mom?"

"No. I mean how hard is it for you? We didn't get much chance to talk alone over there."

"I can't... I'm not... I just don't know what to do." His voice faltered.

"I know."

"No. You don't know. She keeps my life together. We have agreements. And now she is probably going to die."

"You don't know that."

"Well, the doctors say..."

"Dad. You have to keep it together. For her. And you can't step out on her. Not now. Not anymore."

"But Regina hasn't let me touch her in ten years, and Joyce is the only one who understands me."

"Dad."

"What?"

"You can talk to me."

"Okay."

"Gotta go, Dad. Thanks for the phone message."

She loved her father, but she hated his affairs and his anger and his excuses.

I will never marry someone like you, Dad.

This every-other-week-in-Connecticut routine lasted six months. Next month they would graduate.

"So, what do you do in the summers in Seattle?" Her roommate for the training program, Joan, was asking from the other twin bed in the hotel room. She lit a cigarette and took a long drag. They had become friends and would quiz each other about the day's lessons, often giggling hysterically about their made-up answers.

"We build teepees and plow fields," Maryl smirked. Joan was from Chicago and had never been to the West Coast.

"Seriously?"

"No, silly."

"But sometimes we do rent canoes and go paddling around Lake Union. Or go hiking up in the mountains. Hey, do you remember the movie McQ? It was shot in Seattle."

"Yeah, I remember it. But I've never been a John Wayne fan, so I don't recall what it was about."

"Sinister detective stuff."

Joan took another drag and blew it Maryl's way.

"Dammit, Joan. You know I'm just going to have to wash my hair again. I can't stand that stink on my pillow all night."

Joan was humming something. "Hmm hmm, in Seattle…"

Maryl took up the tune. "The bluest skies you've ever seen, in Seattle…"

"And the hills the greenest greeeeeen, in Seattle," Joan crooned, holding her cigarette as if it were her microphone.

They both were in full singing mode now "Like a beautiful child, growing up free and wild…"

A sudden bang on the door.

"What!" bellowed Maryl.

"Knock it off. We're trying to study," someone yelled from the hallway.

"Well, we're trying to sing," Joan yelled back, a little tipsy.

Maryl smiled at Joan with admiration. "You are so ballsy."

"Back atcha." Joan tinkled her ice cubes in the plastic cup.

Joan and Maryl were inseparable, drinking and wise-cracking and being general troublemakers in and out of the classroom.

One Thursday night on the barbeque patio, Frank the VP, walked up to her and Joan. "What are you two lovely vixens up to?"

"We're off to the hot tub," Joan winked. Frank was lean and tan and confident.

He took that as an invitation and followed them. "I'll get some champagne," he called over his shoulder as he veered off to the lobby.

"Criminy," Joan whispered loudly. "He is definitely my type. Dibs!"

Maryl rolled her eyes. "Every guy here is your type." She flicked the end of her towel at Joan's head.

"Oh, and what about you, miss sexpot?" Joan teased her.

Maryl shot her a look. "Unbelievable, Joan. I told you that one thing in confidence and asked you not to repeat my stupid mother's words."

"Sexpot. Sexpot. Sexpot," Joan chanted and skipped ahead to the pool area.

"Shut the hell up," Maryl called after her.

"Shut up about what?" Frank fell in step with her. Maryl felt her face go red.

"Nothing." She looked the other way, still steamed at Joan. She certainly didn't want Joan saying that around Frank.

Frank stopped and faced her. "You know you're doing really well in the program, Maryl. We didn't think you would."

"You didn't think my time in steel-toed boots or the fact that I built awesome cheese sandwiches would translate to greatness?"

They shared a brief moment, smiling at each other for longer than was appropriate, because he was a VP and was, in fact, married.

Joan saw this and gave Maryl a nasty look. She was accustomed to having any man she wanted, but there was just something about Maryl's flaming locks and strong jawline and slim waist that was a magnet to men. "Hey, let's get this party started!" she whooped from the jacuzzi.

The next morning was test day, the day before all twelve of them went home for another week.

"My mouth tastes like an iguana slept in it," grouched Joan, pouring herself some OJ at the breakfast bar before class.

"Well, a lot of things were in there last night. I'm not sure which was an iguana." Maryl kidded her about making out in the hot tub with at least one other inebriated classmate.

Joan shot her an ugly glare but then managed a self-congratulating grin as she remembered.

"Joan. I'm kidding you." Maryl took a step back and looked at her, then took her coffee into the classroom.

While Joan had been swimming with the sharks last night, Maryl was joined by Chris, one of the shyer classmates, who was emboldened by his drink. He sat beside her in a poolside chair and attempted to talk about their class. They both ended up laughing about an instructor who had drawn what appeared to be a giant spider on the board. It was meant to be a database structure, but everyone was in stitches by the time he turned around.

This morning, Chris looked about as awful as Joan did, as he took a seat in class next to Maryl.

"Hey, I heard someone in the hall talking about the test. The answer to question twenty-three is G." Chris smiled at the gift he had given her.

"I heard that." Joan sat heavily in her seat and glared at Maryl.

"What's the death look for?" Maryl whispered to Joan as the instructor began handing out the test papers.

"Bitch," hissed Joan.

Maryl put her head down to concentrate on the test. But she couldn't get that look out of her head. She had seen it before.

Nine

August 1980

When she returned to the Bellevue office after the final training week, Raymond and Kyle popped a bottle of champagne in the office, celebrating that Maryl had finished the program.

She wanted to dance, she was so happy they were celebrating *her* but downplayed it. "Gosh, guys, you don't have to act so surprised that I made it through."

"Yes, but we are!" They laughed.

"What's the biggest thing you learned, Maryl?" Raymond asked as he pulled plastic glasses out of their sleeve.

"That DAMON was developed in a secret storefront in Stamford with sewing machines and pickle jars in the windows to throw off the spies."

"What?" Kyle swung around. Raymond just grinned.

"True story," said Maryl and held out her glass. "Four forty-one Summer Street."

Kyle laughed until he snorted.

"In all seriousness, Raymond Sir, I have to say that I had never paid much attention to newspaper articles about The Information Age. Seemed like some Aquarius Rising marketing lingo."

"And?" Kyle chimed in, glass raised for a toast.

"And there's something to it. We are transforming client data into information. And that information is power."

"Hear, hear." Kyle tipped his plastic glass at Ray and said, "I knew she would eventually get it."

"Gambling, Kyle?" Maryl laughed.

"I only bet on sure things."

They had invited Jean, the cheese shop owner, and Maryl's parents, none of whom attended.

With a pretend drumroll, Raymond opened the mail that had come that day holding Maryl's final grade for the program. She had tied for first place in her class with Joan.

"Isn't Joan the one you roomed with for training?" Raymond asked.

"Ha! More like Joan was her partner in crime," Kyle told Raymond. Maryl had relived some of the more exciting moments of training with Kyle over the last six months. She hadn't told him about the glare or the unsettling behavior of the last day since she figured it was just a hungover response and it would blow over.

"I thought you died," Max said as she jumped up onto the bar stool.

"Ha Ha. Guess what? I just graduated!"

"To queen from princess?" Max joked.

"And I tied for first place in the class, which was so cool. And now all that travel back-and-forth is done and—"

"Hold up, sister. Have a sip of this. It's my new Maryl Muddle."

"Max, aren't you going to congratulate me?"

"This *is* my congratulations. Now drink up and tell me you love it."

"Oh yum. It's so good. Is that ginger beer I taste? Yes, I accept your congratulations." She sipped the gin and lime juice and mint concoction, and yes ginger beer.

Over two more Maryl Muddles she told Max the story of Joan in all its color and drama. Max clapped his hands at one point, and when she was finished, he had one word to say. "Bitch."

A week later, Raymond came into Maryl's office with Kyle. Maryl had papered the walls with tips and diagrams from the class and was selectively taking some down and replacing them with new ones.

"What's up guys?" she asked as she surveyed the wall.

"Did you cheat on your test?" Raymond asked.

"What? No." She spun around.

"Well, apparently this Joan gal wants your name off the wall, saying she was the ace in class and that you cheated."

Maryl froze staring at something that wasn't there. Her mind raced.

After a minute, she said, "What the hell? Why would she do that? Doesn't make sense."

And then she remembered the comment Chris had made that morning. 'The answer to 23 is G.' But Joan had heard it too. *And anyway, the answer actually wasn't G. DAMON wasn't written in FORTRAN. SIMDAR was. DAMON was written in Assembler code. She had chosen the correct answer: E: Assembler.* She said nothing to Ray, but that afternoon she spilled it all to Kyle, her eyes stinging in disbelief that Joan would do that. But why?

"Could it be some kind of jealousy deal? I know how chicks get." Kyle was trying to be of some comfort but was failing.

Kyle was one of the leading technical engineers in the company but also had an MBA. He knew the product inside and out and could talk nerd to the user groups and finance to the CEOs who were only interested in the bottom line. Maryl adored him. He was part Irish and had thick black curly hair, strong brows, puppy dog eyes, and pale skin. They were about the same height, which Maryl called best-friend height. Kyle snickered when she said that.

"But jealous of what? She's a damn smart woman," Maryl answered.

"Come on, Maryl. Look at yourself. You don't have a clue why women would be jealous of you?"

She didn't. She was back to being comfortable around men—men who weren't named Leonard or Lenny or even Leo—so it was easy for her to talk to them. And sometimes that was hard for women who had no brothers or no college guys who had become lifelong buddies. She was fortunate. But guarded.

The next day a dozen roses arrived. From Frank, the VP, and Jeff, the lead trainer. There was a note. *Congratulations, Maryl. Don't worry about politics. You did good.*

She showed Kyle the note. He raised one eyebrow and looked at her.

"Oh shit." Maryl burst out. "Frank." And she proceeded to tell Kyle about the weird hot tub behavior that night at corporate. *So, yes. It must have been jealousy. It must have stemmed from Joan watching Maryl talk to Frank.*

That night she was on the phone to Helen.

"Oh wow," Helen was saying. "That's awful. Don't you want to call Joan and talk to her about it?"

"Come on, Hel. What do you think she would say to me? That she's sorry? That she didn't mean to tell headquarters I'm a cheat?" Maryl spoke too fast.

Helen knew her well, so she fell silent to let Maryl recover from that diatribe.

"Sorry, Hel," Maryl said eventually. "I'm not mad at you. I'm mad at Joan and the situation and maybe a little bit mad at myself."

"At yourself?" Helen asked.

"Yeah, dammit. I let my guard down. I didn't keep my gloves up. She sucker-punched me." Maryl sighed. "Damn. Damn. Damn."

Maryl leaned into the job, and within her first year with the company she was writing a weekly newsletter to all users of the software, instructing them on secret tips they should know to get more out of this software product. She had become a full-blown nerd. One of her jobs was to try to break the program by pushing it to do things her own way, not the way the instruction manual read, which was one of the reasons Raymond had hired her. She was quick to learn and always challenged the rules. Since most clients challenged the rules as well, often accidentally, she was perfect for the tech support role, helping customers get out of a programming mess or get around the rules in the user manual to produce reports they wanted.

But she was a tall, thin, red-headed nerd with crystal blue eyes and a quick wit.

Max told her it was her "balls" that attracted men. They visited often at the bar. One day he said, "I have news!" which turned out to be that he was madly in love with a man he had met and was moving to New York.

"No! Not fair! That's *my* dream, Max. You beat me to it." And they both laughed. She would miss him.

Since Maryl lived in the same town as George and Regina, she saw them often—too often in her opinion—and another holiday season was approaching with its short soggy days, dusk settling in at four in the afternoon. Today, she pulled down into their steep driveway and greeted Joey at the door before shedding her coat. She knew her corporate attire earned her parents' approval and used it to her advantage.

"Well, my buddy Max is moving to New York. He beat me to it." She said as she walked into the kitchen. Regina looked up but said nothing.

"I just saved you from having to ask how my day went." Maryl was trying to say something fun and light.

Regina scowled.

Maryl's mind was humming Donovan's song about the Season of the Witch.

"Mom, you must be feeling a little better. You're up and around in the kitchen. That's good to see."

"Well, who's going to fix dinner if I don't?"

George was watching the news about the assassination attempt on Reagan.

"Hi, Dad." Maryl thought about joining him but pushed up her sleeves instead and started slicing the hard-boiled eggs and chopping celery. Her mother had developed a taste for potato salad, but only if it was made with French's mustard. Not that designer kind. And it had to have celery in it. And pickles. Not just any pickles. They had to be garlic pickles. And olives. The black ones.

It was really a full meal in itself, Maryl thought, and one that her mother would eat. They chopped in silence, as the news anchors talked about the bullet in the brain of the press secretary.

Life is so short. She thought she should say something nice to her mother, so she ventured in a low voice, "You know, Mom, I understand about you and Dad. I hate his philandering too..."

"You don't know anything!" Regina picked up Joey and stalked down the hall.

Donovan was in her head again.

For the next several months, Maryl played tech backup to the sales guys in the office, attending client meetings in A-line skirts and ruffled blouses. She knew her stuff. When things got heated in a negotiation meeting, Maryl had a tendency to stand up, walk to the male client who was trying to low-ball, and say in a sultry tone, "Do you really want to go there, sir? My boss can be a real SOB but the guy over at IBM is worse. Trust me." It didn't always work, but it certainly gained her a reputation.

"Darrell Dizzle?!"

Maryl had on her highest heels and a sophisticated navy pin-striped pantsuit, heading through the maze of cubicles at Boeing Computing Services. She had stopped abruptly and burst out laughing at the name placard on one of the desks. The lessons in ladylike behavior she had been taught at The Assumption of the Blessed Virgin Mary grade school flew out the window. Her noisy outburst caused a man at the copy machine to jerk his head around to look at her.

She lowered her voice to a loud whisper and exclaimed again to Kyle, "Darrell Dizzle? Seriously? That's someone's real name??"

"Could you please shush?" Kyle glared as he motioned to her to hurry up. They were two minutes late for an important sales pitch to one of the biggest clients they could hope to land.

Maryl giggled. "But did you see that nameplate, Kyle?"

The glossy wooden double doors to the conference room were closed.

"Shit," said Kyle under his breath, as he pressed down on the brass lever to open it. He hated being late to anything. Maryl, on the other hand, didn't mind making a grand entrance. After all, she was quite often the only woman to enter a meeting like this and she took full advantage. She smiled at the six men around the table. May the best man win.

"Sorry we're late," offered Kyle.

"That's quite all right," said the gentleman at the head of the table. "I was a minute late myself as I had some last-minute copies to make." He turned slightly toward Maryl with a smirk. "My name is Darrel and I'll be leading the negotiations today."

"Jeez, you can take Maryl out of the country, but you can't take the c—" Kyle started in. The lot was full of vehicles that didn't have parking garage status: dozens of Camrys, Pintos, and Cutlasses. In sharp contrast, the lot at Maryl's office was full of beamers, 911s, Corvettes, and an occasional Pantera favored by all the young startup CEOs on the seven floors of glass and steel.

Maryl cut him off. "I know I know. It was just so funny. I couldn't help it. I mean, seriously, would you name your kid that?"

Kyle just shook his head. "You can be so sophisticated one minute and a small-town gal the next. Which is one of the reasons we get along, I guess." He winked at her over the top of his tan Audi as he unlocked the door.

Kyle reached under his seat and thrust his fist into a green sock puppet. "Oh hey, Darewool. You hab a bewwy funny name." The puppet wobbled in front of Maryl's face. "You almotht cotht me five hundwed big oneth back theww…" continued the puppet.

Maryl let out a belly laugh. One of Kyle's childhood fantasies had been to be a puppeteer. His grandmother had sewn several for him, and he still had four that he cherished. On occasion, Kyle would put on a skit for the office to show how to handle a troublesome customer. These shows were hysterical and were usually followed by beer and wine.

"Okay, okay. Now, where to for lunch, Miss Small-town Redhead?" Kyle started the car.

"Let's have Chinese," she answered. "I thought it was brilliant how you threw in the reference to the recent visit of China's senior leader, Deng Xiaoping, to their Everett facility. That got their attention, though they didn't say much about it, did they? Anyway, it got me jonesing for Chinese food."

Kyle and his wife had divorced a year ago and he had moved to an apartment. According to Kyle, she was a blonde beauty but turned out to be a blonde bitch. Maryl could not fathom anyone being bitchy to him. He was the kindest, funniest, and most supportive man she knew, and they were becoming best friends. They worked closely on most client deals, strategizing about their next steps. Maryl sensed that Kyle wanted to be more than friends, but she was still shy of jumping into anything complicated.

"It's time you bought something with that huge salary of yours," Kyle said one afternoon over lunch. "You need some investments of your own. I know how you want to make your dad proud. He's in the mortgage industry, right? He could get you a good rate."

Maryl had shared little about her relationship with her parents, but Kyle was right. She should start putting down roots and making smart money choices. She needed some investments, and the stock market was not her first choice. She called her college buddy, Fletcher, the one who had put most of his money into real estate.

Fletcher showed up in his handicap-retrofitted Audi and off they went to tour eastside condos.

Maryl navigated, holding the real estate list in her lap, and the third one they toured was a condo she could afford. It was an older building in Kirkland, another suburb, but it was clean and had a tiny view of Lake Washington. A month later it was hers.

Over the next year, Maryl bought four houses on the eastside through Fletcher's keen eye, most of them fixer-uppers, but the market was so cheap that she decided she would become a landlord. In no time, she found renters and borrowed forms for applications and contracts. She was set.

She was actually using her business acumen and doing things that would make her father proud. Doing the *shoulds*.

It was spring and Helen was pregnant again, this time with a little boy to join his big sister, Emma. But when Maryl spoke with her that evening on their every-other-month-if-they-were-lucky phone call, there was something Helen was not telling her.

"What's wrong, Hel?" Maryl asked over the long-distance line.

"Exactly," said Helen slowly.

"Huh?" Maryl was confused and concerned all at once.

"Yes. *Hell.*" Helen sniffed and proceeded to fill Maryl in on Doug's latest visit to the doctor. "He has been snoring a lot more, and we just thought it was sleep apnea and now the doctor is saying he has something wrong with his heart." Her words tumbled out. "He has to have something called CABG surgery, which is Coronary Artery Bypass Graft surgery, which sounds so darn scary, and the doctors here won't do it, so we have to go to San Francisco for a few weeks, and Maryl, I am just so nervous, but I can't let Doug see that, you know."

"Oh no, Hel. That's horrible. I can't imagine what you must be going through." Maryl knew that Doug was her whole world, and without him, she would be lost. "I can come down and be there with you. Why don't I do that? I could help you with Emma."

"No, no. Thanks though." Helen was blowing her nose. "And heck if I'd let you take care of my cat, let alone my firstborn."

"Well, there's that." Maryl was glad Helen hadn't lost her sense of humor, but she was worried about her friend. "Are you sure I can't come be with you?"

"My sister lives down there, so I'll stay with her until Doug is well enough to come home," Helen said. "I just can't believe this is happening..."

When they hung up, Maryl called her college friend, Brad, the neurosurgeon. She wanted to know more about CABG. He explained that the surgeon takes a healthy vein or artery from elsewhere in the body, then attaches one end to the aorta and the other end to the coronary artery past the blocked section. *Yes, Helen. It sounds scary.*

Maryl felt empty. Empty and useless and guilty. Guilty for ever complaining about anything in her life of good fortune and abundance and promise and choices.

Ten

One day in the summer of 1981, Raymond came into Maryl's office and asked her to step into his. Maryl loved this man like an older brother. He was the one who stood up for her in the beginning, urging the VP to look past her wise-cracking redhead schtick and give her a chance at this career.

"Oh no. What have I done now, Raymond sir?" Maryl asked. She had begun calling him that a year ago when it became clear that he believed in her and she trusted him with her career. He would always answer with "Just call me Ray, wouldya?"

Ray was tall, straightforward, steady as they come, and happily, happily married. Maryl, and everyone else in the office, loved Teri. Teri ran the family which included two handsome young boys, Ray's pride and joy.

When a person spoke, Ray would look straight at them with a slightly inquisitive look and wait for them to finish their pitch. He would then answer with as few words as possible or with a question of his own. And his intuition was spot on. Having perfected the guy-next-door demeanor, he would chat it up with female gate-keepers of the highest executives and get the appointment that no one else could. Or he could sit and listen to a long yawn-able presentation and boil it down to one sentence for Maryl afterward, including his assessment of the presenter. He was always two steps ahead. Sort of like Columbo, the deceptively absent-minded and bumbling detective on the surface, but extraordinarily sharp and perceptive underneath.

Sometimes Ray would nod to her in a client meeting, meaning for her to jump in and take the floor.

"We're not here to sell you our product," she parroted Ray. "The first step is to assess any problems you have getting at your data and then see if our product is right for you. We can't take on a client where we know we will fail them. It's not good for our reputation or your pocketbook." Clients loved it. Even Mr. Dizzle.

Maryl followed Ray into his office, jabbering to his back all the way down the hall. "You know I *am* working on the weekly report and will have it to you by end of day. And I've documented that tech glitch so that the users understand it and how we're fixing it—"

Ray stood behind his desk waiting for Maryl to stop. It was a power move that he had taught her: standing rather than sitting when facing someone who believes they have the upper hand.

Maryl grinned and sat opposite him.

"Mel." Ray and the guys had discovered her childhood nickname and liked it. "I wanted to give you some feedback on your work and talk about next steps. You've managed to piss off only a handful of people this past year, mostly within the company so that's good. And your mistakes can usually be fixed by Kyle or one of the guys. So, we have headcount for another salesman in the office. What do you think?"

Maryl looked up at him. "Me!"

Ray chuckled.

"Oh. You *did* mean me. As a salesman. Um, yes. Hell, yes." Salesmen made a ton more money than the tech reps and got to call all the shots.

"Well, hold on a minute. There is more training you'll need and some rules you are going to have to follow—or at least try to follow, Maryl."

Maryl was elated and couldn't wait to share the news with Helen. But she didn't pick up the phone to call her. Not this time. It was too much joy to cram down her throat. Doug was scheduled for his heart surgery in the next week, and Helen had already told her not to come. Her sister was there with her, and she would be fine. It was a common surgery; the doctor had assured her. Maryl stopped at Rite-Aid and grabbed a card for Helen. She sat in her car and wrote it out long-hand.

She drove to the strip mall, pulled up to the blue metal box, opened the squeaky hinged door, and deposited it with a sigh.

Since Maryl was now a salesman, she and Kyle had switched roles a bit: Now Kyle let her lead on the sales strategy and appointed Mark and Dan, the best techies in the branch, to her team. They were unbeatable. Over the next year, they landed Boeing, Puget Sound Power & Light, Ste. Michelle Winery, Weyerhaeuser.

The most rewarding part of the job, to Maryl, was the return visits to these clients once the contracts were all signed. They needed this software. Her company supplied it. She would meet with their internal teams to discuss which of their data loads were most burdensome and inaccessible, then return to the office, and she and Mark and Dan would map out the plans to apply her company's software to the problem.

Dan looked as if he came from swampland, sporting a long red beard and a wide girth. Mark had gotten him a job on the tech team in the Bellevue office since he wasn't making enough money as the bass player in a local band. They both played bass, but Mark was the older, responsible brother.

Together, they made heroes out of the decision-makers who stuck their necks out to buy this expensive system. They trusted her. It felt good.

One day she was finishing up a presentation to a room of end-users, as they called the ultimate users of their software within a client company. She had laid out some options for them about the sharing of data between their customer services, finance, and sales departments. Since Puget Power had commercial as well as residential customers, they needed to compare revenue and demographics across both sectors, so Maryl was outlining an analytic tool they could use within the product.

As the team gathered their notebooks and filtered out of the room, the head of the client services team approached Maryl.

"Hey, Maryl," said Albert. "What are you doing over lunch?"

"Is this a date? What would Becky say?" Maryl bantered back. She had met his wife at a user conference last month.

"No, I was hoping to bribe you with a hoagie if you drop me off at the Alfa dealership on Bel-Red Road. They called to say my car is ready, but Becky can't pick me up for another hour."

"Wow. Nice. Sure! I've always wanted to look at those."

Pasquale Perini was the very Italian lead mechanic of the Alfa dealership. Tall and weather-worn, he greeted Albert in a thick accent. "Welcome. Welcome. Nice to see you." He smiled from Albert to Maryl and back to Albert.

"How long have you been in the States?" Maryl asked as she shook his grease-stained outstretched hand after he rubbed it clean with a rag in his pocket.

"No use." He pointed to his hands. "Grease and dirt from my lovely automobiles. I've been here twelve years, and I'm buying this place from the owner. For my boys."

"Are they still in Italy?"

"Yes. Yes. They are good boys and love cars."

"I do too," Maryl said. "Particularly the nice ones." She motioned to the outdoor lot.

Her interest in the Alfa Spider started when Dustin Hoffman roared up to the gas station in The Graduate.

"Do you want to drive one?" Pasquale asked.

"What?"

"Do you want to take one for a drive?" Pasquale thought he hadn't said it correctly.

Albert had witnessed this exchange, and put his hands in the air, palms up. "Up to you, Maryl. They are just finishing up my paperwork and I'm outa here."

"Heck yes," Maryl said, and Pasquale led her inside to get some keys.

Maryl and Pasquale drove around for thirty minutes, on and off the freeway, only stopping for him to lower the top. She was thrilled. She was sold. She drove home that evening with a shiny new 1982 cream-colored black-top Alfa Romeo Series 3 Spider convertible.

Periodically, Ray would organize a "fun night" at his home, to celebrate the latest wins, or to salve the wounds of a loss. Having just landed the Weyerhaeuser deal, Ray wanted to acknowledge all the players who helped with that victory. Spouses were invited, and there were 22 altogether in Teri's kitchen, where guests gravitated towards the smells of lemon sauce and berry pie, and the charred BBQ chicken saved by Teri from the outside grill.

"Come dig in, guys," Teri commanded, and only the spouses were shy. One of the shyest, Tam, was from Vietnam and stood at the end of the line with Maryl, who had met her before. She was Mark's new wife.

"How is your family?" Maryl asked.

"My family okay but my mother very sick. My husband like job very much. We thank for that. But take care my sister, she five year old, little hard for us."

Tam's mother had been raped by pirates on the boat that was carrying them from Vietnam to Thailand when they fled six years ago. The story was horrible, and the recent news had come out that over 500 Asian refugee women were raped as they were fleeing the war.

As a result, Tam had a five-year-old sister who now lived with her and Mark.

"I'm sorry to hear that, Tam. Is there anything I can do for you and Mark?"

"You very kind." Tam smiled.

And I just bought a shiny new toy of a car. Ain't I a privileged bitch.

Eleven

George had been promoted once again, and they had moved from Bellevue to a penthouse suite in downtown Seattle, overlooking the waterfront. Regina had finished her chemo, and Maryl thought it was maybe a consolation prize for her. Floor-to-ceiling windows, brand-new appliances, and white carpet throughout. She shuffled around the condo like a ghost, aware that George was dallying again.

When Maryl visited, she and her father sat in the living room discussing his business and hers. She was in good favor now that she had a real corporate job and George could brag to his buddies that his daughter was in the technology world. He would pour her a G&T and treat her like they had always shared the Wall Street Journal and had the same viewpoint. Maryl kept the discussions to business only. She would let him be delusional. He needed that now.

"What did you call it again? When companies rent space on your computers?" her father asked her.

"Timesharing." Maryl slurped her drink.

"And how many companies are doing this now?" he asked.

"Are you asking how many clients we have or how many competitors we have?"

Maryl looked up as Regina walked in and sat down with Joey in her lap.

"Well, I always thought timesharing was about vacationing. Why do they call it that? Seems silly to use the same word—" Regina inserted herself into the conversation as she stroked Joey's head.

"Jesus, Gina," her father said. "You have no idea what we are talking about. You've never had any business experience. Just go back into the goddamn kitchen."

Tears sprang to her mother's eyes as she got up and retreated to the kitchen. Maryl did not go to her rescue, other than shooting a disapproving look at her father. It was about time her mother felt the same treatment as she had had for most of her life. She knew it was cruel to think.

She stared at her father, who looked away. "She just doesn't understand me." He sulked. She drained her drink, got up, and left through the elegant elevator that opened to their condo.

Every year, the company honored its top-performing salespeople with prestigious awards. Those who exceeded their quotas or brought in the most revenue were invited to an exclusive event called " theClub." For Maryl, 1982 had been her breakthrough year. Her exceptional performance earned her a spot at the coveted February gathering on Marco Island, Florida, where the award ceremonies would take place. Making theClub was a big deal - it meant recognition from the highest levels of management. Attendees would rub shoulders with VPs and even the CEO, ensuring their names would be known throughout the company's upper echelons.

It was a four-day boondoggle that was accepted industry-wide. Anything could happen. It was not unlike office Christmas parties at their worst. While Maryl was excited about the award, her enthusiasm for the trip battled with the haunting echoes of her previous Florida trip.

She hadn't told Kyle about that awful experience.

"What's up, Mel? I thought you'd be more excited," he said two days before she was to leave. Kyle was proud of her and knew that he was a big part of her success. She had told him so and had even suggested that he should go instead of her, which he thought was odd.

"You deserve this!" he told her with a little too much emphasis. She shuddered thinking back on what she deserved on her last trip to Florida.

"You'll have fun. Just watch out for the crocodiles."

"Alligators. There are more alligators than crocodiles down there," she said without thinking.

Kyle raised an eyebrow. "Well, aren't you the encyclopedia of creepy facts."

"Oh, I researched it a long time ago when I went down to the Keys with some friends," she said.

"Another unknown fact about the Irish lass." Kyle dropped it.

She flew direct from Seattle to Fort Myers, a seven-and-a-half-hour trip that challenged her neck and shoulders, not to mention her patience.

Maryl found her bag at the carousel and hopped the shuttle down to Marco Island. The van driver offered her an icy water bottle. "Sit back and relax, ladies. It's a cool hour and a half ride."

"Oh, you made it too," a woman said from across the aisle. "I like Sales much more than tech support, don't you?" she said to Maryl, who couldn't remember the woman's name but recognized her from training in Wilton.

"Oh, I don't know which I like better, but the sales commission wins hands-down." They laughed and spent the hour talking about the software and their worst client calls. Maryl was glad to have the distraction from Florida memories.

The shuttle van doors swung open, and they tumbled out into the heavy warmth. Balmy. It wouldn't be long before her mop of curls would be a huge ball of frizz. They walked under a large white arbor and into the cool air of the double-story lobby with its polished brown marble floors, beige couches, and large carved chairs made of exotic woods. A tall woman carrying a tray served them chilled champagne under a huge wooden ceiling fan as they waited in line at reception, staring out past the desk to a lush green courtyard.

"And here are the keys to your room," the receptionist drawled.

Maryl, finding herself among the minority of women at the Club, couldn't help but smile at the prospect of having a room to herself. She relished the luxury of spreading out across both beds, one for sleeping and the other for her "stuff" — shampoo, straightening iron, pajamas, underwear, books — knowing all too well the struggle for adequate hotel counter space. Plus, she shivered at the memory of her Wilton roommate, Joan, and wondered if she would be attending. After all, she was the top student in her class, Maryl snorted to herself.

With a cold Heineken from the mini bar, Maryl settled onto the couch with her itinerary notebook, eager to dive into the schedule for the week. Welcome cocktails beckoned at four-thirty on the patio, followed by a brief introductory meeting and year-end report in conference room J, before dinner at one of the resort's restaurants. Evidently, every day of the Club required at least a semblance of business activity to justify the expense.

At four-thirty, she took the elevator down. Spotting the woman from the shuttle enjoying a drink on the patio, Maryl made her way over, only to be intercepted by a tall man in sunglasses and a straw hat. "Hey, don't you write that tech newsletter?" He gave her a flirtatious smirk.

"Indeed, I do, though I've had to put that on hold since transitioning from tech to sales," Maryl answered without breaking stride, noting his self-assured demeanor and choosing to ignore it. *No need to stroke egos on this trip. This is about me. I deserve this* she thought. It was her 'redemptive pilgrimage' back to a place of horrible memories.

As she approached one of the senior directors she recognized from training, he greeted her. "Ah, the thorn in my side. You asked more questions in the six-month training program than all my former students combined."

"Well, nice to see you too, sir. I think. Although your bedside manner could use some work," she quipped, the playful banter easing any lingering tension.

As the meeting approached, they reluctantly made their way to conference room J, the effects of the welcome cocktails evident in the slightly disheveled appearance of the group. VP Frank Ward greeted them with a jovial tone, acknowledging their pasty complexions and advising them to buckle up and slather on the sunscreen for the week ahead. Some whistles came from the crowd.

Maryl turned in her seat to scan the room. She spied Joan to her right, already playing footsies with the guy in the straw hat. She noticed a man in the back row who glanced her way with expressionless eyes. Handsome, but blank. He cocked his head to the other side and looked away.

After the welcome meeting, Maryl joined one of the directors and two fellow award winners, one from Philadelphia and one from Newark, for dinner at the Tanglewood restaurant where she ordered a glass of house chardonnay, and the blackened mahi mahi with sweet potato and vegetable hash with a tropical fruit salsa. Absolute heaven. Across the room, she saw the expressionless man again. But this time he was laughing with others at his table.

"Who is that?" Maryl asked of her table mates, motioning with her napkin.

They all turned at once, causing Maryl to wince, and the director said, "Oh that's Ethan Krahlman, the youngest director ever in the history of Dun & Burkham. Stay clear of him. He's trouble."

"Wait. Dun & Burkham? Why is he at our meeting?"

"Oh! The cat's out of the bag. Part of the announcement at this conference is that D&B is purchasing us, and we will become their computing division."

Maryl found herself restless that night in the luxurious hotel bed. The news of a $500 million corporation purchasing them was heady stuff, but still, Dun & Burkham's acquisition of their company put her on tilt, stirring up a mix of emotions she couldn't quite untangle. On the one hand, there was a sense of excitement at the prospect of being part of a prestigious corporate entity like D&B. Plus, she might finally be able to step out of the shadow cast by her perfect older brother, senior partner of the largest small-town Wenatchee law firm. On the other hand, there was a nagging feeling of apprehension, a fear of losing the independence and freedom she cherished in her current role in her small Seattle branch far from the corporate eyes in Connecticut.

She reached for her phone on the nightstand, feeling the need to share her thoughts with Kyle. As she dialed his number, she couldn't shake the image of Ethan Krahlman from her mind. There was something about him, an enigmatic allure that both intrigued and unsettled her. She couldn't quite put her finger on it, but she had a feeling their paths would cross again.

"Hey, Ky," she greeted when he answered.

"Hey, Mel. What's up? It must be late back there." Kyle's voice was warm and familiar, instantly soothing her.

"I just needed to talk," she admitted, her words tumbling out in a rush. "Did you know about D&B acquiring us?"

"Yeah, I did," Kyle confirmed. "Ray filled me in earlier. It's big news."

Maryl let out a sigh. He listened attentively, offering words of reassurance and empathy. He could hear the shock in her voice. They talked late into the night, their conversation meandering from work to personal anecdotes of the day. Maryl was tempted to ask Kyle what he knew about this Ethan character but decided against it. She updated him on Mark and Tam, suggesting they do something for them. Tickets to the zoo? Pay for a babysitter?

As Maryl finally slept, she was thankful for Kyle's validation, making her feel that, in the uncertainty of the days ahead, she knew she could weather the stormy seas of corporate change. It was nothing compared to what Tam's mother had gone through. And as the first light of dawn filtered through the curtains, she felt a sense of humble gratefulness.

People would kill to have my problems.

TWELVE

The following day at the promised a rare luxury: six whole hours of free time. While some opted for fishing or golfing, the majority gravitated toward the beach, and Maryl was no exception. She squeezed herself into a daringly vibrant turquoise bathing suit, grabbed a towel and water bottle at the pool, and made her way out to the sand. The beach buzzed with activity, from kite-flying to volleyball and the intricate artistry of sandcastle building. Maryl strolled along the shoreline, taking it all in and relishing the opportunity to soak up the sun from every angle, determined to return to Seattle with an even tan.

Midway through her return journey along the sand, Maryl was somewhat shocked by the sight of Ethan Krahlman strolling toward her on the beach. Alone. She inhaled sharply at the sight of him, wearing a simple pair of swim trunks that hung slightly below his pelvis. Yet, to her surprise, he simply mumbled a greeting as he passed, something he might have said to any stranger, his expression unreadable.

Later, Maryl encountered Ethan once more, this time seated on the patio with paperwork spread out before him. Shirtless and shoeless, he seemed entirely absorbed in his task, a dark, cold drink adorned with a lime resting nearby. Maryl offered a casual hello as she passed, headed for the coolness of her room. He didn't respond. Was it his apparent aloofness that piqued her interest? Was that his intention? She didn't know or care as she collapsed on her bed for a short nap before the evening festivities.

The bedside phone was ringing. She picked it up with both eyes closed. "Hello?"

"What, you're sleeping in the middle of the day?" It was Kyle.

"Oh, well, you know there's this thing here in Florida that makes you sleepy during the day. It's big and round and yellow and hot." She yawned. "I don't think we have it out there."

"Very funny. So, are you looking forward to all the pomp and circumstance tonight? Accepting your award for being such a great salesman?"

"Sales *woman*," she corrected him. "And just so you know, there aren't that many of us here."

"It's a common statistic," offered Kyle from his engineering perspective. "The ratio, I mean."

"You are such a nerd, Ky." She smiled into the phone.

"Why thank you, Princess Maryl," he jabbed back. "Okay, I'll let you go get ready for the big night. And let me know what secrets they lay on you tonight about D&B."

"Okay." She hung up.

As evening descended, cocktail hour ushered in yet another business meeting, highlighting the week's main event: the awards ceremony. But first, more about the merger—the takeover—whatever they were calling it.

Ethan Krahlman took the floor to deliver the presentation. His confident stance and easy charisma captivated the room as he effortlessly navigated through the intricacies of the agreement between Dun & Burkham and their company. Maryl watched in awe as he wove together complex concepts with a touch of humor, making the subject matter accessible and engaging. Several people nodded and when he was finished, there was a round of loud applause.

Maryl found herself dumbfounded and impressed by the man she had previously dismissed as handsome but aloof. When the room was clearing, she approached him and said, "Hello. Great presentation. I'm from the Bellevue office."

"I know who you are."

She stared at him and started again. "I noticed you on the patio today."

"And I noticed you." he stared back and returned his focus to his slides.

"So, I guess you were working on this presentation out there?" she commented.

Ethan turned. He frowned at her. "You are really bad at flirting." When she didn't respond, he said. "Do you want to continue this game, or do you just want to go to dinner?"

"Ummm sure," she said a bit too weakly.

"Meet me out front by the taxis in half an hour," he instructed.

Maryl turned and wobbled out of the room, unsure of what had just happened. Once in her room, she stared in the mirror. *What the hell? Is he an ass or a god? And, either way, what am I doing going to dinner with him?*

She changed clothes again and hurried down to the lobby. Ethan was out by a cab, looking at his watch. When she appeared, he jumped in on one side, and she got in on the other.

"The Lagoon House," Ethan instructed the driver.

Ethan turned to Maryl. "Look. Let's set a few ground rules here. I don't play games. You've been checking me out and I've been checking you out. I like what I see and hear about you, but we haven't spent any time together. So, we're going to do that this week, okay? And we'll see where it takes us. I don't like to waste my time, and you shouldn't waste yours either. Are we clear?"

"Crystal clear. But you'll have to be okay with me asking a ton of questions if you want us to have any sort of resolution of this in the next few days." Maryl tried to match his cadence. After all, this was half her adventure, too. "So, first of all, why have people warned me away from you?"

"Because I can be an ass."

"Already noted. And I can be a bitch."

"I'll bet you can be."

"But only as a defensive maneuver."

"Fair enough."

"Where do you live?"

"Philadelphia main line."

"What's a main line?"

"It's where all the prominent Jewish families live."

"I see. I don't come from money. Just so you know."

"Then you'll have to make your own."

"True. Trying. And I'm not Jewish."

"Not yet."

Maryl smiled.

"Why do you live in Seattle?"

"I've been in the Pacific Northwest most of my life, one way or another. Grew up in a small town in Washington, went across state to college, left for some adventures, returned to visit one holiday, and ended up getting a job at this company. There. In that branch. A mistake sort of. Or just a turn of events, I guess I should say. Why do you live in Philadelphia?"

"It's where my parents live."

"You live with your parents?"

"Don't be a smartass."

"Do you like your family?"

"They're my family!"

And there began Maryl's education about Jews versus Catholics, East Coast versus West, and the powers of persuasion.

Ethan paid the driver, and they entered the Lagoon House, greeted by the delicious smells of roasted peppers and parmesan and papaya and lemon and olive oil and butter.

Once they were seated, Ethan softened. "You can have anything you want. The company is buying. God, I'm glad to get away from the group for a while."

"I'm flattered."

Ethan had thick dark unruly hair, a freckled face, wide shoulders, nails bitten down to the quick, a deep rich voice, and thin lips that he never quite closed, exposing two front teeth whiter than the rest. She continued to ask questions as they ate seared halibut, beef short ribs, and vegetable risotto, all cooked to perfection.

Ethan answered everything she asked in a charmingly direct manner, telling her that he was just driven enough to be put in charge of things at a young age, and that he now ran the NYC office, commuting daily by train from Philly. He had plans to take over the Philly office too but with this new transition, he had to wait to submit the request. He asked about her childhood, her parents, her schooling, her siblings, her goals in life, and he even touched her hand for longer than necessary when offering her some of his beef.

After two hours at the table, Ethan suggested they stroll outside and took her by the hand. They talked for hours, laughing at things they had in common: no patience with stupid people, perfectionism, preference for warm vacation venues instead of cold ones, love of the same favorite films, distaste for opera and stinky house pets, and bad breath in general. All the important things.

And they talked about religion. Jewish. Catholic.

"So, I've always wondered about Judaism, Ethan. Mind if I pick your brain a bit?"

"Fire away! And you can tell me about your Catholic stuff too. What's on your mind?"

"Well, I'm actually not a practicing Catholic, as I have many issues with the church, but I can tell you what we—they—believe."

"Fair enough."

"So, I noticed you guys don't really say "God" much. What's up with that?"

"Good catch! Yeah, we're kind of big on respecting God's name. We usually go with "Hashem." It means "The Name," or "Adonai," which is like saying "Lord." It's our way of keeping things respectful, you know?"

"Huh, that's cool. We throw "God" around pretty freely, but we've got other names too, like "Father" or "Lord." I guess we're both trying to show some respect, just differently."

"Right. Hey, I've always wondered about all those statues and pictures in your churches. We don't do that at all. What's the deal?"

"Oh, those? We're not worshipping them or anything. They're more like... visual aids for prayer. And to give a shout-out to saints and holy people. Helps make the faith feel more real, I guess. But yeah, I can see how it might look weird from your side."

"Weird to me but makes more sense now. Oh, and what's the story with the Pope? We don't have anyone like that."

"The Pope's like... the big boss, I guess? He's supposed to be St. Peter's successor, leading the whole Catholic show. But hey, who's in charge for you guys?"

"We've got rabbis. They're like our scholars and teachers. But there's no one big kahuna for all of Judaism. Different Jewish crews might follow different rabbis they respect, but there's no one ringleader for everyone."

"Huh, that's pretty different. But who has the last word on what's right or wrong? Don't you guys feel lost without a leader?"

"Just the opposite. We've got more room for different takes on things. And we love a good debate. There's even a joke: "Two Jews, three opinions!" What about you Catholics?"

"Catholics are more structured, in a control-freak way, in my opinion. Rules for rules' sake. Hey, what do you guys think about the afterlife? We've got the whole Heaven, Hell, and Purgatory thing going on."

"Afterlife stuff is pretty vague for us. We're more about living it up right now, you know? We've got some ideas like Olam Ha-Ba—the World to Come—and Gan Eden, which is like Paradise. But we don't obsess over it like you guys seem to."

"Well, personally I believe in an afterlife. I guess your Paradise is like our Heaven. But, yeah, Catholics do obsess over stuff. At least we're both big on doing good and living right, yeah?"

"We call it Tikkun Olam—fixing up the world. It's all about making things better through what we do. It's a proactive effort to create a just society."

"Interesting. I like it. So how do you translate 'justice'? I mean, do you sacrifice your firstborn to God or something?"

"Very funny, Miss Wisecracker. But yes, that's a tricky one. The Torah states, "You shall not take vengeance or bear a grudge" but we also have a concept called "midah k'neged midah" (measure for measure)."

"Sounds like the 'eye for an eye' concept. That's vengeance, right?"

"Not really. It isn't about personal revenge, but rather a belief that God alone ensures ultimate justice."

"Ah. Right. 'Let God be the judge of that.' I'm sure that was in a movie somewhere. You know, Ethan, I really don't subscribe to the Catholic stuff anymore. Two of the teachers I do follow are Osho Rajneesh and Paramahansa Yogananda, and it sounds like Judaism has some of the same beliefs."

"I have no idea who those two guys are. Why do you like them?"

"Well Osho was into uninhibited self-expression and breaking free from societal conditioning—which I translate to political and corporate stuff—and Paramahansa believed in a balanced approach to everything; Do your spirit work, your meditation, your yoga, but then get at it; Go do your life and your job according to man's rules on this planet."

"So, Osho was into psychedelic mushrooms maybe?"

Maryl chuckled. "You might be right."

"Here's one more question about Catholics. What's the deal with wine in your Sunday ceremony? We use wine for Kiddush on Shabbat and holidays, but it seems different for you guys."

Maryl touched the coin hanging at her neck. "Yeah. It's supposed to be Christ's blood. I know that sounds gross and almost pagan. Catholics believe it actually becomes Christ's presence when you sip it. Sort of like summoning the dead, to me. I've always found it creepy. Not to mention, germy. It's a big deal in Mass, kind of like a replay of the Last Supper."

"You're a funny girl. We don't have anything quite like that, but wine's still pretty important for us – it's all about joy and making things holy."

"I'll drink to that."

"Let's get a nightcap then."

At the end of the evening, Ethan said goodnight in the lobby and asked if they could dine the next night as well. Maryl agreed.

"I don't think I've met a woman like you," he said. "I must say I'm intrigued."

Back in her room, Maryl closed the door and leaned her back against it, and then her shoulders and then her head. *What just happened?* She said it out loud. Looking up at the ceiling she let out a long slow sigh. She had never felt this way.

She woke to the alarm the next morning and smiled and smiled even before she opened her eyes. Ethan found her at the breakfast buffet and asked how she slept, to which she replied, "Without a dream or nightmare."

"And is that so unusual?" Ethan asked.

"Oh yes," she answered. "So, thank you."

"All that good food." He smiled.

"Uh Huh. Must be it."

They sat next to each other at the conference that morning with feigned attention, touching knees under the draped tables, thinking about the next time they could be alone together. When Ethan was called on for an answer, he didn't miss a beat, and always injected some humor in his response. People laughed. He laughed. Maryl laughed. The world was very bright.

They dined together that evening and talked into the early morning. He was a fascinating man who was driven and purposeful and didn't apologize for it. His stance on politics closely followed her own, though his viewpoint was from the East Coast and the places that made history and translated history down to its most raw form and impact on the world.

To him, Seattle was an afterthought. He couldn't understand why, given the choice, anyone would choose the west coast. Maryl countered with stories of mountains – real mountains, not the short hills of Pennsylvania – and deep snow and lush forests and blue skies and clean air and wild animals and cabins and the smell of dirt and grass and sitting in a meadow with a picnic basket. Stories that sounded like made-up stories to Ethan.

"I'm sensing a soft side to the tough bitch," Ethan joked.

"That's not a bad thing."

He told her that he liked the way she wore her hair and the way she wore her clothes and the way she walked and the scent that she wore. Once again, he said goodnight in the lobby, and they went to their separate rooms.

Maryl awoke to sadness, knowing she was going home to the West Coast and Ethan to the East. She got up and sat on the vanity stool and looked in the mirror. The phone rang.

"Don't go home yet." It was Ethan.

"What do you mean?" Maryl asked.

"Don't go home yet. I've rented a suite at a resort in Fort Myers for three more days. Let's make it a whole week together. I'll pay the difference in airfare."

"But...but what about my job? What about my schedule back in Seattle?" She wanted to stay but she was also a responsible girl, and besides, she had to check on her dad and mom. What was she doing? She had to go back to those who depended on her. No, she would go home today. This was just a fling. Nothing more.

"I'll call Ray and make it happen for you, okay? Don't worry about a thing. Are you good with that?" Ethan asked with a kind but all-business voice.

"Um, let me think. I don't know. Give me a few minutes and I'll call you back." Maryl fingered her necklace and spun around on the stool to look out the window. Her heart was so full. This was the man she'd always dreamed of.

She looked in the mirror again. Her ribcage felt too tight. Even though they had never slept together, and she had always been clear with Kyle, she knew that he had wanted more in their relationship, and now she felt guilty, knowing this would hurt him.

First his wife and now me, she thought. On the flip side, she hadn't done this intentionally. It just happened. Was she supposed to pass up this opportunity for true love and go back to a super sweet guy who was "good enough?"

Maryl grabbed the hotel phone and dialed Ethan's room. "Okay, Ethan. I don't think we'll get this chance again. Let's do it. What will you tell Ray?"

"What do you mean? He's a guy. I'll just tell him like it is: You and I are interested in each other and, as long as we're out here, we're just asking for three or four days to see what comes of it. Christ, it's not like we're eloping or doing something illegal. We're just going to sneak away for a few days. I'm sure he'll understand. Besides it's really only two more business days, since the weekend is coming up." Ethan sounded so confident. She said okay and hung up.

And then there was Ray, who probably wanted Maryl and Kyle to end up together. As she pondered Ray's potential reaction to her burgeoning feelings for Ethan, she wondered if he would disapprove. Perhaps even admonish her with a stern lecture? The last thing she wanted was for Ray to guilt her into abandoning her newfound connection with Ethan, or worse, to persuade her to return immediately and live happily—or unhappily—ever after with Kyle, the safe, reliable option. *Safe and reliable?* Kyle was a fine man, a steadfast presence in her life, but he lacked the magnetic allure and spark that drew her toward Ethan. After this week, she couldn't spend the rest of her life with *safe and reliable.*

She needed the exhilarating rush of emotions she felt in Ethan's presence. She yearned to explore this unfamiliar territory, to bask in the warmth of newfound affection without the burden of guilt or obligation. *But could she? Did she deserve it?* In this moment, she craved the freedom to be selfish, to pursue her own happiness, consequences be damned. For Maryl, the allure of what could be outweighed what might be lost, and she resolved to follow her heart on this one. *It was just a weekend.*

Thirteen

"Just a weekend. Yes, but it's still sex, right?" Helen was counseling her friend on the phone. "What about Kyle? I was thinking he might be the one for you...."

Maryl's heart raced and her eyes stung. Her best friend was calling her out.

"I know. I'm a shit!" she replied to Helen, the sage.

"No no. Sweetie, you're not a shit. You're a strong woman with a lot of passion, and nowhere to put it."

Maryl pondered that. Was she interested in Ethan only because of the fiery passion in her gut?

"But what if Ethan is truly the one for me? I'll never know. And I don't want to go back without pursuing it a bit further. I mean we live 3000 miles apart."

Helen sighed. "You are going to do what you want to do, Maryl. Just be sure it's for the right reason. I know you. This could just be another challenge you want to accept. Another adventure. Let me ask you a question: What if Kyle asked you to marry him and the two of you would move to Manhattan and start a company of your own?"

"What?" Maryl had been pacing but sat down on the padded bench at the end of the bed. Helen knew that living in New York City had been a dream of Maryl's since they were kids. A dream that she had stuffed down deep as a someday thing... a Pollyanna thing.

"But he wouldn't," she finally answered. "That's the thing. Kyle is too practical and too steady for that. And I don't even know if he would *want* to marry me. This is getting way out ahead of things."

"Okay."

Before Helen hung up, she said, "You know I believe in you, girl. Why don't you pray on it tonight and then you'll know."

"I'd rather listen to Rush," Maryl mumbled as she hung up.

It was just that easy for Helen. Always. She would pray on things and then take the path that manifested. She believed Jesus Christ was her savior and was helping her every step, so she "let go and let God" with just about everything.

Maryl thought Helen was too trusting in this Catholic God and didn't push hard enough for the things she might want. She just said prayers to the man in the clouds and whatever happened was meant to be. But Helen was smart and not blind to reality, and she was a true friend to Maryl, so she never chided her about it. Much.

With Rush singing Freewill on the clock radio, Maryl pulled a plastic bottle of gin from the mini fridge in the room.

Hell, it's not like I'm a virgin. Maryl was self-talking now—or ratio-nalizing. *And Kyle and I have no commitment to each other at all. And I have my whole life ahead of me. And Ethan knows so much that I could learn about this company... and...* Her thoughts were interrupted by the phone ringing. She looked at the clock. It was probably Kyle. She didn't answer.

That night, Maryl drifted into a deep sleep and dreamed.

The Pope was sitting in the Basilica on the oaken Throne of Saint Peter with its carved ivory trim, looking kindly at Maryl. "Do you want some help with this decision?"

"No thanks," she said. "I know what you're going to say. That I'm already damned because I'm not a virgin and that I could redeem myself by eating that little round bread thing at church."

The Pope responded, "The Church teaches the sanctity of com-mitted relationships and the sacrifices that go along with them. You should seek divine guidance. Get down on your knees."

"Been down that road. Didn't help."

Almost magically, but logically to Maryl's dream mind, the other spiritual leaders she had studied came floating around her with their advice. She was almost certain they could hear her.

Osho Rajneesh with his fleece cap said, "Experience life in all possible ways — good-bad, bitter-sweet, dark-light, summer-winter. Experience all the dualities. Don't be afraid of experience, because the more experience you have, the more mature you become."

"Thumbs up to that," she said. Osho was one of her favorites, as he believed, as she did, that there was no God, but that there was godliness, and that each person makes their own heaven or hell.

Joseph Smith Jr. sat in a stick chair in his starched collar, looking straight ahead: "Seek guidance through me, since God speaks directly through me alone. Consider the commitments you've made. Repent, be baptized, and receive the Holy Ghost."

"Seriously?" she said. "This advice from a guy with thirty wives?"

Paramahansa Yogananda with his huge brown eyes and delicate features spoke to her. "Look within and meditate on this decision. Is the pull to Ethan coming from a place of spiritual growth or egotistic desire? Pursue the path that leads to greater self-realization and harmony for all involved."

"Ugh. I hate what you're saying but you make a good point," she said.

She woke up exhausted with the bed sheets soaked. Before dressing, before even coffee, she sat on a towel on the floor with her heels pulled up under her, closed her eyes, and tried to block out the world.

F O U R T E E N

Ethan had hired a car for the one-hour drive up to Fort Myers and was holding Maryl's hand as they settled in for the trip.

Heading up I-75, Ethan asked, "Do you know about the Ten Thousand Islands south of Marco Island?"

"Really? There are ten thousand islands??" Maryl marveled. "My father would say 'Well, I'll be a hornswoggled toad.'"

"Is your father a hillbilly?"

"No. Not at all. It's just an old saying that his father and probably everybody's father said back in the day."

"Like Great Scott, huh." Ethan grinned. "My ancestors would probably have said "Oy gevalt!"

"I'll have to log that in my brain for later," Maryl said. "Anyway, back to the ten thousand islands...."

"Well, it's a mythical story, but there are hundreds of them, some only a few meters long, and some underwater. Don't you have some old history like that out there in Seattle-land? Oh." Ethan paused dramatically. "That's right. You don't have history out there. All the history is out here on the East Coast."

Maryl jabbed him playfully in the ribs. They had a running jousting session about which coast was best.

"We have Bigfoot," Maryl pointed out.

"Now that's a fairy tale, not a historical myth!" Ethan laughed.

The car pulled up in front of the Hyatt Regency at Coconut Point, and two attendants arrived to open the doors. Ethan walked up the steps and said over his shoulder, "I'll go get the keys."

Maryl squinted against the sun, tenting her hand over her eyes. She wondered if they had laundry facilities, as she had only brought enough clothes for the conference. The hotel seemed lovely, with large squares of patio rock and greenery growing between them on out to the sand. She was certain that Ethan would return with keys to only one room, and she was very much okay with that at this point. Every minute with him was better than the last. Despite knowing him for mere days, she felt a rare and growing ease in his presence. They were in a bubble it seemed. No one else mattered. They were each other's life sustenance.

Just for the weekend.

She had never seen such a lovely suite. The king bed had mounds of pillows and comforters. The bathroom had two plush robes and a dozen towels for each of them. High-end toiletries were all provided, and there was already a bottle of champagne on ice, a fully stocked minibar, and a fruit and cheese basket. And a separate sitting room!

"What? Do you know the owner or something?" She turned her gaze his way.

"Why yes. Yes, I do." He smiled. "My family comes down here a lot."

She didn't need the laundry facilities, as they wore no clothes except swimsuits for the next four days. They slept in each other's arms, they ate in bed, they swam together and read by the pool and ate fruit and drank champagne and lived an unimaginably regal life for those days.

She coaxed Ethan into talking about his family. He had one sister, Ellen, who had a wealthy Jewish boyfriend and a marketing job at a city magazine. They visited their parents' house weekly if not more.

"Ellen is closer to Dad, and I'm closer to Mom, but each would give us a lung if we asked. Of course, it may be the other way around since Mom still smokes a pack a day." Ethan told her.

"There were five of us kids, all 2 years apart. My poor mom. One was born severely retarded, and she's in an institution now."

"I'm sorry. What about your other siblings?"

"Older brother, Steven, a big real estate attorney in the Aggie industry. Then me. Then younger brother, Billy, who is always in some kind of trouble. And then my little sister, perfect Agnes."

"Perfect Agnes?" Ethan grinned at her.

"Not even close. But she was born after the not-so-perfect one and had all her limbs in the right places, so my Mom constantly told her 'You're so perfect' probably even to this day."

"Sounds like an interesting family. Are you close to any of them?"

"Billy and I get along, although he's currently peeved that I sold out and joined the corporate world."

"What does he do?"

"Mostly pot."

"Wow. So different than my family, or any of my friends' families. In the Jewish community, it's all for one, and we take care of our own. Always. No matter what they do or don't do for us. You will want to convert."

"Oh, is that so?"

"I'm sure of it."

"Have you converted most of your previous girlfriends?"

"Didn't have to. They've all been Jewish."

"And I'm not."

"No. You're a shiksa."

"Sounds pejorative."

"My family won't care. They just want everyone to be happy and get along."

"So do you celebrate all the Jewish religious holidays?"

"Well, of course, but they're not really religious holidays like you have in the Catholic Church. They're more like bonding parties, or historical gratitude events that celebrate how far we've come as a body of Jewish people together. Most happen at home and not in a church building. And we reinstate our vows of loyalty and support to each other several times a year."

"That sounds nice."

"It's the way it's been for generations."

"Sounds like the mafia."

"Ha. Very similar."

"I believe that humans are all one race, and fighting over dogma is ridiculous. I also don't believe this Jesus Christ guy was the only one sent to this planet to help us get our act together."

"And how do you define getting our act together?"

"Being kind. Walking a mile in another's shoes, as they say. Leveling the playing field so no one is dirt poor and sick and no one sits on the throne of wealth."

"Hold up. I'm into wealth. I mean, if I earn it, it's mine. And I work damned hard. Doesn't mean I won't share."

"We share a hard work ethic."

"I can see that."

"And I don't think we'll ever have world peace. We live on a planet of win/lose."

"Just like business."

They talked for hours about family and work and philosophy and real estate and money and everyone in the company they knew in common and some that they didn't. They agreed about many things but enjoyed the banter of disagreement about others. It was refreshing, honest, respectful, and freeing.

On the last day together, they were preparing to call Maryl's parents and tell them they had found each other. Finally, they had each found the person of their dreams.

She sat on the bed with Ethan holding her in his arms. "I'm nervous," she whispered, looking at the phone.

"Why? It doesn't matter what they say, Maryl. It's no one's business but ours."

"You're right. You're right. I just think it would take some pressure off me if they knew I finally found someone for a permanent relationship."

"Like theirs?"

"Well, hopefully not like theirs," she mumbled.

"So, they'll be happy for you?" Ethan asked the question that was in her mind.

She dialed.

George and Regina were silent at the other end of the phone.

Then they peppered them with questions on speakerphone. *How long have you known each other? What are your plans? Who is going to compromise and move? What about the religious difference?*

And then a heap of admonishments: *You don't know what you're doing. You are just thinking of sex. You have no idea what real love is. This is totally irresponsible of both of you. Shame on you. We had hoped you were smarter than that.*

Maryl hung up and crashed down from the highest height of bliss to crushing shame and disappointment, and Ethan declared them to be idiots.

On the plane back to Seattle, Maryl stared out the window.

George and Regina weren't the worst parents. They just didn't love each other anymore and hadn't for a long time. In fact, George probably stayed now out of guilt, since Regina had cancer. It had been difficult navigating through their moods and phases, including George having his long affair. It was easy to figure out why they had reacted the way they did on the phone with her and Ethan. Maryl felt foolish for thinking they would be overjoyed for her. But it had been a forceful punch in the gut. She blinked back tears in seat C12, as Mount Rainier came into view, and they began their descent.

"Ladies and Gentlemen, please fasten your seatbelts."

She didn't even unpack when she arrived home, opting to crawl into bed and spend the next two hours sobbing. She was dead tired, emotionally drained, and dreading going into the office the next day. But also because there was a kernel of truth in her parents' blistering rebuttals. She didn't really know Ethan that well. She was making life-altering decisions. And what about her job? What if she lost her job over this?

She looked like hell at the office in the morning. Kyle wasn't there. Something about a sudden client meeting in San Francisco.

Ray told her she looked awful and took her to the downstairs coffee shop to chat. *Did he know about Ethan? Did he know what the D&B purchase would do to their office? Was he mad at her for falling for this guy? Had he told Kyle? What was Kyle's reaction? Why wasn't Kyle in the office?*

No. No. No. Yes. He shook his head but looked her in the eye and told her he just wanted her to be happy. Whatever he could do to help her, he would.

Kyle was gone for two weeks. She tried calling him. She missed him. He didn't answer her calls. Then he came back for a day. Her face lit up when she saw him in the hall, but he looked at her with dead eyes and walked past her with no words. She was crushed. He left again the next day for what Ray said was a special project in California.

Ethan and Maryl spoke on the phone for hours every night, and sometimes during the day. They now had company issues to sort out, given the D&B news. Ethan became more interested in her daily life, and Maryl in what was happening in New York and Philadelphia with the takeover.

They each flew to Chicago for a weekend and stayed at the gorgeous Chicago Hilton with a suite overlooking Lake Michigan. They wandered through the Shedd Aquarium building where the Caribbean Reef exhibit was. Maryl spent an hour staring through the glass at creatures of all colors. Underwater scenes always transported her to a sort of spiritual world where souls floated around like angelfish and gravity could be upside down and everything was love and bright colors. Until one soul got chomped on by another, that was. Scuba diving was on her bucket list for sure. Ethan had no interest in leaving a perfectly paved cityscape.

He came up beside her, slipped his hand in hers, and calmly suggested that she move to Philadelphia and live with him. Turning to look him in the eyes, she saw that he was serious. He held her gaze for just a moment and then looked away and said, "Or not."

"Oh, babe. I wasn't hesitating. Oh... well, I guess I might have been, but yes! Don't think I haven't considered it. I was just waiting for an invitation and now you've given me one. I'm so happy." She kissed him there in front of Nickel, the rescued green sea turtle.

"So that's a yes?" he asked.

She wouldn't give up her career for a man. Any man. She had no friends on the East Coast and no business contacts there. But as black and white as Ethan positioned himself, that would not be a good approach to the conversation.

"Ethan, you know I've fallen hard for you. But I have definite goals for my career, and I'm afraid I'd have to give up my job if I quit now. Especially with no job to go to. And I don't want to work for a competitor. I've already been researching that."

"We can figure it out," he said. "Let's go get some lunch and talk about it later." And they did. For two days they revisited the conversation until they were exhausted. Leaving each other that weekend without a resolution was hard.

Fifteen

Last week, they had talked to exhaustion about the move. Ethan had called and said, "I've been thinking. Why don't I come out there and visit for a few days? See where you live, what is holding you back from moving, and just talk things out. You can show me around."

And here he was. In her city. In her new Alfa. In her real life. For a few days.

"What do you want to see first? The Space Needle? The waterfront? Shall we go up to Mount Rainier? Out to the Olympic Forest? OH. And there's an underground city tour...."

"Hold on. Hold on. Settle down." He looked at her with a huge grin. "Are you trying to sell me on moving HERE?"

She smiled. "I'm just so excited for you to see why I love it here so much."

"And what I'm snatching you away from..." he smiled back. "I see what you're doing."

She sped onto I-5, and then veered onto 405, headed toward one of her favorite restaurants at the top of the tallest office building in Bellevue. From there, Ethan would see Lake Washington glittering in the sun, and Seattle beyond it, with the Olympic Mountains towering to the west. A perfect venue. And besides, she didn't want to just go to her house and fall into bed with him. They would waste an entire day that way.

"What's so funny?" Ethan yawned next to her in the warmth of the car.

"I'm taking you to one of my favorite restaurants, so we don't waste our first day in bed." She shot him a sideways glance as she sped around a shiny black Mercedes. "And why are you yawning? Didn't you sleep in the plane?"

"A day in bed wouldn't be so bad," he teased. "Yeah, I tried sleeping but the guy next to me was snoring the whole time. So annoying."

They sat with their knees touching, gazing out at the view. Luckily, the day was spectacular. "Wow I didn't realize the air could be so clean," Ethan was saying. "I thought it was rainy all the time here."

"We like people to think that." Maryl stirred her drink.

"I can see all the way to those mountains. Nice. So, where's your place? Can we see it from here?"

"Olympics."

"What?"

"You said mountains. There are so many mountains here, Ethan." She teased him. "Those are the Olympics. Behind us are the Cascades."

"Okay smarty pants. Can we see your place from up here on the twentieth floor? And, just to remind you, we have restaurants on the thirtieth floor out there."

She ignored that. "Almost. It's just over that hill." She pointed north. One of the real estate purchases she had made was in Kirkland, a suburb just north of Bellevue. She had sold her condo and moved into the little corner house a year ago, adding a deck on top of the garage that had a sweeping view of the lake.

Ethan ordered a bottle of champagne to celebrate his visit, and they talked for three hours sitting on top of the world in the sun. The company, he said, would have a name change soon, and become D&B Computing. They talked about what distributed client-server computing would mean to the world, and to all the mid-sized companies who couldn't afford a huge IBM mainframe in-house.

He told her about the chess board and who would be let go and who would be promoted, and grinned as he told her of his own new position. He would manage half of New Jersey as well as New York. They ordered a second bottle.

They discussed the European contingency, mapping out how Ethan would interface with them and manage global clients whose Manhattan offices oversaw international branches. And he told her about some of the D&B products that would be folded into their product offerings. Everything made sense.

"But why do they want us—or *need* us—I should say?" Maryl asked.

"That's a good question." He filled her glass. "I'll tell you why. First, they see us as a conduit for marketing *their* products to all our customers. Secondly, they are falling way behind as far as technology goes. They are ancient. We can offer them a huge leap forward in tech and expand their network incredibly. You realize we have computers all over the world now. They will want that network."

"What products of theirs would we be selling?" she asked.

"Primarily their analysis products. Think of it. All of our time-sharing clients could now use D&B's products to analyze their data. On our machines. They wouldn't have to get permission from their MIS departments."

She loved learning about the big-picture strategy of the company and the products and the customers and the executives. He knew so much. She wanted so badly to have an everyday relationship with this man. She would never be bored. She would never tire of his eyes looking into hers, and his hands on her body, and his deep laugh about the things that struck their funny bone the same way.

Now that she had a taste of him, she couldn't go back.

That Sunday afternoon, as she waved goodbye to him in the airport, she knew that the only way forward was to move to Philadelphia and be part of this huge new world in the software industry, and the huge new world of Ethan.

Kyle came back to the Bellevue office after two months and had nothing to say to her, refused to even look at her. He was passively mean, and withheld client info from her, making her job even more difficult. He hadn't responded to any of her messages or phone calls while he was in California. She had obviously sucker-punched him since it was apparent that he had made mental plans for them as a couple.

"Stop calling me," Kyle had said. "Stop trying to talk to me. I don't want to hear anything you have to say."

"But, Kyle," she had said, "I feel like we need to ..."

"Just leave me alone."

She stopped trying. *Am I at fault here? Did I do something wrong? Did I lead him on? Do I owe him something?* She was miserable at the office. She missed his friendship and his partnership at work. It was very uncomfortable for both of them.

Later that week, Ray brought Maryl into his office. She sat down, remembering how fun and flip they had been with each other the last time she was sitting here being promoted to sales. That seemed so long ago now.

"How are things with you? How is your relationship with Ethan?" asked Ray.

"He wants me to move out there, but I don't want to give up my career for any man." She looked up at Ray with a sort of question on her face.

"Do you want to marry him?" Ray asked a logical question.

"Well, I want to be with him all the time, and see if we can live together before I would know the answer to that." Maryl had concluded that a trial run would be best but that would mean giving up everything about her current life just for a test. On the other hand, she had to admit that she loved an adventure.

"Some movement has been made in that direction." Ray looked at her.

"What movement?" asked Maryl.

"We could move you to the Philadelphia office and you could continue your position with the company there. I would hate to lose you, but if you are going to quit anyway, well…" Ray's voice trailed off.

"Is there an open headcount there?" She asked.

"Well, no. But there is a salesman there who is pretty much just skating, and they would really like a ballbuster like you to replace him," Ray said.

Maryl cocked her head to one side, considering this. "Did Ethan have something to do with this?" she asked.

"Well, yes." Ray looked down at his desk and back up at her. "But here's the catch. This salesman in Philly is from a wealthy family in Boston who are friends with the CEO of D&B. He will scream bloody murder to daddy if we fire him out there, so the strategy is for you two to just trade places. He comes here and you go there. It would be handled quietly."

"What's the catch?" She asked.

"If you get out there and change your mind, there won't be a position back here for you to return to." Ray shrugged his shoulders up to his neck and made a sorry face.

Maryl picked up the phone and called Ethan.

"What did you do?" she asked him—a question and an accusation.

"I assume you're talking about the strategy of moving Clarke to Seattle and you to Philadelphia, all on the company tab which allows us to be together and you to continue your illustrious career," Ethan stated in an annoying monotone and then paused.

"Illustrious?" She let that drop on the floor.

There was silence between them for a full 10 seconds.

"Ethan?" Maryl checked to see if he was still there.

"I told you I don't do drama, Maryl. Do you want this to happen or not?"

Maryl continued to be impressed by Ethan's ability to speak fearlessly. She wanted to be that steely and clear and precise about exactly what it was that she wanted.

"Do *you* want it to happen?"

"What the hell, Maryl. Why do you think I went to the trouble of arranging this if I did not want it to happen?"

Maryl considered that she might be being dramatic. She was confused and felt like she was being a baby about this. She shouldn't put this burden on him.

Ethan broke the awkward silence. "I'm sorry, babe. What's the matter? You are a strong woman who knows what she wants. What's going on? Are you having second thoughts about us?"

"No. No, it's not that. I'm having trouble getting my footing on this. There's more to my decision here than for you on your end. I have friends, family, real estate, my job, my office mates. I've never lived on the East Coast. I don't know anyone out there. What if this doesn't work out? So many factors to consider..." she trailed off.

Ethan let out a sigh thick with what sounded like disgust. "Are you serious, Maryl? We have talked about all of this. I know you. You're incredibly strong. You want the same thing I do. For us to be together. You're getting too stressed about this which isn't like you at all. It's black and white. I'll call you in the morning and we'll discuss this in the light of day." Ethan hung up.

Lying in bed, staring at the mint green ceiling that needed painting, she wondered if he was right. Maybe it was just that simple. She loved him and wanted to be with him. These last six months she had missed him terribly. The phone calls were too short.

She missed the way he would touch her hand in person to pause her when she got too stressed or "over-animated" as he called it.

She missed the way he looked into her eyes—her soul—and under-stood her like no one had. She missed the intelligent discourse, the back-and-forth opinions about politics and religion and business. And yes, she missed the feel of his skin on hers and his mouth on hers and his fingers on her...

Monday morning came soon. To convey a solid professional message to Ray, she donned her power suit: a pale blue blouse paired with a navy pinstripe jacket and matching pants. After a dab of perfume on her neck, she shoved her index finger into the back of each high heel, pulled them on, and then left for the office.

"Temptation" by New Order was playing on the radio.

It was catchy and stuck in her head. Please don't let me...

Steering into her reserved garage parking spot, she jumped out, clicked the button on her key fob that locked her Alfa Romeo, touched her necklace, and headed for the elevators. Once inside, she punched the deli floor button, stopping off to grab two coffees: one for her and one for Ray.

"Good morning, bossman," she addressed Ray as she entered his office.

Ray was deep in paperwork but looked up and put his pen down. She offered him the caffeinated peace offering and sat down.

"Yes. Let's do this." Maryl looked at him with blazing eyes.

He would be missed as he had always been her biggest supporter in her career to date. But she wanted to be clear to everyone involved: She was a career woman, loved her job and this company AND she loved Ethan and wanted to be with him. It was a win-win.

"Okay." Ray took the paper coffee cup in both hands, held it for a moment, took a sip, and said, "Consider it done."

Sixteen

"What in the hell are you doing, Maryl? You finally get a decent job, and we think you are moving forward in life, and then you do this. This is just immature and impetuous, and it will never work," George said. "You think he's your knight in shining armor, but he's just a knight on a chessboard like all your other boyfriends. He'll move two steps one way and one step the other, and before you know it, you'll be back here licking your wounds."

Maryl thought about this for a moment, not because her father's words held any truth, but because the reference to chess was somewhat correct. Ethan was a knight. He was the only one on the board who could leapfrog other players and the only piece that could get around blockades. She believed that he was clever enough and powerful enough to be CEO one day.

"Dad, I'm not asking your permission to do this. I'm telling you what I'm doing and hoping that you will at least support me in this move. It's not like I'm quitting my job and running off to Morocco."

"You think you know what love is?" Regina said. It wasn't really a question. "Well, you don't. It's obvious that you don't. How long have you known him? A year? That's not love. That's just sex. Your father and I have been married for thirty years. That's love."

Maryl was crushed and tried to decipher her mother's emotions. She knew George hadn't loved her for all of those years. Was it anger in her voice? Jealousy? Or some twisted form of protection? She couldn't tell anymore. Five kids in ten years, ironing her husband's frayed shirts every night, cooking cubed steak and potatoes four times a week, with Dad's infidelity looming over it all—it must have sucked out her soul.

But fast forward to today, and her father had been promoted yet again, this time to Boston to run Old Stone Mortgage. He had also been elected president of the MBA for the year, an illustrious honor that made her mother feel like she was finally living the prominent life she deserved.

So why is she still so filled with bitterness toward me?

For as long as she could remember, she was her mother's disappointment. No proud smiles, no bragging to her friends, no mother-daughter outings like Agnes got. Just an endless stream of criticism.

How could someone so steeped in faith, so committed to the promise of divine love and forgiveness, harbor such palpable anger?

She wouldn't let Regina poison this moment. Not today. Regina had stolen too many moments, crushed too many dreams. This time, she'd protect her own happiness, even if it meant shutting out her mother.

With as much calm as she could muster, she proceeded. "Mom, I know this is sudden, but I'm twenty-five years old and you need to let me make my own decisions, right or wrong. I know that's hard for you, but please. Can we not have this conversation?"

When the uncomfortable phone call ended, they settled on a plan: half of Maryl's belongings would be shipped to Ethan's condo—on his dime. The rest, including her precious Alfa Romeo, would be moved to their daylight basement with its roll-up doors in Weston, Massachusetts. Her mother had chosen this idyllic Boston suburb with its meticulous landscaping: the white picket fence up front, the sloping backyard, and the stand of birch trees whose silver-dollar leaves rattled in the slightest breeze. Now that was probably more like her mother's dream.

It was the summer of 1983.

Helen remained neutral about it all. Doug had recovered from his heart surgery, and they had just returned from a spring break family vacation to Lake Chelan where they stayed every year at Watson's cottages on the south side of the lake. "I thought about you while I was watching the kids at the pool," Helen was saying. "There was a little redhead girl who kept jumping into the deep end against her mother's wishes, and she reminded me of you."

"Yes, that's me," Maryl said. They talked about Regina, her cancer, her recent behavior, and about the upcoming move to Philadelphia.

"I would always see your mother in church," Helen said. "Even after you stopped going. She seemed so pious like she was bearing a heavy cross."

"Why do you think I loved hanging out at your house so much? Yours was the kind of family I always dreamed about."

"Oh, we had our moments." Helen steered the conversation away from Regina. "You'll have to send me pictures of the Liberty Bell. And the Betsy Ross house."

Maryl loved that Helen didn't judge her. Lord knows there were plenty of reasons to do that these days. She was abandoning her teammates, her properties, her clients, and her friends.

She visited each of her renters and gave instructions to mail the monthly checks to her friend, Fletcher, who would forward them to her. Fletcher had volunteered to keep an eye on her properties.

She knew Dan was bunking at Mark's until he could find a place, so she rented her house to him for the next six months, with the caveat that he couldn't use it for band practice, since it was in a nice young-family neighborhood—one of those they called "up and coming".

She spent the next three weeks calling on her existing customers as a polite transitioning gesture, taking Ray or Mark with her, since Kyle was still spitting acid her way, and Clarke had not yet arrived from Philadelphia to fill this position in the Bellevue office.

Darrel Dizzle had given Maryl the nameplate off his desk as a parting gift and they shook hands warmly. She and Kyle had undoubtedly landed the biggest fish in the sea that year. Maryl knew she was leaving Clarke the crown jewels—a client list that most reps in the country would drool over, with the contracts in place to bring him recurring revenue year over year. He would probably be going to Club next year instead of her, as she had no idea which East Coast clients she might inherit from his territory. But she didn't care. She knew she could turn any situation around if needed and could launch new sales efforts there as she had done in Seattle.

Besides, Ethan was her Club now. He was her biggest fan, and together they would do great things at the company.

SEVENTEEN

Maryl ran down the breezeway when her flight landed at Philadelphia International Airport at three p.m. that Friday in September, and then made a beeline to the luggage carousel, where Ethan was waiting.

"They let you off early!" Maryl was all smiles.

"I let *myself* off early," Ethan said. "Remember, I'm the boss up there."

He had a handful of flowers and grabbed her up and held on for a full minute before she pushed back and looked at him. That man. Her man. His eyes were so intense, scanning her, and touching her hair, and kissing her. She was giddy with excitement bouncing up and down a bit until she thought better of that behavior and settled into a calm sophisticated stride beside him. Ethan paid for an attendant to get her bags and bring them to the car.

"I'm starved. How about you?" Ethan had one hand on the wheel and one holding hers. They stopped at a deli and grabbed Philly cheese steaks because Ethan had made it very clear that cheese steaks made anywhere else in the world were simply imposters. This would be proof.

They pulled off the Schuylkill River Parkway which was studded with pink cherry trees in full bloom and climbed Ford Road to the top of the park where there was one building. Only one. Park Plaza Condominiums. It was a high-rise condo building that arched around the front in a long curve so that all four units on each floor had stunning views. She stared up at the building with its rounded façade and eighteen stories of floor-to-ceiling windows imagining it on a street in Paris along the Champs-Élysées.

"You know, I just moved across the country to live in a place I've never seen," Maryl said to herself as much as to Ethan. "I don't even know if you have a decent shower."

"Come on. I'll show you the place." Ethan grabbed her hand. "And maybe we'll give the shower a trial run."

"Shouldn't we bring my bags?" Maryl hesitated.

"I'll have the doorman bring them up," he said.

The doorman.

She wasn't in Kansas anymore.

The elevator took them to the very top floor, and they walked straight into Ethan's apartment which wrapped a quarter way around the building. She skipped over to the floor-to-ceiling windows and could see the Schuylkill River, Fairmount Park, and Philadelphia city center in the distance.

"You can use this room for your things." He motioned to a room on one end of the condo. "And our bedroom is on the other side."

He tossed the cheesesteaks on the counter in the kitchen, which was in the center of the condo with a swinging door into the dining room/living room area.

Maryl had never seen a place like it in her life. Fifteen hundred square feet, two bedrooms, two bathrooms, a full kitchen, dining and living room. There was a large comfy-looking L-shaped sectional facing the windows, an elegant dining table with a chandelier above it, and a mirrored wall behind it. Ethan came up behind her as she continued to stare out the window and kissed the back of her neck. He put his arms around her and whispered, "What do you think?"

She turned to face him and leaned into him, burying her face in his neck and breathing him in. He smelled of coffee and an earthy cologne she couldn't place, and she wanted him naked right then and there. He obliged.

Two hours later, they sat, partially dressed, on towels in the dining room, devouring the cheesesteaks, still warm, stuffed with impossibly thin sliced beef and sauteed mushrooms and tiny peppers and onions and gooey cheese.

"Pack your bags for the weekend, babe. We're off to the Jersey Shore." Ethan announced the next morning.

"Oh, goody." Maryl didn't know where that was exactly. "What should I pack?"

"Seriously? It's the shore! Don't you do beach holidays out there?" He smiled.

She was happy that her bags were already sitting in the spare room, unpacked, as she dumped the smaller one out on the carpet in a pile. Sorting through, she pulled out two pairs of capris, three tops, two sweaters, flip-flops, and some tennis shoes that could double as beach shoes she supposed. *But they'll be toast after this trip to the sand.*

"How many days?" she called to him in the next room.

"Let's shoot for four. Daniels can't get his knickers in a twist too much over that."

"Oh god. My new boss wears knickers?" They both chuckled.

They took Ethan's BMW along the Atlantic City Expressway East and then Garden State Parkway South. Maryl thought that 55 looked like a straighter shot down to Cape May as she looked at the map spread out on her lap.

"Nah. If we took that route, you'd miss seeing the area around Atlantic City and then the Jersey Shore all the way south from there. This way, you can tell all your West Coast buddies that you've actually been to the Jersey Shore." He patted her leg.

And he was right. This was much different than Ruby Beach on the Olympic National Rain Forest or Cannon Beach in Oregon with craggy rock formations looming out of the ocean and evergreen mountains stretching all the way to the sand. Here little towns overlapped with each other down the coast with wooden boardwalks and mounds of green scrub grasses blown over to one side, and miles of sand dunes forming little hills down to the crashing waves.

"If I stand on the beach, I bet I could almost see up and down the entire coast." Maryl studied the map.

"Yes. It's just one long tan strip of sand."

After an hour and a half, they arrived at the southern tip of New Jersey—Cape May. Ethan pulled up to a stately gray and white Victorian hotel dating back to the late 1800s. The wide porch was overhung with gray and white striped awnings and lots of white windows with black shutters next to a red double door with tall arched glass panes.

"It's like New Orleans," Maryl almost clapped.

Such a lovely building. Maryl entered the heavy doors in a rush to find a ladies' room but stopped in the lobby to take in the ambiance. Deep green velvet couches, the huge black fireplace and gold-framed photos of white ships hanging on the golden turn-of-the-century wallpaper. Off to the left was a highly polished wooden bar with studded leather stools.

She loved it, and it must have registered on her face when she turned to look at Ethan.

"I know. I know. I don't like Victorian. But I thought you would like it for the romance of the place. And it has a lot of history."

She put her arms around his neck and kissed him there in the low light of the red wall sconces, pulling away to find the restroom.

"Our suite isn't ready yet, so the beach attendant set us up in the Adirondack chairs under that pergola on the sand." Ethan pointed with his elbow, balancing a bottle of champagne and an ice bucket.

Being the end of September, the temperature was 61 degrees and a bit breezy, so they repositioned to one large chaise next to the chairs, snuggling together.

The Eagles' *Hotel California* was playing on the beach speakers and Maryl hummed along.

"Funny how a song about a place three thousand miles away is just as relevant." Ethan smiled and took her hand. She squirmed closer to him, tucking her hair behind her ear. She didn't want a mouthful of red curls to interrupt their kissing.

That evening, after unpacking in their charming 300 square-foot king bedroom with views of the ocean, they sat in the hotel dining room with a chilled bottle of South African Chenin Blanc and a plate of char-grilled oysters between them.

"Tomorrow we can walk around the town and up the shore a little way. My family visits here often and I want to stop in a few places."

"Okay. As long as I get you to myself most of the day," Maryl answered. "I mean, I'd love to just lounge around in bed for the morning, catch up on my sleep... and other things."

"Uh-huh." Ethan nodded. "So, besides the activity I believe you are talking about, what else do you have your heart set on?"

Maryl pulled out a brochure she'd snatched from the lobby and pushed it across the white tablecloth. "I know it's a Catholic thing, but I'd love to go see this."

The brochure had a photo of an elegant white building with a red roof, well, several red roofs, and a cross mounted atop one of them. There were about a hundred rooms along an outside U-shaped porch with tall white columns and a green lawn stretching across the middle.

"Oh yeah. Saint Mary by-the-Sea. It started out as a hotel but didn't make it. Back then it took a lot longer than an hour and a half to get down here for holiday. And then it became a sort of nursing home for old black people, and then some nuns from Philly bought it for a retreat house."

"Must have been nice to be a nun back then."

"You're joking," said Ethan. "And then, as the story goes, they wanted their male counterparts, the priests, to come down and have a retreat place too, so they bought a beach house for them."

"Power to the nuns!" Maryl said.

"Well, I really don't want to stay there very long," Ethan said.

"Oh, I think you'll be lucky if they even let you in, Mr. Jewish Main Line," Maryl teased.

The next day Ethan took her on a walking tour of Cape May, its shops, beaches, and bars. He showed her what was left of the wooden boardwalk from his childhood, and the last corner shop still standing where he and his sister were allowed to venture alone for ice cream cones that would melt down their arms as soon as they exited the shop.

The air was clean and brisk, and Ethan kept her hand in his as they walked and joked and talked.

"You know one of the things I like about The Virginia Hotel?" Maryl asked.

"You mean besides the bed?"

"Yes, besides the bed, bubba."

"Bubba now?"

"I like that it is an adults-only hotel. No screaming kids banging on the walls or running in the hallway."

"So, you don't like kids?" He jabbed her playfully and she giggled beside him.

"No, I'm not saying *that* Mr. Weisenheimer. I'm saying it's nice to be able to use the handrail on the staircase without wondering if there are boogers on it. And it's nice to swim in a pool without wondering who peed in it."

"Well, it's not just kids who do that," Ethan countered.

"What? Are you saying you have peed in a swimming pool?" She gave him a fake wide-eyed stare.

"Knock it off."

"So, do you like kids, Ethan? I guess there are a lot of things I haven't asked you yet."

"Like what other things?"

"You know, now that I think of it, I never asked you if you have any kids already."

Ethan stopped on the sidewalk and turned to face her. "What? Why would you even ask me that? You know I've never even been married."

"Jeez. Sorry. Didn't mean to..."

They walked in silence for a few minutes.

"And *this*...this is my favorite ice cream place." Ethan guided her into the shop.

They took their paper bowls of mint chocolate chip and chocolate swirl across the street to the beach and sat in chairs under an umbrella watching the surf.

"You know, we're looking at Delaware."

"That's Delaware?" Maryl pointed across the water.

"Yep. You can almost see Dewey Beach. Most people don't realize you can take a ferry from here to Delaware. Wrap your head around that. Oh, and if you squint, you can also see past Delaware to Maryland down south there."

Maryl realized she didn't know her geography very well, since that seemed impossible.

The day was winding down. Barefoot couples with their shoes in their hands wandered by. The smell of fried fish filled the air. The dunes took on a purple hue in the evening, with the fences, like pitch pipes, rising out of them haphazardly, linked by wire all the way down the beach. Sunken down in their beach chairs, they could barely see the waves.

Eighteen

T he next day, as promised, Ethan took Maryl to tour Saint Mary by-the-Sea. After about ten minutes, she could see that he was bored, so she told him it was fine if he wanted to hang out on the porch.

He wandered down to a newsstand, bought a paper, and returned to the porch of "the nuns' place" as he called it.

Of course, it had been remodeled, but she read the history as she walked through the halls. These sisters had a ton of money back then. Maryl wondered how they got it. Supposedly one of the priests of a Philadelphia parish helped them financially. Maryl felt nauseous, remembering a nun-priest encounter she had witnessed as a girl.

And then in 1941, the government took over the property to use for the army, paying the nuns one dollar per year for it. After the war, six years later, it was in such shambles that the nuns paid for a complete remodel and moved back in.

The Catholic Church. All that money. All that hypocrisy.

That night Maryl couldn't sleep.

"Shh." Her little brother was shushing her, huddled next to her behind the juniper bush down the block from Grandma's. It was dusk and they were spying on the nunnery, which was a grand old brick house on Palouse Street where all the Catholic nuns lived including Sister Lovelace.

On this particular night, Father Brudle, the handsome priest from the parish with his square jaw and blond hair, was holding open the back storm door on the convent, leaning like James Dean against it while he talked in low tones to Sister Lovelace.

Maryl was confused. This was all wrong. The porch light was on. It was the first time she had seen a nun without the coif, and she felt a terrible nausea in her stomach watching what seemed to be flirting. Lovelace was giggling at whatever Brudle was saying and he was chuckling as well, trying to be as quiet as possible.

After a few minutes of this Father Brudle took a step toward Lovelace, and then another. Lovelace looked up at him, and for a fleeting moment, she caught a glimpse of Maryl, peeking out from the bush, gaping at them. In that moment Lovelace's face turned extremely ugly with anger, or maybe it was embarrassment. She shot a death glare at Maryl and went back inside.

"Let's get out of here!" Billy had jumped up and run, but Maryl was rooted in the dirt, stunned and not quite sure what she had seen.

How could a priest and a nun flirt? Weren't they the pure ones on earth? Weren't nuns married to God? And had she just witnessed a sin? And why did she feel like she had been the one sinning?

Maryl would never forget that glare or the feeling in her stomach. It was the beginning of her disenchantment with the Catholics.

Ethan and Maryl fell into a comfortable routine in Cape May – coffee on the porch with the paper, a morning swim, breakfast in the dining room, a stroll on the beach followed by a nap, then cocktails and dinner and the sunset. They stayed an extra day and talked for most of it. What would their daily routine be back in Philadelphia? Would she be interested in accompanying him to the New York City office on occasion? Would she help him conquer the world? Would he support her efforts in the Philly office? What were the parking and train trip plans? What did Ethan prefer for dinners? Eat in or dine out?

Happy they had taken the vacation, and ready to take on the world together, they drove back that Thursday and settled in.

Since the next day was Friday and she didn't have to report to the office until Monday, Ethan took an extra day off and gave her a tour of the city. Maryl had only been to the East Coast for training, and that was in the quiet lush town of Wilton. This place was much different. Old. Some crumbling structures. The streets were dirty in many parts and smelled of pot and body odor. In Center City, the combination of beautiful historical buildings with huge columns and stone staircases next to new ten-story cream-colored boxy buildings with brown tinted windows against the sun was, well, unsettling.

It felt unfinished to Maryl, gritty—like it was a city that had been struggling to change for decades. Busy and dingy with abandoned buildings and small markets and garbage on the sidewalks, dirty brick walls, weeds growing in the gutters, a luncheonette on every corner with signs for quality meats and Pepsi Cola, open markets on the sidewalks with brown paper covers over the vegetables, huge tattered awnings that reached out to the streets, tons of Oldsmobiles and nearly every car on the street was dented or rusted or had a cracked window. Construction made things even dirtier and noisier, especially on Market Street where she would be working.

Every other block had a discount records store with bicycles leaning against the windows on the sidewalk, waiting for their owners to remount and ride home with a new LP in their knapsack. There were pharmacies everywhere that still had deli counters where kids would grab a milkshake or cheeseburger and eat them on the curb while reading their newest comic books. And lots of black people. She had never seen so many in one place.

Ethan headed the car down the Schuylkill and out the Main Line.

"Ah. I see now." Maryl was wide-eyed at the gorgeous properties, beautiful homes, lush landscaping, tall old sweeping trees, clean streets, and upscale shops.

"This is where I grew up," explained Ethan, pointing out so many childhood landmarks that she would never remember them.

She was in Ethanworld, engulfed in his entire life spent here, with him knowing every corner of the widespread city and all the history, and probably most of the people. She was overwhelmed. He grabbed her hand and shook it excitedly. "Let's drop in on my folks."

Holy Crap. Maryl was not prepared. "Wait. Now?"

"Sure. You'll love them. They'll love you." In four minutes, they were parking in front of a lovely old home in Ardmore, with manicured lawns and a sidewalk up to the front stone porch.

Ethan walked right in and sat down next to his mother who was on the couch having a cigarette and reading something. She patted his leg and said "Well. This is your new friend?" as she looked Maryl up and down.

Maryl walked nearer and reached out her hand. "Hello," was all she could muster. Ethan's mother stood up and gave her a two-armed hug, one hand still holding the cigarette and the other holding the magazine. "Welcome to Philadelphia. Are you hungry?"

Maryl looked at Ethan. "Mom, I told her that would be the first thing you asked her." All three of them chuckled and the tension eased. Ethan's father walked in, nodded briefly at Maryl and said, "I can't believe they're tearing down the club on Sixteenth. Did you drive by there, son?"

Both of his parents were loud. Not obnoxious but just inclusive of everyone in the room, and outside of the room, and maybe even those in the yard. They acted as if this was a normal occurrence, Ethan bringing friends over, and it was a reason to get into the refrigerator and bring out leftovers.

"Sit down. Sit down," his mother insisted, as she dragged Maryl into the kitchen. The two men stayed in the living room. The fridge was crammed with jars and bottles and plastic containers and eggs and vegetables. "Here. Put this on the table. Abe just brought these home."

They looked like croissants to Maryl. "Oh yum. Miriam. It's Miriam, right? I love croissants," said Maryl.

Miriam laughed loudly. "Ethan, your girlfriend thinks knishes are croissants!" she called out to the world.

NINETEEN

———◄O►———

Three weeks later, 214 US Marines were killed in a bombing in Beirut, Lebanon. They were on a peacekeeping mission during the Lebanese Civil War. Almost simultaneously, a second bombing occurred at a building housing French paratroopers, killing another 58 people. The attacks were carried out using truck bombs driven by suicide bombers. It was the deadliest single-day death toll for the United States military since the first day of the Tet Offensive in Vietnam in 1968.

International terrorism and the Middle East conflicts came stomping up to the doorstep, taking over news channels and all social conversations about foreign military policy. There was widespread shock and anger, and the holidays were replaced with a state of national mourning with heated arguments about Reagan's military policies.

"We need to wipe out those SOBs," Ethan preached. It was the first time they had a serious political disagreement. Maryl hated all violence and thought it was archaic and uncivilized to solve problems by killing people on the other side of the argument. Once again, she imagined herself as a Ring Girl striding around the boxing ring with her signs: STOP! JUST STOP IT!

The Philadelphia staff welcomed Maryl, which was surprising since all twelve had been together since the office opened. James Hare was the first to shake her hand when she walked in the door. "Who sent you and what do you want with us?" he quipped through his handlebar mustache and quickly clasped his hands behind his back.

Next was Tom, a short soft nerd in large glasses who spoke rapidly and generally under his breath. He didn't say anything to her for the first week because, as Patty the office admin disclosed, he was shy. Later, when Maryl got to know Tom, he refuted that, saying that he just wasn't interested in social chatter. Which was why he rarely went on sales calls.

Patty was the glue of the office of course. A nice Jewish mother hen who would do anything for any one of her *children*. There were other support people in the branch and an often-absent manager, Eugene Daniels, a big fleshy, loud man with matching stories. But harmless, she was told.

James and Tom and Maryl spent a lot of time together in the office and out to lunch. She knew the way to a man's heart, and it was no different with techies. On Fridays, when Ethan took the later train home from NYC, she would take them to the nearest pub and buy them beers. Through them, she learned her way around the politics of bigger players in the database niche and their true product feature advantages. They were both extremely technical in the same way Mark and Dan were, even coding around glitches themselves when clients had issues. And they were both single and available most evenings. Maryl took advantage of that, calling them with questions even on weekends. She adored both of them and they her because she was willing to get down and dirty with the code. She had a lot of "whys", and they had a lot of answers.

One day she stopped in the lunchroom to grab a cup of coffee and listened to Tom and James going after a fictitious math problem from a book on the table.

Twenty-five of King Arthur's knights are seated at the round table. Three of them are chosen and are sent off to slay a dragon. What is the probability that at least two of the three had been sitting next to each other?

"Oh, this one's easy," said Tom. "We just use complementary counting by finding the probability that none of the three knights are sitting next to each other and subtracting it from one."

"Okay, Mr. Math-head." James rolled his eyes at Maryl, and she grinned.

"What is the Roman numeral for the number zero?" James challenged.

James was the trivia king and Tom was the math whiz. They made a great team but had many lively arguments.

"There isn't one. Everybody knows that," Tom responded.

"Okay, here's one. Why does the stock market use the words 'bull' and 'bear?'"

"Because a bull is stronger than a bear," said Tom.

"Well, no actually. That is a false statement. If you pit a bull and a bear against each other in real life, the bear will normally win, because the bull only has its head as a weapon whereas the bear can use his claws and teeth and..."

"James," Maryl interrupted. "What's the answer to your trivia question?"

"Oh. Yes. Well, bulls will whip their horns *up* to swipe an opponent while bears will swipe their claws *down* to disarm theirs."

"I didn't know that," Maryl said. "Do you follow the stock market?"

"Oh, only for the analytical angle. It's fascinating how very few people have figured out how to make a million dollars playing the market. I mean, other than insider trading."

"I'm one of the billions of people who haven't figured that out," Maryl said.

"Insider trading?"

"Very funny."

"I'm with you, Maryl," said Tom. "You know what they say. You have to spend money to make money."

"Yes, but whose money?"

"What?" Tom turned in his chair.

"Whose money can we steal to make our first investment?" Maryl turned with her coffee cup but stopped for a moment, and turned back to the two of them. "Speaking of making money, can you two give me more technical ammo for my sales pitch to these prospects?"

Tom and James grinned. "Yes, ma'am." The two of them followed her to her office.

"This is the best way to sell DAMON to geeks," Tom said. "You know who James Martin is, right?"

Maryl knew from her training that Martin was a British technology consultant who had followed the rise of DAMON and wrote about it.

"Well, Martin put out a challenge to us and our two biggest competitors to solve this problem with our code: *Give a six percent raise to all engineers in the company who have received a review ranking of seven or better.*" James clasped his hands behind his back and rocked on the balls of his feet. "It took a dozen pages of code in COBOL and two pages of code in SIMDAR, but here's the simple code from DAMON:

CHANGE ALL SALARY=SALARY*1.06 WHERE POSITION='ENG' AND AVG(INSTANCE(RATING)) GE 7

Maryl read it aloud. "Multiply their salary by a hundred and six percent *if* their job title is 'engineer' and *if* their review rating is greater than or equal to seven."

"It's so brilliant and so simple," Tom said. "We can write code that reflects what a real human user is trying to get at, in their own language."

"That's why it's called a 4GL - fourth generation language," James chimed in. "It really sets us apart."

Armed with this techie version of features and benefits, Maryl edged her sales wins up significantly in the competitive landscape, directing at least half of her pitches to the geeky guys inside the customer base. She knew the executives always looked to the techies for final review when it came to an expensive decision about which software to use.

"You don't need to know all that technical stuff," Ethan told her. "All you need to know is how to direct your techies during a call. It's like having hand signals in baseball. You're the pitcher. Stay on the mound."

Ethan and Maryl had settled into a routine of bolting out of bed to their separate bathrooms, dressing hurriedly, and racing to the 30th Street Station in her car so he would make the early train to Manhattan. He would grab a bagel and coffee at the station before making his way to his seat in his car on the 7:20. She would stop at the deli in the building for coffee and a bacon sandwich. Every day. And in the evenings, they would do the reverse. Ethan's days were longer because of the hour-long commute each way but it allowed him to get work done on the train, and even some socializing with the regulars who did the same daily trip in the same train car.

The Manhattan office was right next door to New York City's Penn Station. Ethan would bring Maryl to the office at least one day a week to work from there. They would walk up from the trains below Madison Square Garden, stopping at Ethan's favorite bagel stand at Two Penn Plaza to get a dozen for the office. From the 28th floor, Maryl could see the Empire State Building, the Hudson River, and a slight view of the East River as well.

"Do you ever tire of this view?" she gushed to the administrator at the front desk, who handed her a key to the women's room. "When you return, I have a cubicle for you for the day, Maryl."

No one seemed to notice the noise of taxis honking and buses hitting their brakes all day. It was distracting to Maryl, but she never complained because she loved the high energy of the city, the people on the street speaking foreign languages, the taxis screeching to a halt at the curb and then whizzing off with a passenger, the crazy homeless addicts calling out for change "for coffee ma'am" and the general chaos of street vendors and food trucks and newsstands on every corner.

During lunch hours, she would strike out on adventures and roam the sidewalks of this dirty, dark, concrete neighborhood so loud and full of shops and people.

On one such noon hour, she jumped when she heard a woman scream.

"Aargh! He has my baby! He stole my baby! Catch that man!" The woman was large and standing next to an empty stroller, waving her yellow purse at the crowd and pointing with the other hand. "There! There! The green hat!"

She was screaming loudly now. "I turned my back for one minute! One minute!" Maryl heard the guilt and pain in her voice.

A few people looked over their shoulders to catch a glimpse of the woman but then kept walking. No one did anything. Hands in pockets or clutching their Styrofoam takeout boxes, they hustled on with their lives, heads down, not making eye contact.

Maryl stood frozen on the sidewalk, watching this happen. She hadn't seen the baby snatching. *Should she go talk to this woman?* She turned around and ducked into a sandwich shop, shaken to the core that a crime like that could happen in this city and be so ignored. As if it happened all the time.

"Yeah. That stuff happens all the time. You just have to ignore it." Ethan was riding the elevator down with Maryl to catch the train home.

"But Ethan. Holy shit."

"Yeah. Last week I saw a taxi run over a bicycle courier and he didn't even stop. And people just went on their way. No one wants to look at that blood and gore in the middle of their workday." Ethan looked a little bored with the conversation. "By the way, I got us a joint bank account at Manny Hanny. We can both contribute and build up some vacation funds. OK? Here is your signature card. You can just sign it and drop it off on one of your noon adventures."

"What's Manny Hanny?"

"Manufacturers Hanover Trust Bank."

It took Maryl an entire day to get over the stolen baby and the dead courier. Her mind and all of her senses were on overload.

"Quite a difference between Manhattan and Philadelphia, huh?" Patty said the next day after listening to Maryl's story. She was born and bred in Philly. "You won't see that here."

"But what about all the mafia activity and the gangs here?" Maryl had watched the news last night about the murder of Angelo Bruno and the Philadelphia Mafia's internal struggle to fill that top power position.

"Oh, that's just South Philly," Patty brushed it off.

"Mostly around Moyamensing and Southwark." James had been eavesdropping and joined the conversation.

"The what and what?" Maryl giggled.

"Ever heard of H. H. Holmes?" James asked Maryl, pulling on the ends of his handlebar mustache.

"Uh…no?" answered Maryl tilting her head with a grin and crossing her arms, ready for a forthcoming story of history from James' weird brain.

"He had a huge house and offered it as hotel accommodations for tourists in Chicago for the 1893 World's Fair."

"Not getting the connection here, James."

"He had a torture chamber in the basement, and he killed about two hundred people there – everyone who ever stayed at his place."

"What?" Maryl stared at him. "That's horrible. How did he get away with that? Didn't people wonder why no guests ever left??"

"Oh, he also had an autopsy room and a crematorium in his basement. He would torture and murder them and cut some of them up into pieces and toast them or sell the bodies to medical schools."

"James. Is this a joke? Is there a punchline?"

"No, no. True story."

"Connection?"

"Oh. Right." James smoothed his upper lip with his thumb and middle finger. "He had another business and murdered that partner for the insurance money. So, it was either insurance fraud or murder that he was hanged for. My guess is the latter."

"James. The connection to present-day mafia?"

"Oh, yeah. Philly had a rather imposing prison down in Moyamensing, and Holmes was hanged there. That's what I remember about the town."

Maryl cranked her head at the ceiling and ran her fingers down her throat, suppressing a giggle. "Good to know, James."

"Oh, and the guy who built the prison? He's the one who designed the dome for the US Capitol building, and the wings for the House and the Senate." And with that, James made a popping sound with his lips and did a pirouette.

Maryl howled. Patty was shaking her head as James wandered back to his desk. They had both forgotten all about the original discussion of current gangs.

"Argh I'm so tired," Ethan said when she picked him up that April evening. "You won't believe what Daniels did today. Such an idiot."

"You mean my boss?" Maryl kept her eyes on the road.

"For now." Ethan stared out the window. "I mean, what an idiot. You know that deal he's working on at Atlantic Electric? He wants to give away an entire application. And technically, I could claim that client. I could. And they would like me a lot better than Daniels, I can tell you that."

"Ethan, what are you talking about?"

"There's a huge professional services contract that D&B could get for this one application they want us to code for them. The capability isn't in DAMON yet, so it should be labeled as professional services. But no. Daniels wants to have corporate throw it in for free for some kind of goodwill or something. The guy shouldn't be allowed to run a district."

"This wouldn't have anything to do with the fact that our office gets revenue credit for a system sale and yours get credit for any professional services added onto it?"

"What? It doesn't matter who gets what, Maryl. My point is that Daniels is an idiot. I tell ya I should just take over the Philadelphia office and run that. You and I would be unbeatable. You understand the tech side and revenue. And of course, then *I* would be your boss." He let out a laugh and jabbed her.

"Nice cocktail hour on the train?" She smelled it on him.

"You have no idea how stressful my days are, babe. And this commute kills me. I deserve a pop on my way home."

"Ethan. Your commute? You go straight from my car down the stairs and into your favorite train car, and at the other end, you take an escalator to the floor with the bagels and an elevator up to your office. That's not a bad commute."

"You don't understand. It's doing it day after day after day. You think it's fun and easy because you've done it a few times. Well, let me tell you, the fun wears off fast."

"Whatever you say. Hey, speaking of fun things, do you want to go see a play this weekend?" she started.

"Stop, stop. Pull over here. I want to get the Times. Right there. Right there." He liked to settle into his chair after dinner and read the paper. Just like his father. And his father's father, she guessed.

"You are certainly a creature of habit, babe." She pulled away from the curb and headed home.

"You know it," he said absentmindedly as he flipped through the sections.

She figured maybe she'd ask him again over dinner.

Twenty

E than's friends were all from high school or college. They all went to Penn State and were huge Nittany Lions fans, and subsequently Joe Paterno fans. Football season, which ran from August to November, was all about the NCAA teams, unlike where Maryl was from. In the Seattle area, it was all about the Seahawks and the professional teams, so she had never watched a Rutgers or Temple or Boston college game, let alone Penn State.

During the season, everyone gathered at Ethan's on Saturdays to watch. Barbara Kohlberg and her beau Jake always brought a large crockpot full of Cholent. She was a thin, giggly true redhead and Jake was in law school now, dumping his real estate career last year to try something new. Maryl was fond of Barbara, who was the sweet innocent type.

"So how are you liking Philadelphia?" she had asked Maryl the first time they met.

"It's been great and not so great," Maryl confided. "I love my job, but the city itself is pretty nasty, don't you think? And I don't get to see Ethan as much as I thought I would because of his job…"

"Isn't your job the same as his?" Barbara had interrupted.

"Well, no. I do sales in the Philly office here and he is the branch manager up in the Manhattan office. He manages all the mess up there. And all the techies too. So, as you may know, he's not much of a morning person when we leave for his train, and by the time his day is over and his commute is complete, he's pretty exhausted. We don't have much of a couples' routine together, except for falling into bed at night." She sighed.

Barbara had reached for her hand and held it a moment. "Well, it'll get better. Ethan's a great guy. You two just need a vacation together."

Maybe Maryl thought to herself. *Or maybe I need a vacation of my own.*

Caleb and Sarah Stein were friends of Ethan's from Penn State and seemed to share a lot of inside jokes. She was a good cook and usually brought a casserole. Caleb was a stock trader on the floor at PHLX. They were the only ones in the group who had a child so far—a darling one-year-old daughter named Chloe whom Maryl had yet to meet.

Simon Weisshal and Susan Blumsteiner were newlyweds. He and Ethan had played baseball together back in grade school. He ran a gym on the ground floor of a downtown office building. Every Saturday, after their morning workout, Susan and Simon would go next door to the deli and pick up a box full of Rugelach, since Ethan had a sweet tooth. The cream cheese and apricot preserves were his favorite.

And then there was Nathan Sternheim, who was a tall thin sad-looking boy who had lost his parents in a car crash and, along with his sister, Muriel, had inherited millions. He was the chips and dips guy.

They were all Jewish.

"Hey, Maryl," Barbara called out as she walked through the door with both hands full of goodies and her purse over her shoulder. Jake trailed her, reaching to take off his cap.

"Here, let me take that," Maryl greeted her with an awkward hug trying not to spill the wooden bowl of shrimp and cocktail sauce.

These Saturday gatherings would begin with everyone in the living room before the game started, sorting out cocktails and arranging the noshes, with lots of commenting on the current view out the windows. Autumn showed in all its glory from the 18th floor, with thousands of trees in the park below glowing yellow and rust and green. The guys would bring each other up to speed on their weekly job dramas, and the girls would complement each other on their new outfit or hairstyle or manicure.

But once the game started, the women dutifully retired to the kitchen. It was tradition apparently. Maryl discovered this on the first game day of the season, as she settled in between Nathan and Ethan on the couch. After ten minutes of banter about the players, Ethan nudged her and said, "Why don't you go help the girls in the kitchen?"

The Saturday "kitchen parties" with the girls were foreign to Maryl. She had always watched the games with the men, first her brothers and father, then her beloved Kappa Sigma fraternity buddies in school, and then with Kyle and Ray and Teri. Sure, she would help Teri in the kitchen, but it was all part of a great room, and they could whoop and holler at a first-down from the counter.

Barbara, Susan, and Sarah were educated, capable women. They each had a career: Susan was a divorce attorney, Sarah worked with Ethan's sister in the marketing department of Philadelphia Magazine, and Barbara was a dental hygienist. They had known each other for years.

"Oh, by the way, Muriel is having a party next Sunday and she says, 'No pork' so we'll have to bring chicken or something else," Barbara was saying. "Muriel is Nathan's sister." She nodded to Maryl. "She wants us to see her new garden in Bala Cynwyd."

"I'll have to check with Ethan. That's dinner day at his parents' house."

Barbara made a round "O" with her mouth and nodded. "But this will be more fun for you!" she whispered deviously in Maryl's ear. "Where's the wine opener?"

That Sunday, Ethan and Maryl stopped by Miriam and Abe's for breakfast, in lieu of dinner, since they were headed to Bala Cynwyd for Muriel's party. Abe was watching Hill Street Blues.

"Dad, why are you watching that crap?" Ethan said as they walked in the door.

"He's so sick of WCAU today, the drought in Kenya, and all the news about gay people getting AIDS, I think he's just taking a mental break," Miriam said from the kitchen.

"And what about the Iran-Iraq conflicts? Can't let us forget that bullshit." Ethan sat down with his father, grabbed the remote, and switched the channel to football.

"At least the price of gas has gone down a bit since last year." Maryl joined Miriam in the kitchen.

"Why couldn't you come to dinner today? We always do dinners on Sunday, you know," Miriam stated.

"Oh, Muriel wanted us to come see her house in Bala Cynwyd. Apparently, she's done some remodeling and put in a garden."

"Well, that will be fun. And her brother Nathan's a sweet young man, too. They were both lucky to inherit that Sternheim fortune."

Miriam served a steaming hot Matzo Brei and Maryl had never tasted an egg casserole so luscious. She topped hers with sour cream, while Ethan piled on applesauce and cinnamon sugar. After that, she couldn't even think of more food at Muriel's. They said their goodbyes and Miriam bellowed after them, "Tell Muriel hello and when's she going to find a nice boy and marry him?"

Ethan rolled his eyes. "We are *not* asking her that." He opened the door for Maryl, who had dressed a little more casually than a normal Sunday – designer jeans and a new white ruffled blouse with a navy sweater. She had tried to tame her red wad of frizz, then tied it up in a band, but Ethan had wanted her to wear it down. He told her she looked nice.

She brought a green salad, the least dangerous dish she could offer. However, she did bring all the vegetables in separate baggies—peppers, mushrooms, carrots, celery, cucumbers—just to be safe, and two kinds of dressing.

They walked up the porch steps and at the door, Maryl could see over Muriel's shoulder into a modest, comfy living room and a steamy kitchen. It had been her parents' house, Muriel explained later, and she and Nathan shared it now since they were both single. "It has plenty of space with three bedrooms," she was saying, "...and when Sarah and Chloe moved out, it just made sense for Nathan to move in."

"Oh," said Maryl, thinking she was already supposed to know this background. "Makes sense." She was helping Muriel set out dishes. *Maybe Caleb had been in the armed services? Vietnam? Or maybe they split up for a while?*

"So, Sarah lived here? Are you related?"

"Oh, no. I had just inherited this house, and poor Sarah was going through some major struggles. It was really easy to have her here since she's so quiet and is such a great cook. Did you have a chance to wander through the gardens she put in? Lots of herbs and healing plants. She even planted a small cherry tree and we had the first fruits this season!"

"Sounds like it was a win-win. How long was she here?"

"Almost two years. She stayed here until...well, until she was better."

"Better from childbirth?"

"Well, not exactly. She just needed to stay somewhere else for a while... She was getting some help to keep herself safe." Muriel quickly changed the subject. "That was so nice of you to bring a salad. You didn't have to bring anything."

"Of course I did. I am another mouth to feed."

As the aroma of poached salmon wafted from the kitchen, the ten friends gathered around the big patio table, where Muriel had strung holiday lights to make it look festive. Two tall porch heaters radiated welcome heat and Inky, the cat, snaked through the twenty legs, looking for love and snacks. The cat monitored the deck for Gefilte fish droppings, which Muriel was serving with horseradish to start the meal. Next was the salmon with cucumber dill sauce.

"You've outdone yourself, Muriel," Jake chuckled, eyeing the crispy Brussels sprouts.

Barbara chimed in, "Speaking of outdoing, did you guys see the new mural on South Street?"

The conversation flowed as freely as the kosher wine, touching on Philly's art scene and the Eagles' latest game.

"These sprouts could convert a vegetable hater," Ethan declared, reaching for seconds.

"Okay, Mr. Picky Eater." Sarah shot a look at Ethan. "Remind me to give you a custom piece of dessert I made for you… one without raisins."

A wave of stifled laughter rippled through the group, and in the commotion, Nathan accidentally dumped a buttery sprout on his "Rocky" t-shirt. "Dang it," he muttered, eliciting more poorly concealed smirks and giggles.

When Sarah brought out the Tzimmes cake, a collective "ooh" filled the room. "Now that's a sweet end to a perfect Philly night," Susan sighed contentedly, fork poised for the first bite.

As the evening wound down, chairs scraped against the decking as the friends reluctantly rose from the table. "I think I need to be rolled out of here," Jake groaned, patting his stomach. Ellen stretched, stifling a yawn. "Sarah, that Tzimmes cake was to die for," she said, giving her friend a quick hug. The group shuffled towards the front door, as Nathan continued to lament his stained shirt.

Sarah and Caleb followed Ethan down the porch steps. With a smile that teetered between sweet and sinister, Sarah present-ed the specially wrapped dessert to Ethan. "Enjoy," she purred, nestling against Caleb.

"Hope we got the dosage right, honey," Caleb quipped. Ethan's face remained carved in stone as Sarah's shoulders circled in a slow-motion shrug.

Maryl carried the half-empty salad bowl out the door and waved to them.

Dishes crashed in the kitchen. Maryl set the bowl on the porch step and followed Ethan back in to check out the commotion. Nathan was on the floor with whipped cream in his hair and the black-and-white cat licking his fingers. "Dang this cat," Nathan complained.

"Oh, you know Inky is your favorite," Muriel said, wiping his hair with a paper towel. Nathan stood. "Oh well, I needed to take a shower this week anyway."

Maryl saw Ethan looking at a framed photograph of a man who looked like Caleb in military uniform and medals that had been pushed back on a shelf in the bookcase. It looked like the kind of framed photo you would see on a casket at a funeral. "Is that Caleb's father?" she asked no one in particular.

"No, actually that's Caleb," Muriel said. "He was a handsome pilot, wasn't he?"

Ethan quickly collected Maryl and led her out to the car, making it a bit difficult to retrieve the salad bowl. "What's the hurry?" she asked Ethan.

"No hurry. It's just time to go."

TWENTY-ONE

In late September, they all piled into a party limo van and headed three hours across the state to Beaver Stadium in University Park. The Nittany Lions, with an 11-1 record, were playing East Carolina who had a 2-9 record and, with those odds, the van full of fans were already celebrating a sure win. In fact, there was a pot with each of the guys betting on the point spread. Ethan put in two hundred-dollar bills like it was chump change and bet a 5-point spread.

Sarah, already tipsy at mile twenty, was the bookie, keeping track of who put in what. Maryl watched her closely, wondering what her story was. She could tell that Sarah wasn't particularly fond of Ethan, avoiding him when she could. With her husband as Ethan's best friend, that must have been hard on her.

Caleb threw in $50 and bet a seven-point spread, smirking at Ethan. "Okay Krahlman, you're on!"

Maryl was happy to sit next to Nathan in the back while Ethan did his life-of-the-party thing in the front and kept everyone laughing… and drunk. Nathan had a shy smile watching his friends argue politics and repeat themselves as the cooler emptied.

"So, 'Ethan's new girlfriend from Seattle'…are you Jewish?"

Maryl took a moment to answer. She looked at Nathan to see where this question might be coming from. "No. I'm a recovering Catholic." They both smiled. "But I'm certainly learning some Yiddish."

Her favorite new word of the week was "meshuggeneh" even though Ethan had used it against her when he said, "You must have been meshuggeneh to think you could wear that to the client meeting, babe." She had worn her favorite orange zippered jacket with her black skirt and tights, and he said she looked like a Halloween pumpkin. She had laughed it off and went on to tell Ethan the funny story of Darrell Dizzle. Ethan had simply shaken his head.

Maryl, with 50,000 other fans, had cheered for the brand-new Seattle Seahawks in the year she graduated. But this was a different story. It was LOUD and raucous and competitive, and she was sure there were more than 100,000 people there. Ethan ordered beers for everyone, warm peanuts and hotdogs, and a pretzel with mustard for himself.

She hadn't mentioned that today was her birthday, thinking that Ethan would remember. She was wedged between Ethan and Caleb and could barely hear over the roar of the crowd. The two boys discussed work over half-time. "We're introducing currency options," Caleb shouted to Ethan. "You should get in on it."

Ethan shot back "Oh, so I can gamble on the yen and the pound sterling?"

"No, man. If you wanna buy that yacht you always talk about over in Germany, they're gonna make you pay in Deutsche Marks. Hedge your bets, man. You never know what's going to happen with the dollar." Caleb explained.

Maryl broke in. "What exactly is the PHLX?"

Ethan answered before Caleb could. "Philadelphia has its own stock exchange, babe. Can you say that about Seattle?"

"And…" Caleb cut in. "It's the oldest stock exchange in the country. You are living in a place of illustrious history, ma'am." Caleb was on his fourth beer, but she knew he was trying to rescue her from Ethan's sarcasm.

"What was your college team?" Caleb continued the conversation, leaning in so he didn't have to yell above the half-time band.

Ethan cut in. "She went to University of Washington, home of the loser Huskies. I never even heard of them before I plucked Maryl from that little town."

"What are you talking about? We finished the season eleven and one last year!" Maryl protested.

Ethan ignored that and said, "Babe, don't say *we*. You're not Seattle anymore. You're East Coast now, where all the winners are."

Why are you being such a brat today? Because we're with your friends?

The crew left the game early, as the Lions were ahead, and they had imbibed to the limit. Caleb sat up front with the driver and promptly fell asleep. Sarah stared dreamily out the window, while Ethan and Simon talked heatedly in the next two seats.

"No, no, Ethan. Listen. Listen. I heard you and Caleb talking about money stuff, but trash is where it's at now...speshly hash trash," Simon was saying.

Ethan laughed out loud. "Hash trash?"

"My dad works at talk cigars in Jersey and there's something big going down. He says some big company is buying them and airbuddies gonna make gobs uh dough." Simon was drunk. "We should ask Caleb to hook us up, huh."

"Your dad changed jobs? I thought he worked at that environmental company."

"He does. That's what I'm tryin' to tell ya. Listen. Listen."

"Okay, okay. But how do they make money off trash? Is this one of your stories with a punchline?" Ethan hadn't seen Simon so sincere.

"Oh well, it's all because of the new enwiring... enwental.. . ruglations they're going to pass next month. Super fun." Simon slurred. "My dad says companies are scrambling to clean up their hashards...their *hass*ards or they'll be paying huge monies in money fines. Super fun."

"Oh. Okay, buddy. Super fun. Well, I'm going to rest my eyes, okay?"

Maryl had been watching the conversation and tried to determine whether it was a friendly one, as Simon was being so insistent, and Ethan was clearly brushing him off. She leaned forward, intending to offer him a kind word to counteract Ethan's callousness. "Simon..."

Ethan shook his head at her and swiped his flat palm quickly across his own throat.

She sat back in her seat and joined the other three ladies sipping the last bottle of champagne in the cooler. *Poor Simon. He is really trying to convince Ethan of something. Wonder what.*

She filed it in the back of her now-tipsy brain and focused her attention on Sarah. She was a strange one, quiet but with an attitude of aggression somehow. Maybe it was motherhood, or maybe marriage issues. At halftime, Sarah and Ethan had volunteered for beer-and-peanut replenishments. As Maryl had to pee, she had joined them. It was an awkward walk with them, and she felt tension but dismissed it as simply a mismatch in personalities.   But was there something between them that caused the contention? She would bring it up with Barbara on another day, or maybe the next time she saw Ellen.

"Oh, sorry. What?" Maryl looked at Susan who asked the question again.

"So, how long have you and Ethan known each other?"

"Well, we have known each other for over a year now, but most of it was long distance you know." She almost felt embarrassed, sitting in this limo with little in common with any of them, even Ethan. "But he still forgot it was my birthday today." It just slipped out, and she regretted it immediately.

Susan whispered, "Yikes. So how are you two getting along?"

"Fine, I guess." Maryl knew Susan was a divorce attorney so this line of direct questioning was probably normal for her. But she felt uncomfortable telling her about her growing concerns. On the other hand, these were the only friends who knew them both and she was going to be spending a lot of time with them.

She had found a bottle of Valium in his bathroom and was freaked out about it. "Have you ever taken Valium?" she asked. "I mean, do you know what it is?"

They looked at each other and then at Maryl. "Yes. A lot of us do. Don't you?"

"Oh no. *I* don't," she continued. "I'm just trying to figure out why Ethan might be taking it."

"Yeah, it's not a big deal. It's for anxiety," offered Barbara. "I wouldn't worry about it. He must be under a lot of stress at work."

Slumped in her seat, Sarah mumbled something that sounded like "knight in rapist armor" which caused Maryl to crank her neck and stare. Sarah was drunk, or over-medicated, or both.

"What was that?" Maryl asked.

Sarah turned and looked out the window as if Maryl weren't there.

Maryl looked back at Barbara to see if she had heard Sarah's words. Nothing. *My mind is playing tricks on me*, thought Maryl. *I haven't told a soul about that.*

US Route 322 had been a slow mess leaving State College, as it always was after the games, and the guys had fallen asleep in the front. But the winding road after that was picturesque with rolling hills of green and now the van crossed over the Susquehanna River Bridge in Harrisburg. Churning brown water below them, both sides of the river green and the sky so blue.

All is well. She forced herself into positivity. *I'm a very lucky girl.*

Soon they would reach the I-76 and be almost home. She chuckled at "the I-76". Where she came from, the interstates were called by their number. I-5 or I-90. But here, people added a "the." The I-76. The I-81. The I-74.

They dropped onto the I-76 and soon were in Philadelphia, and then up Ford Road to home.

She was humming the theme song to Rocky in her head.

TWENTY-TWO

It was a Wednesday which meant her boss, Eugene Daniels, was in the office all day. He sauntered in and dropped into the chair facing Maryl's desk.

"How's it going, eh?" Daniels asked casually. No one called him Eugene. Just Daniels. For her first week, she thought that was his first name. He was a large pasty man with full lips that were unintentionally pouty, with his bottom lip always pushing on his upper one, giving him a slightly dopey look.

"Great," she said.

"I hear some of the guys are calling you Mel, for short."

"You can call me Maryl," she answered. She still was unsure why Ethan had pegged Daniels as an idiot so she thought she would distance herself for now.

"How was your weekend?"

"Great. We went to the Penn State game. Is that where you went to school?"

"Boston. Boston College."

"I see. My folks moved to Weston not too long ago."

"Oh. That's a pricey little hamlet, eh?"

"Charming."

"Yes, I spend a lot of time up there fishing with my college buddies. We used to catch some huge bass in the Charles River."

"Ew, I thought the Charles was polluted."

"Myth," he said as if he'd answered that a million times. "But what we really love is catching those big stripers off Martha's Vineyard. I've got some photos in my office if you want to check them out."

"Stripers?"

"Striped Bass."

"What did you major in at Boston College?"

"Just liberal arts in general," he said. "I thought about majoring in theology."

"Yeah, I'm a recovering Catholic," Maryl deadpanned.

Daniels stood. "Well, I'll let you get back to it. Welcome to Philly."

He was a sweet guy, Maryl thought. *Wonder why Ethan thinks he's not.*

She thought she might check in with Clarke.

"Hey, Clarke."

"How's my chair?" Clarke asked.

"Warm."

"Gross."

"Hey, Daniels just came in and sat down to tell me about his fishing prowess, mainly with those big stripers."

Clarke chuckled. "Isn't he something?"

"Anything I should know about him other than he's a good Irish Catholic boy and Ethan is not?"

"That's pretty much it. But you know, I'm from Boston so I have a soft spot in my heart for Daniels. In fact, he's even been up to Dad and Mom's with me. So be nice to him, okay?"

"Like I wouldn't be?"

"Hey as long as I've got you on the phone, do you mind if I ask a few questions about the Darrell Dizzle project here at Boeing?" It was a complex application since there was so much propriety surrounding the data and the fact that several departments wanted to share it.

"So, how about they modify the structure of that part of the data-base, and we just do a schema reorg for them?" Maryl suggested.

"Mark says that will throw off the report writing they need to do," Clarke said.

They talked for another forty minutes. When she hung up with Clarke, she was missing that client, that office, and her buddies there.

"Say hi to Mark and Dan for me, Clarke."

"Will do. And oh, tell Daniels "Go Eagles" for me.

"Football?"

"No, silly. Hockey."

A week later, Maryl was in Daniels' office discussing the upcoming Squibb trial with James. "We need this one. Ethan thinks it's his territory, but it's not."

Ethan argued that the company was founded in Brooklyn, had a bio lab in Syracuse, and a large facility in Lawrence, which was basically a suburb of New York City.

Daniels argued that New Jersey, especially Princeton and Lawrenceville was his territory. The feud was on and Maryl was in the middle of it. "So, it's up to you two to bring it on in. I'm counting on you."

"Got it," said Maryl. She was looking at a photo of a sweaty hockey team on Daniels' bookshelf. "Oh, that reminds me. Clarke said to tell you 'Go Eagles'."

Daniels burst out laughing and pointed to the photo. "*That* is the Boston College ice hockey team, the Eagles."

"Ah. Now it makes sense," she said. *Not a bit.*

"You know, Clarke is a hockey player as well," Daniels said. "In fact, Clarke's dad and Len Ceglarski are good friends. They take Clarke and me to the games up there a few times a season."

Maryl and James had blank looks, so Daniels continued. "Ceglarski is the head coach of the Eagles. He also went to college with Clarke's dad. We all share the same alma mater. He also happens to be Hockey East head coach of the year. Next time you talk to Clarke, just yell 'Frozen four eighty-four, eh?'"

Now I get it. Clarke. Daniels. Clarke's father. Boston. No way was Ethan going to break up that band.

She was talking this through with James as they strategized over a beer in the breakroom later that afternoon. Maryl thought they had Ethan dead to rights on this one, but James interrupted her celebration. "What you have to know about Ethan, in a business sense, is that he is always two steps ahead, maneuvering in unexpected ways—which is good in that it keeps the competition off balance, but bad because no one in *this* company knows what he's about to do next. He keeps everyone on their toes, and not always in a good way."

Maryl thought about it. "You mean Ethan is the knight on a chessboard."

James stared at her. "Exactly. So, we need to be just as cunning."

Twenty-Three

Sunday came.

Maryl had showered and was sorting through a box in the spare room when Ethan shuffled in. "Whatcha doin?" he asked. "I'm headed to the lobby for the paper."

This wasn't the first man she had shared space with. But it was the first stranger. In a strange house. In a strange culture.

He read the Washington Post and insisted that the only way to drink coffee was with cream and two sugars. She still read the Seattle Times and drank her coffee black. He wore black slacks or khakis and loafers every day, while she wore jeans, tight t-shirts, and tennis shoes every chance she got. His idea of a great night in was ordering pizza and watching sports from the couch. Hers was cooking a great meal and sitting at the table talking. If she got control of the remote and turned on a movie, he would go into the bedroom and read.

She was trying to blend their lives together, as she thought that's how it should work. But she still had her things in boxes in the other room. None of her books on his shelves, none of her clothes in his walk-in closet. Her toiletries still sat in the black train case she carried back and forth from the bathroom to the spare room, which Ethan had begun calling *her room.*

Was she doing this subconsciously? Or was she waiting for him to suggest that she move all the way in?

She hadn't wanted to blast into his life and upset his routines, thinking that she would do that over time. But as time went on, it became more awkward. She saw how tidy his closet was, but a jungle of shoes occupied the floor. He hadn't cleaned out any drawers in his bathroom for her—she was still using the guest bath by the front door. The kitchen had all the utensils for cooking, but none of the ingredients. Not even baking soda.

She felt she was renting space in his house. In his life.

Every Sunday they went to dinner at Miriam and Abe's. Ellen would be there with her beau Zach, who looked like Tweedle Dee to Maryl. She couldn't figure out the attraction for Ethan's sister, as she was gorgeous and fun and had a promising career in marketing. But the more couples she met on the East Coast, the more she learned not to judge so stridently.

Here on the Main Line, it became apparent to Maryl that wanting to marry a wealthy man was viewed as a practical objective, not a stealthy giggle, and financial stability was highly valued. Jewish men were not seeking a glamorous porn queen with big breasts and perfect teeth; Instead, they wanted a dependable Jewish wife who would allow them to shine in public but be a needy little boy in the privacy of home. They wanted a partner like their mothers, capable of cooking, cleaning, raising children, and managing the household. They, too, desired security—the security of a good wife and a stable family.

Maryl had learned to wear a nice blouse and skirt on these Sundays, and she always brought flowers, since her cooking skills were not appreciated at these gatherings. Chicken and potato salad were not only too casual but not at all kosher. And she had not mastered brisket yet, so there was that.

"Come in. Come in," Miriam said, as Ethan led through the door. "Oh, you bring such pretty flowers. Did you get them at Good Grocer? You know, they get them from Mitchell's Nursery, so you might want to go there sometime and get them direct. He has a nice little business."

Jewish, Maryl presumed. "Sure." Maryl gave her a sweet smile.

The warm aroma of freshly baked challah filled the air. The table was set with Ethan's grandmother's delicate white China on a crisp white linen tablecloth. Maryl was always afraid she would stain that cloth with a slip of a fork, or a clumsy brush of the candle sticks.

"We're serving your favorite, Ethan," Miriam called from the kitchen.

Maryl glanced at Ethan on the couch. He mouthed "brisket" to her.

She walked over the thick red and black carpet and sat next to him. "Your mother spoils you," she said.

"Well, I *am* the firstborn son. And she made matzo ball soup in your honor. Have you ever had it?"

"I don't think so."

"You'll love it."

They sat at the table, and Abe brought out a steaming platter of brisket, already falling apart on the plate. And then out came the potatoes, honey-glazed carrots, and green beans. Maryl was in heaven.

Abe sat at the head of the table. Normally, Ethan sat at the other end, but since Zach was there, and he was so large, that seat was his for the evening. Ellen sat to his right and loaded his plate for him as the dishes were passed around.

Barbara was beginning a tale of her worst client of the week and already had people laughing. "And as Dr. Klein leaned over and gave him the punchline of this joke, the poor patient laughed so hard that blood and drool sputtered all over Doc's face and gown. It was so gross."

Jake patted Barbara's leg and said, "But honey, tell them the news."

Ellen's eyes widened and she sucked in her breath. "Oh my god... are you...?"

Barbara giggled. "No. No. I just got a big promotion. The community college wants me to teach dental hygiene two nights a week, and

Dr. Klein gave me a raise so I wouldn't even think about leaving the clinic."

"Oh. Ha." Ellen breathed. "That's great. Congrats. So, are you going to teach and keep doing your job?"

"Yes. I think it will be fun."

"And when I get *my* degree, she can quit both," Jake chimed in. The room was silent for a minute. Barbara immediately served Jake more potatoes.

Wanting to save Barbara, Maryl cut in. "Jake, I've been meaning to ask you—What is the biggest difference between practicing real estate and litigating it?"

"Power," Jake answered. "Seriously though, there are so many things to fight about in real estate: seller's disclosure statements, property lines, easements, and then every inch of a house in the inspection reports."

Maryl chimed in. "Yes, I'm having a hard time keeping track of it all in Seattle."

"What do you mean?" asked Barbara.

"Well, I still own several houses back there."

"You do?"

"She's a slumlord." Ethan laughed. "And we'll be getting rid of them soon. She's never going back."

"Aww, that's so sweet, Ethan," Barbara gushed.

No, it wasn't. Maryl tried to smile.

Jake jumped in to save her. "Well, actually, Ethan. Real estate is a great investment..."

"Yeah yeah yeah. But not in cowboy and Indian territory."

Stung by Ethan's comments, Maryl tried to ignore him. "Yes. I like balancing my portfolio with some real estate. Plus, I like houses and land. Seems to me, there won't be enough to go around in the future."

"She's a true cowboy," Ethan said. "Ma, what's for dessert?"

"Cinnamon-apple kugel, of course." Miriam and Ellen cleared the dishes as Maryl excused herself to the bathroom down the hall, needing a moment to process Ethan's behavior. It bordered on being mean. When she left the bathroom, she couldn't help noticing that the door was ajar in the room across the hall. A corner bookshelf held an array of tchotchkes, reminiscent of grade school keepsakes, and among them stood a photograph. The image captured a young Ethan, his arm draped around a slightly smaller boy who bore a striking resemblance to him. A cousin, perhaps?

That night, when Ethan and Maryl fell into bed, he took her in his arms.

"You know I was just kidding around at dinner tonight, right?"

"Sure. And I was kidding back."

"Well, I know you're a strong woman and can take it. That's one of the things I like about you."

"One?" Maryl remembered a similar conversation with Kyle eons ago and felt a little guilty thinking of Kyle while she was in bed with Ethan. Events had certainly flipped in a few short years.

"Hey, where'd you go?" Ethan squeezed her and whispered, "Let's not use your diaphragm tonight." He kissed her deeply. She was so touched that she nearly burst into tears.

"I'll be right back," she whispered and headed for her bathroom. *Maybe being around his family had made him start thinking of having his own children? Maybe the way his family had come to embrace her meant that she had officially been accepted and they could move on to the next step.*

Whatever the reason, she slid back into bed, held his face in her hands, and kissed him tenderly, slowly peeling off her panties. Ethan took his time as well, placing his fingers between her legs and slowly touching her in circles the way she liked until she began a soft moaning. He kneeled over her, taking each of her breasts into his mouth, one at a time, and then back to the other one. She was delirious and could feel his member rock hard against her thigh.

"Are you ready, babe?" he moaned.

"Yes. Yes. Yes," she said and arched her back, taking the full length of him slowly at first and then begging him to thrust.

On the way to the train station the next morning, she assumed he would make some mention of their love-making the night before, but he was silent. She had risen early to make him a cup of coffee the way he liked it, cream and two sugars, and he sipped it and tried to read the paper at the same time.

"Damn!" he swore as she took a turn too sharply.

She grabbed a paper napkin out of the console and offered it to him. "Sorry. Hey, I meant to ask you, do you have a cousin who looks like you? Maybe a little younger?"

"What? No. Why?"

"Oh, I just saw a photograph at your folks' house and—"

"You were snooping in the bedrooms? Are you serious, Maryl? What kind of person does that?" Ethan jumped out of the car and slammed the door, making his way down to the train.

The Philly office was abuzz with talk of the MOVE explosions and the block of houses that went up in flames the night before. Police had dropped a bomb from a helicopter out in the Cobbs Creek neighbor-hood and allowed it to explode, killing six adults and five children. Firefighters were told to stand down while two city blocks of houses burned.

James and Tom had rigged up the large monitor in the conference room to tune into the news channels.

It was unclear whether MOVE was a Christian, naturalist organization or a black liberation group, but the police had labeled them terrorists and had evacuated sixty-one neighboring homes, with the full intent of burning the entire neighborhood down, leaving 250 people homeless the next morning.

Philadelphia was in shock.

As the story pieced together, it turned out that the attack was definitely planned, as 500 police officers had shown up to clear that one home, shutting off the water and electricity to force them out.

Five hundred cops. To move a dozen people out of one house.

Maryl couldn't wrap her head around it. This was brutal. The rest of the office sat in silence for the next few hours watching the news unfold. Several called their families, knowing they would be in shock, too. Maryl called the New York City office, but Ethan was in a meeting.

An hour later, Patty handed Maryl a message from Ethan. *Go on home. I'll take a cab. Need to hold a quick branch meeting.*

She understood. At home, she shed her work clothes, poured a glass of wine, and noticed the message button blinking. She punched the button.

"Ethan, this is Caleb. We gotta talk about this before the market opens in the morning. Call me tonight."

When he walked through the door later that evening, wiggling out of his sports jacket and flipping his loafers into the corner, she brought him the chicken dinner she had prepared, and sat beside him on the couch.

"Can you believe it?" she began.

"What?" He looked at her.

"Ethan. MOVE. The MOVE explosions and deaths. Right here in our backyard."

"No. It's not right here in our backyard. It was over in Cobbs Creek. Nowhere near here. Bunch of black activists. Good riddance."

Maryl was stunned.

"Ethan. Are you serious? Oh my god."

"Don't be dramatic, Maryl."

"Then… then… what was your emergency branch meeting for?"

"It wasn't an emergency. It was just the only time everyone was in the same room. We're moving some clients around. Judy is going on maternity leave."

"Oh. I didn't know she was pregnant."

Ethan screwed up his face. "Yes, you did. I told you."

She let it drop. *Was this what Valium sounded like?* She stood to clear his dishes.

"Can you bring me a soda?" he called after her.

"Sure. Oh, by the way, Caleb wants you to call him back."

Two weeks went by. December was looming, and with it, Hanukkah. Maryl was distracted by that new holiday and was in touch with Barbara and Ellen about what she should know, and do, and wear, and bring.

"Just wear something nice," Barbara said over a late-morning coffee that Sunday. They were at The Village Bagel in Ardmore, so Maryl could hop over to Miriam and Abe's by one p.m. "And it's your first Hanukkah. No one expects you to bring food, and there are plenty of big mouths there who will love telling you all about the traditions."

"I hope I finally get to meet Chloe. Do you think Sarah will bring her?" Maryl had yet to meet Sarah's daughter.

"Oh, no. Chloe isn't coming." Barbara said it so fast that it surprised Maryl. And then, "I mean, they are, uh, well, Chloe is a lot to handle for Sarah. And besides, Chloe is so little, and it's… well, it's a solemn day."

"Hanukkah? But isn't it a celebration? Like Christmas?"

"Well, yes, but it's at Miriam and Abe's, so...." Barbara flipped her eyebrows up and changed the subject to Jake.

"How's Jake doing in law school?" Maryl asked, thinking the conversation about Sarah was an odd one. *After all, hadn't Ethan said that the Jewish holidays were more about families than dogma? Why wouldn't a young child be invited?*

"It's hard," Barbara answered. "He wants to go into real estate law since he knows so much about it, but none of his classes are about that. So, he's partly bored and partly overwhelmed."

"Which puts him in a weird mood at home, I suppose?" Maryl was feeling solidarity.

"Not really. He's such a sweetie. I try to make sure everything is calm at home. Clean and calm. So he can study. But yeah. Some days he just wants to put his head in my lap and escape."

"Nice. The great escape," said Maryl. "I feel for him. He's so lucky to have you."

Barbara flashed Maryl an appreciative smile, while Maryl wondered almost aloud if Valium might be the group's drug of choice.

Twenty-Four

"Are you seriously going to work in that?" Ethan was on an angry morning rant about something at work. Maryl had on her brown wool skirt and matching jacket with an ivory blouse that tied in a bow at her throat. "You need to go shopping with my sister."

Home life was becoming more difficult. She dreaded being alone with Ethan. He was surly and distracted but wanted her home with him whenever they weren't at work.

When she picked him up at the train station one evening, she was five minutes late because of traffic. Handing him his evening cup of coffee, she leaned over to kiss him hello and he jerked his head away from her.

"God, you went to client meetings today with that breath? Jesus, Maryl." She didn't open her mouth again the whole way home. From then on, she kept breath mints in the car and in her purse. *Were her clients and fellow employees also grossed out by her breath? Why hadn't anyone said anything?* She was embarrassed and spent a lot of time going back over the past week and her interactions in her head.

"And this coffee is cold." He put it down dramatically in the cup holder and looked out the window. "Jesus."

She clicked the gate fob on her visor, and steered into the parking garage, widening her eyes in the sudden dark after the bright sunlight of the city.

"I'll get out here. See you up there." He opened the door, escaped, and slammed it shut.

Asshole. He's such an asshole.

"Hey," she called after him as sweetly as she could through her clenched jaw, "Can you please check the mail on your way up? I'm expecting the rent checks."

She parked, gathered her coat and briefcase, tossed his full cup of coffee in the waste bin by the door, knowing she should have emptied the liquid out first, and clicked the elevator button.

Upstairs, she changed into jeans, poured a vodka tonic, and started dinner. Ethan liked vegetables sautéed in olive oil. She complied. Carrots and beets rolled around in the hot pan as she pushed them with the spatula.

What the fuck? What am I doing wrong? Why is he being such a dick to me?

She had worked up a full diatribe, but when he walked in the door, he headed straight for the bedroom and shut the door. No words and no mail.

She turned off the burner and knocked on the door.

"Ethan? Ethan, we need to talk. Ethan!" She turned the knob. It was locked.

What the hell? Should she ignore him, as he was doing to her? Should she break down the door? Was he crying in there and didn't want her to see?

She could not imagine him crying.

On her way to the kitchen, she stopped and looked at the phone, remembering the odd phone message from Caleb. She'd ask Ethan about it later. Or maybe not.

Maryl settled into the only piece of furniture in the second bedroom and dialed Ethan's sister.

She had met Ellen on a few of their weekly dinners at the parents' house in Ardmore. She was the female version of Ethan, bigger than life in a small room, same humor, same laugh. On more than one occasion, she had hugged Maryl as she said goodbye. "You're one of us, now! And we take care of our own."

"Hey, Ellen. It's Maryl. Hope I'm not interrupting your dinner."

"Oh hi! No, no. We're done with dinner and Zach is doing the dishes. What's up, girlfriend?"

"Well..." She paused and breathed into the phone.

"Ethan's getting to you?"

"Well, I just don't know what's going on with him. One minute he's great and the next minute he shuts himself in the bedroom and won't talk to me. I don't know what I've done to deserve the silent treatment. I keep going over our interactions in the last few weeks and I can't figure out his behavior."

Ellen was silent for a minute.

"I don't think it's anything you've done, Maryl. Ethan has bouts of depression. I guess he didn't tell you. I'm sure it will pass. Don't worry about it." Ellen was overly upbeat. "So what's new with you?"

Taken aback by Ellen's savoir-faire, Maryl mumbled into the phone. "Umm good. Everything is good. Except for this of course. I just can't..."

"Well good then. Hey, we should grab coffee one of these weekends. Let me know. Gotta go check on Mr. Dishwasher. Talk soon!"

And with that, she hung up, leaving Maryl to wonder about that family and the ease with which they swept things under the rug.

Much later, after dinner was cold and packed into Tupperware in the fridge, he emerged, said nothing to her, and turned on the TV.

"Ethan." Maryl wanted to start the conversation.

"Not now," Ethan said without taking his eyes off the television.

"But I'd like to talk to you."

Turning to look at her with furious eyes, he gave her an ugly once-over and said "You look like hell." And turned back to the tube.

"Ethan. Just stop it. Goddammit. Why are you being such an ass? Is it something at work? Something I did? Just tell me. I don't like this Ethan that you are showing me. We're partners, but lately you're just mean and hurtful, and I don't deserve it. So just talk to me!"

"You wouldn't understand." He stomped back into the bedroom and slammed the door.

She met Ellen for coffee that Saturday morning, wanting to know what it was that "she wouldn't understand."

"So, tell me about your job at the magazine," Maryl said. "It sounds fabulous." She knew that Philadelphia Magazine was an old iconic publication, and if you worked there, you knew everyone who was a big deal in Philly. Or had been a big deal. Or was about to be a big deal.

"Well, it's not really that glamorous," Ellen began. "Most of my day is spent calling on companies who will advertise in the magazine. I have a lot of repeat customers, but I have to keep sweetening the pie for them."

"Like how?"

"Like every holiday I usually set up some sort of discount for a bigger commitment on their end. For instance, if Aldus Stores will sign up for twelve months of full-page ads, I'll give them two Sixers season tickets."

"The Seventy-Sixers?" Maryl's face lit up. "And then, in return, they must take you to the games with the second ticket, right?"

They giggled.

"So, the Sixers give season tickets to the magazine?"

"Yes, well once a year we do a full-page interview with one of the popular players, so that's the trade."

"And you get to attend that interview?"

"Sometimes!"

"So, not to pry, but how do they pay you for all this work? There must be a lot of pressure on you to keep the old clients and bring in the new ones."

"No kidding."

"Sounds like you and I have similar carrots in our jobs."

"Commission," they both said in unison and laughed out loud.

"I mean they do pay me a bit of salary, but most of my motivation is the commission, yes."

"Well, heck, woman. If the magazine ever gives you Sixers tickets, I'm your plus-one."

"Oh, believe me, I suddenly have a lot of friends during basketball season."

"Including Ethan?" Maryl teased.

"Well, Ethan and the guys usually get their own season tickets."

Of course, they do.

"Makes sense." Maryl hesitated but then asked as casually as she could, "So, hey, the other day at your folks' house I saw a photograph of a young Ethan and another kid in baseball uniforms. Is that a relative? They look so much alike."

Ellen put down her coffee and watched the black liquid circles until they settled. "Well, yes. That was our brother, Evan. Ethan's twin."

Silence from both of them, now caught on an island of awkwardness, with the hum of the coffee shop all around them.

"Was?" Maryl ventured, and when Ellen stayed quiet, she tried to back out of the conversation, but how? "I'm so sorry, Ellen" was all she could think of.

"No, it's okay, Maryl. It's just been a long time since anyone brought it up. They were very close. Evan didn't really want to play baseball, but Ethan talked him into it. You know how Ethan does that. And the second game of the season, Evan caught a fast pitch right in the face and died instantly at the plate. He hated batting. He was afraid of the ball. Ethan would take him to the batting cages on weekends, but it didn't help. He just...he just dropped. Right there in front of everyone. My mother started screaming and then everyone was screaming, and Ethan was standing over him. Next thing we know, Ethan grabbed a bat and went after the pitcher and all hell broke loose. They had to call the police, and the ambulance came and he just... he was dead...right there."

"Oh my god."

"Yes. I mean it's been years, but Ethan just never got over it. He blamed himself of course. He started picking fights at school for no reason, and his grades were awful, and he quit the team. Mom and Dad finally took him to a counselor who told him to join the swim team, so that's how he ended up in that sport. Even to this day, he goes to the pool, and when he can't, he takes really long baths. Sometimes I hear him talking to Evan while he's in there. It's creepy but I guess it helps him."

"Ellen, I had no idea."

"No, I guess he wouldn't have told you yet." She dabbed at the corner of one eye and then said, "So, how is *your* job?" as if the biggest bomb ever had not been dropped between them. "Ethan says you're a pistol."

Maryl took a sip of cold coffee to absorb the abrupt segue.

"Well, just like you, I'm scrambling. Trying to get up to speed on the customers that Clarke sold and researching the market here for new prospects. It's daunting."

"Well, I'm sure Ethan is a big help there. We've grown up here. He knows all the players."

And is he one himself? Maryl swallowed the question before it escaped, feeling guilty for even thinking it, now that she had more insight. Instead, she said, "He's so busy with his own branch."

"I think if Ethan had the choice he would prefer to manage the Philly branch," Ellen said. "It's close to home, he knows the market, his commute would be easier, he could hang out with his buddies more. You might have noticed that for all his bravado, he's kind of a homebody. I think a lot of us just really like it here in Philly and we don't mind staying in our neighborhoods with our friends."

"We take care of our own." Ellen's words rang in her ears.

"It's a nice family feeling," said Maryl. "The west coast is more about moving away from your parents as fast as you can, and striking out on your own, I think."

"Was Walla Walla like that?"

"Well, no," said Maryl sheepishly. "I think I was one of the few who escaped from there. But then again, my family wasn't as tight-knit as yours. I love the closeness you have with your parents and your brother."

"Well, you're part of our family now," Ellen patted her hand, and then, "Can you believe that Hanukkah is almost here?" Her eyes were dancing and her black curls bobbing. She loved a party. "Are you excited for your first one? Wait, is this your first Hanukkah? I hope so because mom and dad always make a big deal out of it and everyone has fun."

"You, in particular, right?" Maryl smiled, teasing her almost sister-in-law.

"Haha. You guessed it!"

She was closer to understanding her man and felt a little closer to Ellen after today, but she needed to take her time stepping through this minefield that was Ethan. All excuses aside, he was still an asshole. Maryl hummed her way back to her car with Paul McCartney.

whisper words of wisdom, let it be...

Of course, she wouldn't let it be, but she didn't feel like a train was bearing down on her anymore with no escape from the tracks. She had a better understanding of him now. She could maneuver.

Twenty-Five

⸻◆⸻

Fast forward to Tuesday.

"Well, I talked to Keith at corporate and he thinks they could add four fields with dropdowns," She was on the phone with Ray.

"Okay, nice work, champ," Ray and Maryl kept in touch, particularly about the Seattle clients.

She was glad to be working directly with Ray again, even though it was a bit clandestine. She could sense that he was happy about it, too.

"This will solve the one issue that Boeing is having with all that shared data," Ray said. "I'm thinking Puget Power could use this tool as well. It will help make their reports look like reports instead of lines on green paper. Will Keith prioritize this for us?"

"It depends on the revenue. How much can we get from Boeing for this additional capability?" She asked.

"I can probably get another $50,000 from each.

"Hmmm. $100K would pay for another coder, right? Corporate should justify that." Maryl's brain was jumping. "You know, Ray, we should make this into a real product and sell it to all our clients globally. They're all going to need an easier way to structure their reports, right?"

Ray was chuckling.

"What?" Maryl was visualizing Ray's face with his teeth showing and his eyes squeezed nearly closed in a grin. She suddenly realized that Ray was the one who was her true knight. Not the knight in shining armor type, but the knight her father talked about. The one who showed her how to jump over the other players on the board. Not like Ethan, who jumped people for power. Ray was a strategic thinker and maneuvered around and over the issues for win-win outcomes. He had a deep sense of fairness and could walk in another man's shoes.

"Well, there you go again, tiger. It is great that you brainstormed this fix for us, but remember, this is Bellevue office revenue for now. Just be patient, OK? I will get you the credit when it's time."

"Okay okay. I'm not worried about that, Raymond Sir. But it *is* a good idea to make it into a real product, right?" Maryl had a tight grip on her idea now.

"Yes. Yes. That is a good idea. But I doubt if corporate is going to change direction in our product design any time soon." Ray knew that submitting a 'good idea' to corporate had to have teeth. "So, here's what we can do. Let's fly this under the radar until Boeing and Puget Power incorporate it, and then bring that success to corporate. Until then, it will just be an additional professional services add-on for these two customers, OK?"

"Sounds like a plan," Maryl was nodding.

She trusted Ray completely.

She had kept in touch with Clarke, who had taken over her clients in Seattle, and she was still copied on several of his online messages back and forth with Boeing. Yesterday, Clarke had written her directly. She didn't see it until Saturday:

"Hey Maryl. How's my Philly girl? Can you give me a call about the issue Boeing is talking about on that mail string? I need to figure out this one part of their agreement about access to their data on our machines. I think they are confused about how we give them that access. Frankly, I am too."

She woke him up, forgetting the three-hour time difference.

"Jesus, Maryl. It's six a.m. here and it's Saturday." Clarke growled and then yawned.

"Well, I love you too, Clarke. Let's talk about Boeing."

"Let me at least get a cup of coffee." His voice was a bit softer, and she could hear him rustling his covers, fighting with his robe or whatever he was wearing.

"From reading back over their messages, I think the confusion is that they thought 'access' meant we would let them code some things into our software. It seems they want their data structured a little differently..." She jumped right into the meat of it.

"Hold on. Hold on. I can't find the damned coffee filters. Where the hell does she keep them?"

"Try a drawer close to your coffee maker, Clarke. That would be my guess."

"Okay, got it. Now what were you saying about data structure?"

"Well, when we sold them our software, we loaded a bunch of their data onto the 360, right? So, they could get at it remotely and have a ton more processing power through our system."

"Yeah. Yeah." Clarke was making clattering noises at his end.

"So, by any chance, have they recently loaded other data into our system? Like, data from a different department?"

"Well, yeah. We did a big load for them last month. I guess that wasn't obvious in the mails."

"Okay. Okay so, evidently, they are now trying to merge that data? Does that sound like what's happening?"

"Could be," Clarke now slurping loudly.

Maryl sighed, exasperated by Clarke's nonchalance.

"Clarke, how close are you to the data system we structured for them?"

"I'm not. Not my job. I leave that to Mark and Dan. Why?"

"Okay, so why don't I call Mark and see what he thinks? I'm sure it's a data access issue."

They chatted about the office for a minute. Clarke and Rena, the secretary, were an item now.

"How's Kyle?" Maryl ventured.

"Oh, he moved back down to the Bay Area and is working on another product of ours. Some kind of IC circuit designer product." Clarke didn't know the history of Kyle and Maryl, nor did he care.

Live long and prosper, Kyle. You were always a lovely gearhead. She gave him a mental farewell.

"Okay, buddy. I'll figure this out and talk to Ray, eh?" She said it because it rhymed but also to give Clarke a smile in return for waking him up. She hung up and called Mark.

"Hey," mumbled Mark, the morning after one of his music gigs. "Yeah, you're spot on, Maryl. They want to get some reports out that are a little tricky. We're leaving the contract politics up to Ray, but Dan and I have been trying to code around the software restrictions here at our end. We need corporate to change a piece of the basic reporting code, and I think that's a long shot."

"Got it. I figured as much. So how *is* your brother?"

"Dan is Dan," Mark said. "He has a girlfriend now."

And that was nerd Mark's entire explanation of his brother's life.

Maryl recalled the many hours with the brothers back in her Bellevue office days, poring over the application, learning from them the logic behind the structure and the code. They loved having a Salesperson who wanted to know how everything worked, and she loved that they would take the time (at any time day or night) to answer her questions.

"Good for him," Maryl was signing off. "Tell Dan hi for me. Oh, and let's not be telling people that I'm helping with this Boeing fix, OK? Politics and all that."

"Yup. Got it," said Mark and hung up.

Maryl had taken pride in her painstaking work on the Boeing deal and wanted to see that account stay active and happy. Clarke didn't mind having her involved so long as he got the revenue credit. Which he did.

She sent a progress update message to Clarke, which of course he wouldn't read until Monday, telling him she would handle this through Ray.

And then she leaped into action.

She knew that Darrell Dizzle read his messages on the weekend, so she fired one off to him. He called her right away.

"How's my namesake?" he chuckled.

"I'm slowly being sucked into the historical world of the U.S.," she replied. "I'm telling you, there's a huge difference between the east and west coasts."

"Yes, I went to school in Boston if you recall."

"Oh yes. That's right," feeling foolish for forgetting that fact about him. "Tufts, right? You were going to be a doctor?"

"Almost right. I was going to get my medical degree and work internationally for ARAMCO. Either that or IBM. And here I am at Boeing. Who knew?" he chuckled. "So..." He paused. "You want to fix our problem?"

"Well, I don't think it's defined as a problem, Darrell. I think it's more of a communication issue between our companies and I apologize for that. As you know, we are *not* IBM and we're sort of learning from our customers as we go. But I'm pretty sure we can get you a solution." She spent the next half hour going over her plan, and they hung up with a commitment that she would work this out with Ray.

The next day was Sunday. In the spare room at 3900 Ford Rd, Maryl had pinned up seven large sheets of butcher paper which she had taped at the edges, and she was drawing boxes with interconnecting lines, half-listening to Ethan on the phone with Caleb, she assumed.

"No...Hey, are you forgetting favors?... What do you mean? You made out on that one, and you know it, man. Her father owns half of

Atlantic City. Yeah, so you owe me. Just get me in on that IPO. Right. I'll catch you later."

Sarah crossed Maryl's mind once more, bringing with it a trail of peculiarities. Half the time, Sarah was a bright witty part of the group, and then she wasn't. She would retreat into a slightly slurred state of dead expressions and long sighs. Also, given the group's close-knit nature, it struck Maryl as strange that she had never met Sarah's daughter, Chloe. Equally puzzling was Sarah's habit of leaving Chloe with Muriel during their Saturday game days at Ethan's. The recent memory of Ethan retreating to the bathroom for a private phone conversation with Sarah only added to the growing list of oddities.

She was still drawing lines with a long ruler, most of them horizontal, with more connecting vertical ones, when Ethan leaned against the doorway with his coffee.

"What are you doing?"

"Well, I'm not buying stock in a startup."

"What?"

"Oh, I just overheard you on the phone. Who's going public?"

"Hey, I can't divulge my secrets." Ethan grinned, avoiding the question.

Maryl stood up straight and looked at him. "Hey, can you get me a mailbox key? I don't know what's going on with the renters. I haven't seen any rent check in three months, but Fletcher swears he sent them. Have you seen anything come through for me?"

"No, babe, but I'll keep an eye out for you. And they only give each unit one key, so..."

"Alrighty then. So, what am I doing? I'm putting together my tables and datasets in this design for a new tool. Clarke and I were talking about the Boeing contract, and I think their issue could be solved if we looked at it a different way..."

"Argh, why bother?" Ethan shrugged and walked back to the living room. "Just let Clarke figure it out."

Maryl, with pencil and ruler in her hands, came to the door and said "But Ethan. If we just add about five more fields to this ..."

"Just do your own job," he yawned. "Besides, corporate will never agree to coding new rules in the database schemas."

"Why do you say that?" Maryl was insulted.

"Because you're nobody."

"What? Nobody? You mean I'm not a coder sitting there at corporate? Or do you mean I'm a salesman and not a tech support person? Or do you mean I'm a *girl who doesn't understand the code*?"

"Yes. Yes. and Yes. As far as corporate is concerned, your value is tied to the revenue you bring to the Philly office. That's all. Stop trying to be a hero in another district. I don't know why you still talk to those guys, anyway."

Maryl returned to her project, more determined than ever to figure out a fix. It was the right thing to do, given that she sold them the system and it wasn't doing what they thought it should.

Miscommunication is the root of so many problems, she thought to herself.

The if-then-else logic of her drawings took her down a complex stairway of boxes and lines and arrows, and it was midnight when she realized she needed sleep. She would take a photo of it in the light of morning and fax it off to Mark and Dan.

"But Maryl, that field always has to be numeric. That's fixed in our system to ensure data integrity. And since Boeing is a government contractor bound by all sorts of other data rules, we need to keep that field as is because it converts every number they put there into a percentage value. It can't have any alpha characters." Mark was looking at the photo of her design she had faxed.

"Hmmm. So, what if we added another field that was alpha and linked the two of them? I think an alpha field would make the report writer more useful to a wider range of our customers, don't you?" Maryl was at her desk on her 3rd cup of coffee.

"Only if we could ensure the integrity of the data in each of the other tables that is affected. It would work for Boeing since we know how their data is all related by now. But we would have to customize it for Puget Power I think."

Maryl knew that Mark knew his stuff. "Okay, thanks. You're right. I'll rethink this and get back to you." That night she drew two more options on the butcher paper. The solution was beginning to take shape.

TWENTY-SIX

T he week of Hanukkah arrived.

Maryl smoothed her skirt nervously as she followed Ethan into his parents' warmly lit dining room. The air was filled with the comforting scents of savory brisket, sweet noodle kugel, and the unmistakable aroma of frying latkes.

"Maryl, welcome." Miriam hugged her. "We're so glad you could join us for this Hanukkah dinner. I know it's a bit different from what you're used to."

Maryl smiled genuinely. "Everything smells amazing."

As they settled around the table, Maryl took in the festive decorations—the delicate lace tablecloth, the glittering silver menorah as the centerpiece, and the dreidels scattered among the plates. Abe stood at the head of the table, holding a small prayer book.

"Before we begin," Abe said solemnly, "we light the menorah. Tonight is the fifth night of Hanukkah, so we'll light five candles from right to left, adding one each night. This reminds us of the miracle of the oil lasting eight days in the temple." He directed this toward Maryl, and she appreciated the backstory.

He struck a match, touching the flame to the shamash, the central candle, and began reciting the blessings in Hebrew. Maryl watched, transfixed, as he used the shamash to light the other candles, their warm glow dancing across the faces of Ethan's family and friends.

Barbara shot her a smile and a nod from across the table. "It even gets better when the food comes," she said in a loud whisper.

As the blessings concluded, Miriam passed around platters piled high with crispy potato latkes, accompanied by bowls of sour cream and applesauce. "Latkes are a Hanukkah staple," she explained to Maryl. "The oil we fry them in is another reminder of the miraculous oil."

Maryl took a bite, savoring the perfect balance of crunchy exterior and fluffy interior. "They're delicious," she murmured with a mouthful.

The conversation flowed easily as they enjoyed the rest of the meal - tender brisket, sweet kugel, and roasted vegetables. Ethan's younger sister, Ellen, entertained them with tales of her new marketing project at the magazine, with Sarah chiming in when Ellen left out a funny part.

As the plates were cleared, Abe produced a worn velvet bag filled with chocolate coins. "Gelt for the family!" he announced. "Time for dreidel."

He explained the rules to Maryl - each player takes turns spinning a four-sided wooden top, the dreidel, winning or losing these coins based on which Hebrew letter faces up when the dreidel comes to a stop. Nun for none, Gimel for all, Hey for half, and Shin for put one in.

Maryl was caught up in the laughter and friendly competition as they played, teasing Ethan as his pile of gelt dwindled. For a moment, she forgot the complexities of their relationship, lost in the simple joy of a family celebration, surrounded by her new friends.

As the evening wound down, Miriam Krahlman pressed a small gift into Maryl's hands. "Just a little something," she said. "We're so happy to have you as part of our Hanukkah."

Maryl blinked back tears, touched by the gesture. She met Ethan's gaze across the room, seeing a flicker of the man she'd fallen for beneath the surface. *If only this warmth, this sense of belonging could last beyond the glow of the menorah's flames.*

But as Ethan turned away, his attention drawn by a comment from Simon, Maryl felt a familiar chill. The magic of the evening faded, replaced by the stark reminder of the challenges she was facing.

She clutched Miriam's gift a little tighter, drawing strength from the love and light of this new family, even as she knew she couldn't depend on it forever. Maryl had her own miracles to make, her own flames to kindle - and someday soon, she'd find the courage to chase them.

On the way home, she slid her hand over to his thigh and said, "So, it turns out, I'm pregnant."

Ethan kept his right hand on the wheel and his head propped with his other hand, elbow on the window ledge. His index finger twitched over his lips for a moment, but he said nothing.

The next five minutes of silence were unbearable.

"I know a guy," Ethan said finally. "He'll take care of it."

"Ethan, I'm not sure I want *that*. Let's just talk about it."

"What's there to talk about? We now know that you can bear children. Just not now."

"But you were the one who asked me to take out my diaphragm. I thought that meant you were ready to move forward in our relationship. Have a baby. Start a family."

"You thought."

"What does that mean?"

"It means I wanted to see if we could. I'm not going to marry someone who can't have kids. And besides, Maryl, this is not the time to have a kid. I'm on the verge of getting promoted again, and you need to focus on supporting me in that and of course, your job. Not a good time. You should know that."

Maryl knew it was the logical thing to do, given their work schedules and the elephant in the room. *Were they going to stay together?*

This was the first time Maryl had actually faced that, wanting so desperately for it not to be true. She moved here to be with him. She gave up her old life for this one, to love and support this powerful, handsome, intelligent man who was moving up the ladder quickly. Surely, she could help him escape his demons and transform back into the loving man he used to be. And soon they would both be promoted and would reign as the power couple, moving the company forward as a team.

But now she realized she was delusional. That had been their spoken dream. It was not playing out that way. Ethan's behavior was becoming a deal breaker. He didn't believe in her. And at this point, she didn't even think he loved her.

The next day Ethan announced "I've arranged things for this Thursday. Your appointment is at two o'clock. I'll drive you."

On Thursday, Ethan went to the clinic with her. The receptionist seemed to know him. "Just fill this out please," she said, looking at Maryl with kind eyes. Ethan handed her a check, looked at Maryl, and said, "I'll be back in an hour."

As she lay on the table with the bright lights glaring at her, she felt nothing. No guilt. No anxiety. She just wanted it to be over. Of course, she would terminate. If she brought a child into this world, she certainly didn't want it to be his.

"No thanks," Maryl said to the nurse who was inserting a line into her arm. The nurse did it anyway and said through her mask "Just in case." Maryl had decided she deserved any pain she might experience.

The nurse looked at the doctor who nodded. The procedure began like a pelvic exam with something large and cold inserted into her. Then a machine noise and Maryl shrieked and arched her back and went black.

The next thing she felt was the nurse's hand on her arm. "Time to wake up. Everything went fine. Your clothes are on the chair. We'll see you out in the lobby."

Maryl cried without knowing why. Her uterus cramped, and she doubled over. There was blood on the sheeting. The nurse had left a large Kotex pad on the chair. She dressed slowly and walked gingerly to the lobby, lowering herself carefully into the plastic chair, and sat down on the big wad of cotton pad in her pants.

No sign of Ethan.

She waited ten more minutes, in excruciating pain. The nurse finally came out with two Tylenol and a paper cup of water. "Here," she said. "Your husband just called and asked us to call a cab for you. Something about his office."

Maryl stared at her. "Unbelievable."

The nurse looked at her. "Are you okay?"

"What? Of course, I'm not okay," Maryl snapped. "Did he say anything else?"

"Well, yes. He asked an odd question. He wanted to know if it was twins." The nurse shrugged, patted her shoulder, and said, "Your cab will be here in ten minutes."

Maryl swallowed the pills and groaned again. "Nurse?" The woman turned around. "How can you tell? I mean if it were twins."

"Unless someone needs us to examine the contents of your uterus, we just let the material flow into the receptacle. We don't normally see it."

In the cab, she wondered if she was a horrible person. Tears streamed down her face as she wondered if the child who had chosen her for a mother would try to find her again, in another life, another world.

One of Osho's sayings flashed into her mind: "Don't be afraid of experience, because the more experience you have, the more mature you become."

For two days, Maryl stayed home, emotionally and physically drained. She felt numb and knew it was something like post-partum depression. The nurse had warned her. But why was she depressed?

She had sidestepped a disaster. She would have no lingering ties to Ethan when she left him.

"Hey, Robert. This is Maryl, your landlord. I'm just calling again to check on the rent that is past due. Can you please call me back? Thanks a bunch." She might as well get that issue taken care of, so she left the same message for the three other renters.

Robert called her back immediately. "Hey Maryl. I'm confused. We've been sending our rent to Fletcher on time every month. I just ignored your last message since my bank says you've deposited all three of them."

"Hmm. Really."

"Is there a problem?"

"I don't know. Can you verify the address you're mailing to?"

"Care of Ethan Krahlman at 3900 Ford Road in Philadelphia."

"Yes. That's correct. And is it my name on the endorsement?"

"I can't tell. It's always the same scribble, though."

"Okay. Thanks. Sorry for the confusion."

She called her bank. No, there were no deposits for those amounts in her account. Stolen? Or was Ethan cashing her checks? He wouldn't do that.

She spent the next two days working on the butcher paper drawings of her new product idea, distracting herself from the intense cramping and forming a plan in her head. She needed to get away from Ethan. That was clear.

A week went by. They barely spoke. When she asked him again about the checks, his only answer was, "Really, Maryl? I told you to get rid of those rentals."

TWENTY-SEVEN

———◦○◦———

The data center at Lawrenceville's 280-acre campus was bright, with shiny linoleum floor squares between the huge black humming machines that held all the drug formulary data, sales data, clinical trial data, government regulations, consumer data, marketing and revenue numbers, and data about the employees who made it all happen.

Together, James and Maryl had sold Squibb on a trial because DAMON could be installed more quickly than FOCAL4 or SIMDAR, their main competitors, but also because they liked Maryl's team. James and Tom were brilliant goofballs who always told the truth to the clients, sometimes making Maryl wince at the disclosures that endeared them to client teams.

They were working on a case-tracking system for Squibb's clinical trials. With so much sensitive data, Squibb wasn't allowed to store that data on the timesharing machines at corporate, so James was going to load DAMON2 onto Squibb's machines. He had brought the large black tape reel in his bag, and they spent the better part of the afternoon in the air-conditioned data room. It was an exhausting day, and James and Maryl headed for the train home.

"I should have brought a sweater," Maryl complained to James as they boarded the train. "That was so cold in there."

"I didn't really notice," James said. "I was sweating bullets that I was doing the install correctly."

They settled into seats facing each other, Maryl turning her nose up at a-b-c gum on the windowsill. "So gross," she said in disgust.

"Here, trade seats with me so you won't have to look at it," James said, standing. She was reluctant to make him stare at the wet glob all the way back, but she succumbed. "Only if you let me get the first round."

"Such a deal." He grinned as she got up and headed for the bar car. Returning with eight tiny plastic bottles of gin and two cans of tonic, she pulled out the plastic cups she carried in her bag for just such days.

"So do you want to talk about work or home?" James absently licked his mustache, while spilling the gin when the train lurched out of the station. "Oh gosh darn it," he muttered.

"Gosh darn it?" Maryl smirked. "That's the best you got?"

"Well, it's better than 'Praise the Lord' which is what my first wife always said instead of a swear word. Used to drive me absolutely nuts."

"Yeah, I have a friend like that." Maryl's thoughts rolled around to Helen, and she wondered how Doug was doing. Life sucked.

"Okay, I'll start," James refocused her. "So where do you suppose Squibb is going to get a half mill to afford this after the trial — with all the crap they're buried in right now?"

"Oh hell," Maryl began. "These big pharma companies have just raised drug prices again. It's ridiculous. I'm sure they have tons of cash. Who *is* running the government, anyway? All the stuff we learned in econ classes was some sort of fantasy structure, never to be followed in real life. And don't get me started on the insurance companies."

"Whoa. Hold on a second, lady. Where is this coming from? I was talking more about the recent recall of their vitamins and all the new generic drug competition now that patents are expiring."

"That's a good point, James. I'm sure Squibb has something up their sleeve, like the takeover of one of their competitors, or some new drug under wraps in development."

James let it drop but continued talking. He knew something was wrong, and he knew it had to do with Ethan. To lighten the mood, he launched into one of his history trivia stories.

"You know," he began as usual. "Dr. Edward Robinson Squibb was a local. Yep. He graduated from Philadelphia Jefferson Medical College."

Maryl rolled her eyes. "Here it comes."

"Yeah, and he was the true original pain reliever."

"What? You mean he produced the original pain reliever..."

"No, I mean *he* was. During the US-Mexican war, they were doing operations on all the bummed-up soldiers without anesthesia."

"What?" Maryl shifted in her seat. "*Our* soldiers or captured soldiers??"

"Well, both probably. I don't think doctors were allowed to discriminate. You know. 'Do no harm' and all that."

"So, what's the story." Maryl was impatient as usual. "He created Bufferin and was the hero?"

"No, no. Squibb didn't come up with Bufferin for another hundred years. I'm talking about ether. Squibb was the one who found a way to produce ether using steam distillation while working at the naval hospital.

"So, they just knocked out the soldiers with ether for their surgeries then? Wasn't that dangerous?"

"Sort of. But evidently, his method distilled it down to safe levels. I consider him a hero for that, as I don't like pain *at all*." James slicked his mustache down.

"Well, it still sounds dangerous."

"Oh, it was. I forgot the funny part. Dr. Squibb bought a brownstone in Brooklyn and started his first little manufacturing plant there, ending up burning himself quite badly and nearly burning up his whole business."

"Quite funny." Maryl was a little surly with her comment.

"Okay then. Moving on to the home life conversation. How's it going?"

Maryl responded by unscrewing the cap of the second plastic gin bottle. She dramatically tossed back a huge gulp. "Oh god," she sputtered. "I wanted that to be comically symbolic, but this stuff is harsh without the tonic."

James laughed out loud. "Yes, like rubbing alcohol. Only more genteel." He stared a hole into her.

"Ethan is such an ass, James."

"Well, there are several of us who could have told you that."

"Why the hell didn't I see it?"

"Because you fell in love. Been there. Done that. Not judging."

"Do you know that he wanted to have sex with no protection, and I got pregnant last month?"

James stared at her, feeling uncomfortable now.

"And then he just drove me to the abortion clinic when I announced it to him."

"What?" James frowned.

"Yeah, Prince Charming just wanted to see if I *could* get pregnant. That was his reasoning."

"You have got to be kidding me."

"And at dinner last Sunday at his parents' house? He stopped all the conversations and announced that we were going to play a game of guessing the designer labels around the table."

"Well, that must have been fun." James looked out the window. "And such a thought-provoking topic."

"It wouldn't have been so bad if I had paid attention in fashion school."

"You? You went to..."

"No. I was just being sarcastic. Hell no. I don't follow designers or their labels. And he announced that I would go first. I had to go around the table and guess which designer made each blouse or shirt.

It was humiliating. And no one came to my rescue." Her eyes stung with tears.

"Probably because they are all scared of his wrath, just like at work." James shook his head, looking down at the filthy floor where he had spilled the gin.

When he looked up at her, he saw tears. "Hey. Let's get you something to eat, Maryl. You didn't have much lunch and now we're on our third G&T."

James was alarmed. He had never seen this warrior of a woman even close to tears, not even after the toughest client situations. She was Miss Logic, Miss Balancing Act, Miss work-around-any-problem. He hurried back from the bar car.

"Here, have some pretzels. That's all they had unless I wanted to wait."

She chewed one, now with the true weight of all that she had been putting up with. She felt like the blood was draining out of her—too heavy to stand. Her stomach ached and revolted. Vomit sprayed all over the seat where James's coat was and all over the floor including both their shoes. Maryl couldn't hold her head up. She went down hard, hitting the floor and sliding in the vomit.

"Oh shit!" James grabbed at her arm to pull her up but was sliding too, not able to get his balance. He sat again and tried to use leverage against the other seat to pull her up. The woman in the bay across from them got up, threw a handful of napkins at James, and fled for the next car. He dabbed at Maryl's face and mouth with the napkins, but it was a job for a towel. Or even two. Getting her on the seat, he laid her down and bolted back to the bar car, insisting on two towels, which he used to sop up the area.

Another wave of vomit hit him in the chest.

When the train pulled into the station, he put his coat around her and dragged her off the train as best he could, shouldering his own briefcase and her bag. It took him ten minutes to maneuver into the station and deposit her on a bench, where he sat for five minutes weighing his options. She was out.

Should he call Ethan to come for her? On the heels of her stories, he didn't want Ethan to be anywhere near her. Should he call a cab and have them deposit her at 3900 Ford Road, hoping the doorman would know what to do? Should he take her home to his apartment and risk the wrath of Ethan?

He decided on the last one.

"Ethan, this is James Hare," he was speaking into the phone at eight p.m. "Maryl is with me. She got pretty sick on the train, and I thought the best thing to do was to bring her here to let her recover. We can figure out what to do in the morning. And don't worry. There is nothing going on here."

"What do you mean, sick?"

"Well, she didn't have much lunch, and nothing for dinner on the train, and you know she's kind of a lightweight. We probably shouldn't have had a drink on the train, but it was a really grueling day at Squibb—" James trailed off, knowing he was just making noise.

"Fine," said Ethan and hung up.

Maryl spent the entire night and most of the next morning on James' couch with cold towels on her face and neck. James had taken off her shoes and jacket but didn't want to go any farther, even though her clothing needed laundering. She was still dry heaving in the morning. There was a plastic trash can on the floor by her head, just in case, and there were several of those 'in case' moments.

"Oh, I think I'm gonna die!" Maryl moaned. James chuckled from the kitchen. "No, seriously, James. I think I'm dying."

James poured a glass of Gatorade and handed it to her. "Now, promise you'll vomit in the trash can and not on the carpet if this doesn't want to stay down."

It didn't.

James didn't call Ethan that morning. He figured if Ethan cared enough, he would call James.

He didn't.

Twenty-Eight

———◆○◆———

Around noon, Maryl thought she might be able to make it down to James' car. "Are you sure you don't want me to take a cab home?" Maryl asked, hoping he would say that, yes, he was sure.

When Maryl was inside the apartment, James turned to her and said, "This conversation about Ethan is not over. We need to get you out of here."

"I know," she said. "And James. Thanks for taking care of me. That was above and beyond."

"Just put it in my next review," he joked and turned to the door. "And the silver lining was that you barfed in my bag *after* the DAMON tape was safely installed at Squibb. I don't know how I would have explained to corporate that I needed a duplicate."

Maryl smiled weakly. She went straight to the bathroom, stripped off her clothes, thought about burning them, and stepped into the shower.

Maryl wrapped a towel around her hair and padded over the carpeted living room to the room that housed her clothes and boxes. Entering the room, she felt something was missing.

"Shit!" Maryl yelled. "Shit. Shit. Shit!"

There were no butcher paper drawings on the walls. Only the tiny corner bits stuck to the pushpins. Gone. Every one of them.

She ran to the kitchen garbage can. Nothing there.

She ran out to the hall to the garbage chute. What was she thinking? It wouldn't be in the chute. And besides, she was naked except for the towel on her head. She threw on her sweats and punched the elevator to the basement. It was in none of the large stinky bins.

This was intentional. This was war.

TWENTY-NINE

Tom was staring at his coffee cup in the break room. James had just relayed to him all that Maryl had told him about Ethan's behavior.

"I think he's a narcopath," Tom said slowly.

"A what-what?" James blinked at him.

"It's a narcissist crossed with a sociopath."

"Since when did you…"

"Oh, Colette was doing research for her psych class, and she showed me a new book that just came out by some guy named Otto Kernberg."

"Made-up name?" James snickered. They both snickered.

"But get this. The tick-off list is: disregard for others, lack of empathy, need for admiration, aggression, brutality, master manipulator, and someone who truly believes their existence benefits everyone around them."

"Brutality?"

"Well, I translate it as being brutal in his words. You've witnessed that yourself, James."

I need to address something unforgivable that has come up in our Comcast trial. It appears there was a coding mistake that a sixth grader would have made. Jesus! They are on the verge of a huge acquisition that will double their reach. James. Tom. I expected more attention to detail from both of you. What the hell? When I take over this branch, heads will roll for this kind of idiotic mistake.

The words still stung, as he had bellowed that in front of the NYC and Philly teams. On that day, Maryl had jumped to her feet to defend them, but Ethan had spun around and said, "Sit down, Maryl. This isn't about you."

"Yup. That's Ethan," James now stood and shoved his hands in his pockets, so his elbows were locked in place. "So, we need to get Maryl out of that situation, Tom."

"What do you suggest?" Tom asked.

At one minute after five, they closed the door to the conference room and opened the paper to the classifieds, scanning for apartments close to the office.

"Here's one. Here's one." James was stroking his mustache excitedly. "It's on Seventeenth and Green. Let's go look at it."

He dialed the number in the ad, and soon they were walking up the concrete steps to the building. Tom looked up to the belvedere on the third floor.

"Well, that's cool. Wonder if that is inside the unit we're looking at. She would love that. Heck, I would love that."

The rental agent came up behind them with the keys. "Yes, that's on the upper level of the apartment. It's a lovely little unit and won't last long."

After the tour, James signed the lease agreement and got the keys. They sat in his car looking at the building. "It will be a bear moving her in with all those stairs."

"Well, the good thing is that she doesn't have a bed or any furniture. I know she pretty much lives from boxes in the spare room."

Tom gaped at him. "But she's been here almost a year. Why hasn't..." He trailed off, knowing it was an unanswerable question.

When Ethan came home from work that evening, Maryl didn't wait for him to close the door behind him.

"Why did you tear down my papers?"

"You don't need to be doing that work for Seattle."

"I'm doing it for myself, and you had no business throwing it away."
Ethan rolled his eyes "Are you done?"

"Oh, I think I'm done. I think *we're* done."

"Don't be so dramatic."

That night, Maryl slept on the couch. When she woke, Ethan was already gone.

Maryl took the next day off and tried to reconstruct the product outline. It was slow-going. She called Mark in the Bellevue office to tell him about the diagrams.

"Oh, don't worry about that. Dan and I have been able to reconstruct most of it from your fax. Thanks. Now if corporate will humor us with..."

"Oh, sorry, I gotta go, Mark. Someone is at the door. I'll call you later."

Tom and James were standing in the hall with boxes and tape and the dolly from the lobby.

"Ma'am we are here to escort you to your new digs." James entered Ethan's apartment. Tom was behind him, wide-eyed at the 180-degree view.

"My new digs?"

"Yes, you're moving. You can't keep living in the company of such an ass."

"Such a liar," Tom chimed in. "We have a U-Haul parked downstairs. Ethan is at a conference in Wilton, so we have today and tonight to get you out of here."

"But where to?"

James put a finger to his lips dramatically and whispered, "It's a secret." In his mind, he actually wondered if Ethan had bugged his own apartment. Maryl followed his thinking and put a finger to her lips as well.

"By the way, before we leave here today, I need a favor. Do you know how to copy and save a phone message?"

Eight hours later, James handed the keys to Maryl, who opened the door to a deep green room, with a black and white kitchen beyond, and a tiny, almost spiral, staircase. She was overcome with emotion.

"And wait till you see the best part." Tom was excited about the top floor that he called the turret. From there she could have her morning coffee and watch the sun come up over the city or sip a cocktail after work and feel safe.

Maryl was overwhelmed by this act of support and friendship. "I don't know how you guys pulled this off. Thank you so much."

"And one more thing!" James ran back out to the truck and returned with a folded mound of butcher paper. "Found it under the bed in Ethan's room."

"I hate to say, 'I told you so'," her father was saying.

"But you just did." Maryl sighed, more to herself than to her parents who now sat in judgment on the blue flowered sofa in Weston. She hadn't kept them up on her painful life with Ethan over the last six months. She had wanted her father to focus on her growing successes in the high-tech world. Her brother, Steven, was still a hotshot lawyer, but he was in a tiny town back in Washington state. Maryl was now in a big city, and she shared that with her father in a sort of unspoken bond. When they talked about traffic, it was insane traffic, a chaotic mess of steel and concrete, turnpikes with the sheer volume of vehicles an overwhelming nightmare to the uninitiated.

Logistically, Steven could visit Dad by taking I-90 all the way across the US, traversing twelve other states for about fifty hours in one of his Porsches but he never had, nor would he. Maryl, on the other hand, could hop Amtrak and be in Boston five hours later for thirty dollars.

And so she had.

They had been sitting in the living room for an hour while Maryl told them selective stories about Ethan's true character. Regina held Joey in her lap and stroked his head rhythmically.

"I'm just afraid he will become my direct boss, and then what?"

"Maryl, stop feeling sorry for yourself. Go downstairs and start going through your boxes. You're going to need more of your things now." Regina stood and shuffled toward the kitchen—her go-to escape room. Joey followed her on his short little legs.

"I *know*, Mom. That's why I'm here."

Her father followed her down with a glass of Jim Beam and soda. "Maryl, I know you want your stuff now, but let's look at this practically. You don't really know how long you'll be in Philadelphia, right? What if Ethan does take over the office? You might have to move jobs or even cities."

"Yeah. I know. I know." Maryl looked around their basement, with Dad's workbench on one end, and her boxes of dishes stacked neatly at the other with her couch, table, chairs, and bed. "Maybe I'll just quit and come live in your basement." She was half joking.

"Well, I could start putting out feelers for you. Just in case. You know, here in Boston or back in Seattle, with my buddies." He had no harshness in him. No reproach for her. He was being kind.

Her earliest memory was her father smiling at her as she cavorted on the thin rug of the living room trying to make him laugh, with her mother sitting rigidly next to him not smiling at all. His eyes were dancing in the kind of mirth that made Maryl feel so loved, so special, so safe. He didn't say 'Now, that's enough' or 'Run along and play with your brothers' or anything that her mother would have said, and likely wanted to say right then and there.

What had happened to him to turn him so tacit over the years? He had been so kind to her as a child. Firm but kind.

At that moment she wanted to curl up on his lap and sob, like when Petey Elmhurst turned her down for the Sadie Hawkins dance freshman year. Or when Wilcox had jerked her knee socks down in seventh grade so everyone could laugh at her hairy legs. Regina hadn't let her shave – anything – until senior year in high school. "No need to. Who is going to see your body?" Regina had said.

"Thanks, Dad." She crossed the room and put her arms around him. "Ethan wanted me to get pregnant, Dad. And I did. I thought the next step was marriage. But then he just drove me to a clinic to get rid of it."

George pulled her out to arm's length and studied her face. "What?" and after a moment, "Jeez don't tell your mother." He paused and then, "You know her cancer is back. They are giving her a year maybe." He looked at the floor.

Maryl froze. Here she had been complaining about things in her big-girl life, her corporate life, her career, her love life, and her mother had no life left to complain about.

George cleared his throat. "So, I think maybe you should just rent furniture – I'm sure they have those places in Philadelphia – until you know what you're going to do. I think that's the best plan."

Maryl nodded. She was numb. In fact, maybe she wanted him to be making decisions for her right now. She just wanted to sit down and think about death, and where her mother would go, and if she would be nicer on the other side.

"Okay. But I do need some of this stuff, like my bedding and a few dishes."

"Well, we'll ship them to you, or maybe your mother and I will drive down with them in a few weeks."

"Thanks, Dad." In that moment she was his little girl again.

"Let's go upstairs and see what your mother is feeding us."

Maryl stayed for three days and slept through most of them. She didn't do any more complaining. She helped with laundry and vacuuming and ironing.

When she arrived back in Philly to her new, but bare, apartment, she opened her suitcase and found one of the three pairs of her father's old boxing gloves. There was a hand-scribbled note, "A swift counterpunch should work."

THIRTY

Beverly was the admin in the New York office. She was on the phone with Patty in Philadelphia. "No, he needs the file on Atlantic Electric. The one with their new contract," she told Patty.

"Well, can't he just get it from Daniels? Aren't they in the same district meeting up there?" Patty was hesitant to give Ethan any files that were the strict business of the Philadelphia branch. She was a good gatekeeper.

"He says he needs it now and Daniels is on vacation," Beverly was insistent.

"Okay," said Patty, and hung up. She walked around the reception desk and into James' office.

"Why would Ethan need the AE file?" She stood with her hands on her ample hips with her head cocked to one side.

James looked up. He stared at her for a second and slowly shook his head. "That guy." And then, "Well, Patty, it might take you a long time to find that file, right?"

James beat feet to Maryl's office and repeated Patty's question: "Why would Ethan need the AE file? Right now. Today. Up there at the DM meeting?"

Maryl stood, crossed her arms, and looked out the window. For a moment, she stared at the large black fly crawling up the glass. "Some kind of way out."

"Out of what?" James said.

"His head. His anger. He's planning some sort of revenge."

She paced on the worn office carpet. "And, we know Ethan wants this office, and the only way that could happen is if Daniels gets moved out of the way."

"So, we're talking murder here?" James joked.

"Jesus, no. But what's next down the list from there."

Patty appeared at the door again, looking pale. "That was a call from headquarters. Mr. Daniels has been in a boating accident up near Martha's Vineyard where he went fishing. He's in the hospital."

The next morning, a company-wide message went out stating Ethan was the new boss of the Philadelphia office—at least temporarily until Daniels recovered.

James, Tom, and Maryl sat in the breakroom with their coffee cups.

So, Ethan had known before they did. He certainly lost no time.

That night, Maryl duct-taped her pillow to the wall, put on her father's old boxing gloves, and punched the pillow until the neighbor banged on the wall.

She called Helen. "I'm so pissed! I can't believe they are letting him take over!"

"Well, does anyone at corporate know what's going on between you two? I mean personally?" Helen asked. Maryl thought about that for a moment. "Because how would they know that it's a bad thing? You said yourself that he's a brilliant guy and does well there."

"True." Maryl stared at the pillow on the wall. "And if I said something now, it would just be an HR issue from a girl with a broken heart."

"That's right."

"Fuck," Maryl said and changed the subject, "So, how is Doug feeling?"

"Oh, he's much better. The surgery was really successful."

"Hey, Hel. I know this isn't a new subject for you, but do you ever just sit and think about death? And where we go? I mean, the whole heaven and hell thing. Don't you want to talk to people who have died and come back? Technically died and come back? And see what they know that we don't?"

"Well, sure. But where is this coming from, Mel?"

"Oh, Mom's cancer is back."

"Mel, that's awful. I'll say my rosary for her tonight. And yes, I wonder about the afterlife as well, but I just trust that God will take care of me when I get there."

After they hung up, Maryl tossed and turned in bed, dreaming and waking and wondering which was real. She was in the ring with Ethan, who was punching her in the stomach. Blood was streaming down her legs. The gloves on her hands were all bloody. *Dad will kill me for getting these so dirty.* Ethan pulled her close and put his arms around her and then punched her in the ribs. He was two completely different people. Her father appeared suddenly. "Don't let him tie you up. Keep punching!" Maryl threw a punch and Ethan went down. "I hate you." Helen jumped into the ring. "No, you love him." Ethan stood up but this time he was her father. George punched Maryl on the jaw, sending her teetering back. "I told you not to let your guard down!" Maryl took a swing at him, missed, and then her father was carrying her on the sand in front of the cabins where they used to vacation.

Soaked in sweat and still half asleep, Maryl took a swing at the alarm clock.

"Shit." It was late. She hurried to shower and get to the office.

She met James in the hall, who motioned toward the breakroom. "Coffee?" he said. Tom and two other techies were already there.

"I have an interview tomorrow," one of them was saying. "I'm not sticking around with that ass in charge."

Ethan burst into the outer office lobby and demanded, "Everyone in the conference room."

Maryl's pulse pounded in her head, and she wanted to bolt to the corner trash can and throw up, but she was frozen in place. She hadn't seen him since the day she moved out except for last night in her dream. She was shaking.

THIRTY-ONE

I f fear was Ethan's intent, it was effective, as ten people scrambled into seats in the conference room. No one had expected him to take over so soon. Tom and James flanked Maryl as they entered the conference room.

"Okay, listen up. As you know, I'll be taking over the office here until Daniels returns, or until corporate realizes they should just give me this office as well as New York." He laughed at his own joke but no one else did.

He continued. "Maryl and Tom, I want you in my office after this meeting to bring me up to speed on Squibb and AE and the DOE. We need to close those."

"James needs to be in that meeting," Maryl said.

"Actually, he doesn't. James is no longer a member of this team as of today."

The room fell silent, and all eyes were on James, who turned red and stared at Ethan. Glared was the more apt word.

"What?" Maryl broke the silence. "What do you mean? Where is James going?"

"Nobody cares." Ethan continued the glare-down with James.

James slowly rose from his seat, smoothed his mustache, looked at Maryl briefly, and left the room.

"What the hell, Ethan," Maryl started.

Ethan whipped around to face her. "What makes you think you're not next?"

Maryl pushed her chair back.

"Sit. Down." Ethan checked her.

"Surely you want me to attend to client business. I'm going to keep my appointment at Atlantic Electric." She stood as tall as she could and wobbled out of the room.

"Get down to the train," she hissed at James who was pacing in the lobby with his briefcase. "We're going to AE." They ran to the elevator with Ethan in pursuit and made it before he punched the buttons.

Ethan strode back into the office and announced that he was ordering lunch for the whole office. "You're my team now."

James and Maryl sat facing each other in the train car to Egg Harbor City. They each let out a breath when the metal doors slid shut.

"What the hell?" Maryl began. "Did you do something I don't know about?"

"I moved you out of Ethan's apartment."

"Oh, no. I'm so sorry, James. Yes, that's probably it. He's so vengeful."

"So, how should we handle AE?" James asked. "I think I've just been fired."

"No. No, you haven't. Not yet. You haven't heard a peep from HR yet. And Ethan didn't speak the right words to fire you. Technically."

"True. Okay, we'll go in and pick up where we left off last week. Did you bring the paperwork for them to sign?"

"Soitenly," James said, chewing his mustache. "First thing I did when I left the conference room."

Maryl could tell what he was thinking, and it wasn't anything light.

Atlantic Electric had trialed the products of all three competitors, FOCAL4, SIMDAR, and DAMON, and had decided on DAMON since it was so much faster to get up and running. And Maryl could tell that they liked James and his work ethic. It was going to be a great client.

"You know they were originally called The Electric Light Company of Atlantic City." James began his trivia recall.

"No, I did not know. Sounds like a band."

"Yep. Sort of. Back in 1886, a band of five guys put in two hundred and fifty dollars each to start the company."

"Wow. Risk takers. Wonder how much two hundred and fifty dollars was back then. I mean in today's dollars."

"Roughly two thousand six hundred forty-eight dollars and ninety-four cents."

Maryl burst out laughing. "Thanks for the levity, my friend. I'm still shaking from Ethan's takeover drama. So you like AE, don't you? I mean, like a lot. Why is that?"

"Road Runner." James looked out the window.

"Road Runner?"

"Yeah, the only other company I can think of with two names that both start with vowels is ACME Industries, which always reminds me of The Road Runner."

Maryl rolled her eyes. "And the other, less important, reason?"

"Well, I do like Feehan, their chairman, and the environmental stuff he's into. No one in Jersey can buy an air conditioner unless it's eight EER, and he's cut way back on their plans to construct new plants."

"EER?"

"Come on, Maryl. You know this one. Energy efficient rating."

"Ah. Another double vowel thing."

"But you know, this area down here wasn't always environmentally conscious. When we pull into Egg Harbor, you might even see traces of the huge toxic waste dump that was here."

"Ugh. When?"

"In the last ten years."

"What?"

"Yeah. It was called Price's Pit. Over nine million gallons of chemical waste were disposed of at this site."

"Why did people let that happen?"

"I suppose because they didn't really know what was happening. Just like at Love Canal and Valley of the Drums. Awful stuff. After the Superfund project got going, it became part of that."

"So, is it cleaned up now? I mean, can you drink the water around here?"

"Not so much. Here's our stop."

They sat in the VP's office at AE, signing the final contract. Maryl would get the credit against her quota, and it would be a notable triumph for James, albeit a parting one.

As they all shook hands, James said, "Thanks, Philip."

"Actually, James," Philip said, "I'm surprised to see you here." James and Maryl both stared at him. "I mean, I'm happy you're here, but I just got a call from your new branch manager saying you were no longer on the project. *That* I was not happy to hear."

"Can I speak frankly?" Maryl asked.

"Of course."

"There is some testosterone going around in the office with this new manager and all...."

"Oh, I see." Philip paused a minute and looked at the floor, rubbing his chin. "So, Maryl, how do I get James back on our project? He knows so much about it, I'm afraid we'd be up a creek without him."

Maryl looked at James, knowing that he really clicked with this client. "Well, the truth is, James might soon be available for hire."

"Yes, I just might be," James chimed in. "And I love this project, as you know."

"Excuse me," Philip said. "Can you give me a minute?"

James and Maryl sat in the chairs in his office and raised their eyebrows at each other.

"So, my first question is, do you think they make the coffee with local water?"

"Very funny, James. So, do you think he has an opening? Would you take the job if he offered you one?" Maryl asked quietly.

"Depends."

"On salary?" she whispered.

"On job description."

Philip came back into the room with some forms.

"Well, James, we created a headcount last month to support this DAMON installation, so I *do* have a position I could offer you. Should we talk?" He handed James a formal job description for the position.

"Good. Well, while you two chat, can I just use your fax machine?" Maryl excused herself.

She was *not* going back to the office today, so she faxed the signed contract directly to corporate sales. No telling what Ethan might be taking credit for.

"Shit, I can't believe this," Maryl said in the cab on the way back to the train.

"Which part?"

"All of it. That Ethan blew into the office today, and that he humiliated you in front of the team, and that he is unmistakably out for revenge, and that we now know he was going to try to claim the AE contract for himself."

"Yeah."

"And most of all—that I could lose you! You are the backbone of my team! He knows that! It's all my fault that he is doing this to you. I am so sorry!"

They boarded the train and sat silently for the first ten minutes, pondering what this would mean.

Maryl's mind wandered back to her trip down here to Cape May. It was only a few miles away but lifetimes ago. The drive down had been so lovely, and the weekend had been dreamy.

"So, what are you thinking?" Maryl broke the silence between them.

"I listened to that phone message you had me copy. It's now on my computer. What did you need it for?"

"I'm not sure yet," Maryl said. "There's definitely something shady going on though. I can just feel it."

"Oh, I completely forgot." James drew several envelopes out of his briefcase and handed them to Maryl. "I must have grabbed all the mail on the counter when we moved you out of Ethan's. Sorry. It looks like some of it is Ethan's."

"Oh. Okay, thanks. I'll look at it later."

"I can tell your brain is working on a plan."

That evening, Maryl picked up the phone. "Hello?"

"What the fuck do you think you're doing, Maryl?"

"How did you get my number, Ethan?"

"I'm your boss now. I know all your information."

"What do you want?"

"Where are you living?"

"Not really your business."

"Come on, Maryl. I don't want it to be this way. We're the power couple, right? Why did you move out? You could have just told me you were leaving."

"Ethan, can we not do this?"

"But I miss you. Why don't you let me come over? We can talk it through."

"No, Ethan. And I have to go. It's been a long day."

"Oh. Right. Congratulations on AE."

She hung up and ran to the bathroom and retched. *Dammit. He's not going to win this. I won't let him.*

She sat on her bed, furious. Out of the corner of her eye, she saw the pile of mail James had given her. Scanning them, she saw one from Manufacturers Hanover Bank addressed to both Ethan and her. Inside was the latest checking account statement. She stared. Twenty-eight hundred fifty dollars deposited. Six times. Twenty-eight hundred fifty dollars written out to Sarah Stein. Six times.

What? What was going on? That was the exact amount of the monthly rents from her four houses in Seattle. Fletcher had sworn that he sent them. He'd been right all along. Somehow Ethan had... *The joint account he had me sign. Back then. In the beginning. When I first moved here. So, he could deposit checks made out to me and write checks with his own signature. He had planned this from the beginning.*

From the damn beginning?

What was going on between Ethan and Sarah?

THIRTY-TWO

The following morning, Maryl called Barbara.

"Why the hell would Ethan be sending money to Sarah?"

Barbara hesitated for a few seconds. "I don't know."

"Well, he's mailing her a check for twenty-eight hundred fifty dollars every month."

"What? Did you ask Ethan?"

"I moved out."

"What? When?"

"Just after he drove me to the abortion clinic and left me there."

"Maryl! What the hell? Why didn't you tell me?"

"It was humiliating. All he wanted was to see if I could get pregnant."

"Jesus. This is Sarah all over again."

"What?"

"I thought maybe you knew, but obviously I just let the cat out of the bag."

"What the hell are you saying?"

"Ethan did the same thing to Sarah, but she decided to keep it."

"That's Chloe?"

"Yeah."

"But she's married to Caleb."

"That was the deal. Ethan was furious that she wouldn't have an abortion, especially since she had turned, well, a little unstable, and Caleb had always had a crush on Sarah, so they all made a deal.

They got married right away. Long distance, because Caleb was in the Navy."

"So that must be why Ethan told Caleb he owed him a favor." She thought for a minute. "Does Sarah's father own half of Atlantic City?"

"You might say that. He owns a ton of buildings down there."

"Thanks, Barbara. That explains so many things. Oh, and I need Caleb's number."

"Now, Maryl. Don't go stirring things up."

"No, it's on another subject. About stocks."

"Got it. Just a second. Here it is."

"Thanks, Barbara."

"Okay and let's get together soon Maryl. Where are you living now?"

"In an apartment in the city."

"Got it. Mums the word."

"Thanks. See you soon."

Maryl hung up and sat down. Her rented furniture hadn't arrived yet, so her bed was the go-to perch. She threw her arms back and sank her head into the pillows, staring at the ceiling to put all the pieces together after that call.

She hated to, but she had to spend time in the office that day, whether Ethan was there or not.

"Hi, Patty," she said as she got off the elevator.

Patty smiled. "We have a reprieve. He's in New York today."

"Hey, can I have the key to his office?"

"Absolutely not." Patty winked, handing the key to Maryl.

"Morning, Tom," Maryl said. "Can you help me with something?"

"Sure." He pushed his glasses up on his nose. "What is it?"

"I need to see Ethan's messages, especially a few months ago." Maryl unlocked the door.

"To? From? Keywords?" Tom was already seated in Ethan's chair with his fingers typing away.

"To or from Caleb or Stein, or anyone at PHLX."

Tom turned wide eyes toward her.

"How about this one?"

It was from Ethan to Sarah: "Caleb doesn't have to know about the extra money. That $2850 every month is for Chloe's college fund. That's just between us. Because I'm a good guy, not because you're demanding it. Now, please stop harassing me."

Tom and Maryl looked at each other.

"No, let's keep looking," Maryl said as she filed that away in her brain. *What?*

"Okay. This might be what you're looking for."

100,000 HGEN Buying Toxix Tech

Maryl stared at it.

"Tom, can you look up HGEN ticker symbol?"

"Not on Ethan's computer. Let's go back to mine. Do you want me to print this one for you?"

"Yes, please. And make sure the date of the original message is on it."

HGEN was Hargess Energy Ltd in Chicago. But who was Toxix Tech?

Maryl dialed James at AE, where he was loving his new job.

"Hey, James. How are things?" Maryl said over the phone.

"Weird. It's like I changed uniforms but doing the same thing with the same people."

"Funny. Hey, I have a question. Do you know anything about Hargess Energy? I remember you were telling me about chemical spills and hazardous waste. Does it ring any bells?"

"Right. We were talking about chemical waste on the way to Egg Harbor. No, it doesn't ring a bell. Why?"

"Well, I probably can't tell you why, now that you are a client. Don't want to mess things up any further."

"That's all I get?"

"Well, let's see. How's the coffee?"

"Very funny. Talk to you when you decide to tell me more." James hung up.

"Tom, let's look up Toxix Tech," Maryl said.

"Way ahead of you. That's one of the companies tagged in the superfund." Tom was typing.

Super fun. Simon had said super fun on the way back from the Penn State game. Maryl had thought it odd at the time, but he was drunk. *What else had he said?*

Tom typed and Maryl watched. "Wow, Toxix Tech used to be called ToxiGuard. It certainly has a sketchy past for having the word 'guard' in the name. What were they guarding? Industrial waste hydrocarbons? Yuk."

"I remember that," Tom said. "Back in 1977, there was a huge explosion in Bridgeport, and I think some people were actually killed."

"Why would anyone want to purchase a horrible company like that?"

"That's probably what Ethan is banking on, excuse the pun," said Tom. "But this article says they have some innovative way to clean up hazardous waste. Sort of a chemical that eats chemicals."

"How recent is the article?"

"Last year."

"Hmmm. Wonder why Ethan is so interested in them now."

"He's not. He's interested in Hargess. Look, their stock is in the tank." Tom pointed to the screen.

"And if this innovation catches fire, then Hargess stock will soar."

"And I would suggest that Hargess change their name once they buy them."

"Why?" Maryl asked.

"ToxiGuard sounds like 'toxic art' haha. Or talk cigars."

"Talk Cigars. That's it. Simon's dad works for Toxix Tech. That's what he was telling Ethan after the game. Ethan had insider information. Tom, you're a genius!" Maryl said and ran back to her office, leaving Tom looking pleased but a little bewildered.

"You're welcome," he called after her.

Back in her office, Maryl was telling herself to settle down and breathe. Now Caleb's phone message to Ethan made sense. *We gotta talk about this before the market opens tomorrow morning.*

She felt bad for Caleb Stein. He would end up in the middle of this if Maryl made a mess. And she was going to make a mess.

Paramahansa would frown upon her joy at impending revenge.

I have the information. And information is power. She touched the coin at her neck, wanting to call her friend to share what she knew. But Helen would not be joyful. Helen was a peacemaker. Paramahansa would be proud of Helen. But Helen only had eyes for Jesus.

Maryl was on hold. She didn't know what time the SEC opened, but she was on hold at seven a.m. Bernadette had placed her there, promising to transfer her to the proper person.

The proper person was going to put Ethan in jail.

"Yes, I would like to submit an anonymous tip regarding someone I believe is involved in insider trading," Maryl told a Mr. Baker at 7:22 a.m.

"And what is this person's name? Please spell it for me." Maryl did as she was told. "And which companies are involved?"

"Hargess Energy and Toxix Tech or ToxiGuard."

"And what are the circumstances around your suspicion?" Maryl explained as much as she knew. "And you have confirmed the trade?"

"Well, no, I haven't. How would I do that?"

"That's fine. We can do that at our end. And who did you say his broker is?"

Maryl hesitated.

"That's fine. Here's what will happen next. We will collect information from the Exchange to corroborate your claim, and if there is cause to pursue it, we will refer the case to the DOJ. Any questions?"

"And then what happens?"

"Then they would put together a prosecutorial team and work with the FBI."

"Will he be arrested?"

"Ma'am we don't know that yet. Any more questions?"

"Will anyone be notifying me of the progress?"

"No, ma'am."

Maryl hung up at 7:33 and dressed for work. She dressed for war.

When she stepped off the elevator, she saw that his door was open.

"Maryl, can you come in here?"

Shit. Her heart pounded so loudly that she could hear it. She hated this roller coaster.

Ethan stood. She didn't sit.

"We're moving Tom to corporate. Thought you'd want to know."

"Why?"

"Because he requested it, and that's where nerds belong."

Maryl turned to exit. She couldn't believe she had ever respected this man.

"What are you going to close this week?" Ethan asked.

"Don't know yet. You have my weekly prospect report."

"Well, you better get to it."

You will look good in an orange jumpsuit.

THIRTY-THREE

"Hi, sweetie." George was on the phone. "Just wanted you to know that we're moving back to Walla Walla."

"What? But you just got settled in Weston."

"It's been nearly two years, Maryl. And your mother has pretty much given up on treatments and just wants to go back to her hometown for the end. I think I owe her that much."

"Yeah. I guess." At that moment, she felt connected with her father in a way she hadn't felt since childhood. "I'm so sorry, Dad."

Loss was not a stranger to her father. He had grown up poor on Lynden Street with his own father dying in a tuberculosis tent in the backyard by the garage. His mother made ends meet by starting a bakery in the neighborhood, and George had worked there to afford college. Nanna died when Maryl was about four and her only memory of her was from a photo.

"I bought a condo there and the moving truck comes next week. And don't worry. I've rented a storage unit here in Boston for your car and furniture. I figured you could get them whenever."

"This is so fast, Dad."

"Mmm. The whole thing seems so fast."

"Do you need me to do anything for you?"

"No. I just wanted you to know. Your brother already knows since he's handling your mother's will and all that."

Her brother, Steven, was an attorney and also their mother's executor. He called her that evening. It would be months until it was settled, he told her, and he hadn't wanted to comment on what the trust contained. Perhaps he didn't know.

THIRTY-FOUR

"Hey, Ray. I have an idea." In her usual I'll-deal-with-the-bad-stuff-later mode, Maryl was back to business.

"We've been approaching the Boeing issue as if they need a better report writer. But I'm thinking more like a crosstab or data analysis tool. That's what I was trying to chart out in the diagrams I sent over to Mark and Dan."

Ray was silent.

"Hello?"

"I'm here. Let me put you on the speakerphone. Mark just walked in."

"Hey, Mark."

She could hear Mark slurping his Coke. "How many Cokes are you up to per day now?"

Ray chuckled. "He actually put a mini-fridge in his office. I think it holds about fifty of those."

"Hey. Gotta stay awake somehow."

"So, the band's back together?"

"Sort of. It doesn't really work with one singer and two bass players. We're looking for a drummer. But yeah. We did a gig last night at a bar down in Renton."

Ray chuckled. "Mark's new hours are ten to ten unless he has a gig."

"That's par," Maryl said. "Hey, Mark, I'm thinking that the features that are in VisiCalc or Lotus 123 might be the ticket for the Boeing fix. But not stand-alone. Sort of a mix of spreadsheet and crosstab features since it would give them the contingency tables and more cell control."

Ray cut in. "We can't really use someone else's software product and pass it off as ours, you know."

"Right. But what if we coded some of those features into DAMON?" Maryl posed.

"That's corporate's call," said Ray. "And I'm sure Boeing's need doesn't trump the Bank of America features wish list."

"Mark, could you and Dan take my diagram and do a mock-up? At least a spec doc for us to present to corporate? Ray? Would you okay that?" Maryl asked.

She could see him shaking his head through the phone.

"Only if it doesn't interfere with ..."

"Our other clients," Maryl finished his sentence. "We know."

THIRTY-FIVE

"**W**hat's wrong, Hel?" Maryl couldn't translate the garbled message on her phone that night, so she had called Helen back.

"It's Doug. He's gone."

"Missing gone?"

"No. Gone gone."

"Oh shit. What the hell happened? I thought he was doing okay."

"Well, after all that, it turns out his heart just wasn't strong enough."

"Oh no. Oh no, Hel. Okay, okay." Maryl's mind was racing. "I'll catch a flight out as soon as I can."

Helen didn't argue. Next, Maryl called corporate and told them she'd be working out of the Bellevue office for a week or so. Then she called her dad.

"Hey, Dad." She was leaving a message. "Helen's husband just died and I'm coming out to be with her for a bit. I thought I might drop in on you guys too. But if you're not settled yet, I can probably just stay at a motel."

She flew into SeaTac airport, and Mark picked her up.

"Sorry to hear about your mom and the cancer."

"Yeah."

"Dan and I lost Mom about five years ago."

"Oh, I'm sorry, Mark. Was it sudden?"

"I guess you could say that. She suddenly didn't want to live any-more."

"Oh, shit."

"Yeah."

"I guess I'm lucky that I'll get to say goodbye to mine. Although truth be told, I've always been closer to my dad."

"I remember that. He could be a bear, though."

Maryl smiled. "True."

The Courtyard Suites was within walking distance of the office, but Mark said he'd pick her up at 7:30 the next morning in case it rained. She would spend two days there and then drive to Walla Walla for the funeral.

The Bellevue office was much the same as when she left, but several skyscrapers now blocked the mountain views. The three of them sat in the conference room and drew and erased and drew and erased for the next two days, emerging with a spec sheet and a mock-up on paper.

The night before she left, Ray and Teri took her to dinner.

"I'm so sorry about your mom," Teri was saying.

"Well, it sounds odd to say that I'm going to Walla Walla tomorrow for a funeral, and it's not my mom's. My best friend's husband just died. So, it will not be a happy trip on any front."

"That sucks," Ray offered. "At least you are okay."

"But *are* you okay?" Teri's gaze went right through Maryl's eyes and into the back of her brain.

Over the next hour she poured out a synopsis of her life in Ethan-world, and having done that pity party, she felt entirely stupid, naïve, and embarrassed.

"Jesus, Maryl." Ray looked at her. "Why didn't you tell me?"

"Because. You know. I got myself into this and I figure I have to get myself out of it. No one's fault but my own."

"And there she is." Ray reached for the check. "This one is on D&B."

Before heading out to Walla Walla the next morning, Maryl stopped by the office, as Ray had requested.

He shut the door to his office. "Okay. Here's what I know. Somehow Ethan has a copy of your diagram of your product specs that you sent to Mark, and he has been lobbying Frank to make it a new product line under his own name."

Maryl stared out the window at the side of the new parking garage going up. She stared a long time. So many cranes.

"As if it is his idea, Maryl."

"Yes. I heard you." She gripped the arms of her chair with such force that her knuckles were white. Another minute went by. Ray studied her.

"God dammit." Maryl sprang to her feet. "That asshole."

"So, what's your next move?"

"I'm going to my friend's funeral." She walked out the door.

The trip from Seattle to Walla Walla was two hours of two-lane winding mountain roads and then three hours of long straight gray asphalt. Ellensburg, then Yakima, through Flint and Zillah and Sunnyside, and on to the Tri-Cities, and finally Walla Walla. It was nice this time of year, as crops were coming up everywhere—peas, barley, corn, alfalfa—the normally dull brown fields a soft lush green along the road. And once she hit the Wallula Junction, the high heat hit her. And the wheat fields began. Just two feet high but green-gold and swaying in a slight breeze. Golden up to the sky, it was a yellow and blue day as she neared her childhood town of 24,000. The radio played Sade's 'Smooth Operator' followed by Carly Simon's "You're So Vain" and Maryl belted out every word at the top of her lungs.

With time to think, she came up with a plan.

En passant capture of the knight.

Thirty-Six

I n 1859, St. Patrick's Catholic Church consisted of poles covered with wood shakes and had no floors and only one bench. The first mass was said to a small group of soldiers, and white and Indian women. It was the year that Walla Walla got its name and the year that the local army captain was ordered to carry out the forced displacement of the remaining Walla Walla and Umatilla Native American people to the reservation in Oregon, under the threat of hanging.

So typical of the hypocrisy of the Catholic Church Maryl thought as she and Helen now sat in the front pew of the Gothic brick rebuild of 1881.

Soaring ceilings and grand alcoves filled with candles and statues, all drenched in colors of the stained-glass windows sliding across the church as the hour progressed. The choir was singing Salve Regina in a cappella Latin which translated to something like 'cry now' and 'cry more now' and finished with 'go ahead and sob'.

Helen's son and daughter sat next to her, all with sodden tissues, standing and kneeling as the priest directed. Maryl went through the motions for her friend's sake, but inwardly breathed her prayers to the souls she knew were hovering there in the church, even Doug's, in hopes they would take care of Helen and selfishly, would take care of her in the coming months.

If Paramahansa were here, he would say *A human being falsely identifies himself with his physical form because the life currents from the soul are breathed into the flesh with such intense power that man imagines the body to have life of its own.*

It was difficult for the human beings in this pew to look at Doug's body and not think he might sit up and hug them once again, that he might reach up and pat their cheek, or squeeze their fingers as they gently touched his cold hands.

Hundreds of people filled the community room after the funeral and Helen greeted each of them with a hug. That night, after her kids had gone to bed, Helen and Maryl sat on her couch with a cognac. Helen didn't normally drink brandy, but Maryl had insisted.

"What is there to say, my friend?"

"Not one thing," Helen said.

"I'm thinking I'll come back in a month to be with you after all the mourners have gone back to their lives."

"Oh, I'll be fine, Maryl. You're the one with the busy life to get back to."

"And I need to be grateful for it."

"But you're not?"

"Not always. I'm such a greedy bitch, you know. I just want all the happiness all the time."

Finally, she had made Helen giggle a little as she blew her nose for the hundredth time.

"I'll go see Mom tomorrow and that will be more than enough grounding."

Maryl parked her rental car in front of the garage. The flower boxes on either side held dried-up daisies and a few spindly roses. They weren't part of the condo association's responsibility. Regina had insisted that George install them. The neighbor woman, Rosalyn, greeted Maryl with a wave and walked the twenty steps from her own perky garden to speak to her.

"They are not looking so good, are they?" She noticed Maryl staring at the dead and dying flowers. "Sometimes I put a little water on them since I know your father doesn't think about it now…"

"I appreciate it, Rosalyn. And Dad says you've been collecting their mail when he forgets, so thanks for that. So, how is Dad doing?" Maryl asked.

"He has his good days and his bad days. Like we all do, I suppose. You know I watched my husband die last year, and it was so hard. I'm still not over it. I still reach for him in the bed and yell at him in the next room. It's hard."

"I can only imagine, Rosalyn. I wanted to thank you for keeping an eye on him."

"Oh, no problem, honey. It gives me something to do."

"Well, thanks. Here's my direct number in case there's anything I need to know."

"Okay, honey. I'll keep it by my phone."

George answered the door to the condo and said nothing as Maryl entered. She could tell he hadn't gotten any sleep the night before.

She dropped her things in the slate entryway and put her arms around him.

"Be sure and pick those up," he said, as he broke away and wandered down the hall to the living room. He was back to being a stone wall.

Following him down the hall, she smelled the stink of cancer, the smell it leaves on your skin, the smell that never comes off. Figuring her mother was still in bed, she pulled open the heavy curtains in the front room, exposing the sunny back patio and the tiny rose garden.

"Oh, please don't," she heard her mother's voice, although she almost didn't as it was quiet and pitiful and had no energy behind it.

Regina lay on the white leather couch wrapped in a wool blanket, sporting a wool beanie, and now holding a pillow over her eyes. Joey was next to her.

"Oh, jeez, Mom. I'm sorry." Maryl rushed to close the drapes again.

Her mother didn't move for a minute but then poked a sock out from under the blanket. "Oh, I suppose I should get up anyway," she whispered.

As she sat up, Maryl was shocked at how tiny she was. The large water bottle she reached for could barely fit in her hand, and Maryl jumped to grab it before it toppled.

"Here, Mom. Let me get that."

"So, what brings you to town?"

Maryl stole a look at her dad, but he was at the dining room table staring at nothing. George hadn't told her.

"Oh. Well, you remember Helen. Her husband died, so I went to the funeral yesterday."

When Maryl's eyes adjusted to the dim light, she saw how sunken her mother's eyes were. The bones in her hands looked like a skeleton's.

"I look pretty great, don't I?" Regina pronounced every word slowly, watching Maryl look at her. She was only sixty but looked eighty.

"Oh, Mom." She wanted to hug her, hold her, and tell her she was sorry for everything she ever did to make her mad, but that's not what they did in her family. Not even now.

"Come sit closer, Maryl. Let me have a look at you. I don't know where I left my glasses."

Death. Cancer and death. That was the smell. Maryl switched to shallow breathing.

"Hey, Mom. Can I fix you guys some dinner? Are you hungry?" She tried to change the subject.

"No, your father fixed me some cottage cheese this afternoon."

"How about you, Dad?"

George got up from the table, poured himself a drink, and walked through the slider out to the patio. "I'm going to go check on the pool."

To keep himself busy, her father had volunteered to check the security gate on the pool every evening. The pool was fifty yards away, across a perfectly mown lawn crisscrossed with tidy sidewalks. But George didn't use the sidewalks. He preferred to meander across the grass in his topsiders and check on everyone's gates and wave to neighbors, especially if they were widows.

"Your father is pretty lost right now." Regina stared out the window after him. "Maybe you could come around more."

"Okay, Mom," she said as she stood, wanting to exit before a heavy talk was introduced. "I gotta go, but I'll see you soon."

THIRTY-SEVEN

Once again, Maryl coped with reality by throwing herself into the technology.

"Now, I just have to put some revenue projections to this, and we can submit it," Maryl said. She was in the Bellevue office the morning before her flight back to Philadelphia. "My premise is that at least fifty percent of our existing customers will want a tool like this, and they each would spend between twenty to fifty thousand for it upfront, with annual renewal licensing to the tune of maybe ten thousand. What do you think?"

"Sounds like a good start, but those might be optimistic numbers. Let's pencil out what the development costs will be, and then back into the revenue numbers we'll need to support that." Ray was at the whiteboard.

In the next hour, they came up with some reasonable numbers, a development timeline, and revenue projections. Maryl would be able to sketch out a presentation on her flight back and have Patty type it up into slides.

"Maryl, with everything that's going on with Ethan, why don't you let me present it for you?"

"Thanks, Ray, but I have to do this myself."

"Well, at least send me your presentation as soon as you get to Philly."

"Okay, but why?"

"Just trust me."

Ray erased the board. "And be as detailed as possible with your F&B section."

"Will do, Raymond Sir."

She knew the features and benefits statement would make it hers and not just a random idea from a customer. Ray had her back.

Tony was assigned to support Maryl's clients since James was gone. A tall thin blond kid with a pimply face and large blue eyes that were often rimmed with red from staying up late with his video game buddies.

She spent a lot of time out of the office at AE and Squibb and the DOE public school system, now that they were all signed clients, and she could usually bring Tony up to speed on the train.

"How can the Department of Education afford DAMON when they can't even hire enough janitors?" Tony asked her one day on their train commute.

"Janitors?"

"Yeah. None of our schools are clean at all. It's gross."

"Who gets them dirty?"

"What do you mean?"

"Why are they so dirty that they can't be cleaned properly by the janitors?"

"They just are."

"Tony, you know we're in the middle of a huge crack epidemic, and high school kids are being recruited as dealers. Where do they hang out?"

"I don't know."

"Yes, you do. In the schools where they can sell the shit."

"So, they should hire more janitors."

"So, they should clean up the crack problem and they wouldn't need more janitors." Maryl shook her head. "Let's pivot and talk about this call, shall we?"

Maryl thought back to her post-college days, her hippie days, and wondered if she'd been equally naïve back then. Now she was living in mafia territory, within a drug epidemic of major proportions, Reaganomics, an escalated arms race, the AIDS epidemic. She was in a movie with lots of bad guys and very few good guys.

On the ride back from the DOE meeting, Tony struck up an odd conversation. It had been clear to Maryl that Tony worshipped Ethan.

"I think Ethan likes me."

"Why do you say that?"

"Well, you're the best salesman, er, salesperson on the East Coast, and he assigned me to you. That says something."

"Tony, how long were you at corporate before coming here?"

"About 3 years, I guess."

"Had you met Ethan before coming here?"

"Not really. But people at corporate told me about him."

"I see."

"And I'm into baseball too, so we have that in common."

"Baseball?"

"Yeah. I was a pitcher, and he was a first baseman. Not at the same time, of course. Or the same place."

"Obviously."

"Man, if his brother hadn't died, they would have been pros by now."

"You think so?"

"Yeah. They said Evan didn't really want to play ball, but he was so talented that Ethan talked him into it. And then that screaming pitch. I guess if I had to die, that wouldn't be bad. It was so quick."

Maryl stared out the smeared window of the train for a long time, marveling at the number of people who admired him. Did Ethan used to be one of the good guys?

Thirty-Eight

Several weeks passed. Maryl wondered if she should call the SEC again to check the status of her claim, but when she returned to the office that day, Patty handed her a pink message slip with a number. She looked at Patty for some explanation, who simply raised her shoulders and eyebrows at the same time.

She closed the door of her office behind her, which she never did, and dialed.

"Miss Marks. Thanks for returning my call. This is Detective Renner at the FBI. Do you have a moment now to answer a few questions?"

"Right," Maryl answered, not sure if it was a prank.

"Can you tell me about the relationship between you and Mr. Krahlman?"

"We...He was my boyfriend, but not anymore."

"Did you report him out of spite?"

"What?"

"Did you have an ulterior motive for this claim of insider trading?"

"What are you talking about? I caught him doing something illegal and I reported it."

"And do you have other friends who are doing illegal things, Miss Marks?"

"What? Like what?"

"Anything you can think of."

"The only other person I know who might be involved in this is his broker, but I already gave his name to the SEC."

"And that would be Caleb Stein?"

"Yes."

"And what is your relationship with Caleb?"

"He is a friend of Ethan's. I met Ethan's friend group when I was living with him." Maryl's cheeks were getting warm. "And he is also the one who made a secret deal to marry the woman who Ethan knocked up."

"Ma'am. Again, what is or was your relationship with Mr. Stein?"

"What are you asking?"

"Ma'am, did you have a personal relationship with both Mr. Stein and Mr. Krahlman?"

"What?!"

"Ma'am, if you had a personal relationship with both of these men, it leads one to believe that it could be a personal vendetta at your end."

It did, now that she was saying it out loud. She was angry. And now she was angry at this line of questioning. What was he implying? That she had a sexual relationship with Caleb? Why would his mind jump to that?

"No," Maryl responded. "I did not have a personal relationship with Caleb Stein. Let's get back to Ethan Krahlman."

"Ma'am. I'll ask the questions if you don't mind."

"I'm just saying that, in addition to being a cheat and a narcissist and a bully, he is also... he is also an insider trader. I think you should know those other things about him. That's the point here, right? To understand why Ethan would do this? I mean, a bad guy is a bad guy, no matter how many sins, right?"

"Sins, Miss Marks?"

"I meant crimes."

"I see." Mr. Renner continued, "And how did you come by the audio tape recording between Mr. Krahlman and Mr. Stein?"

"It was a message on our answering machine when I was living with Evan. I mean Ethan."

"And that one message led you to believe that Mr. Krahlman had insider information? I have listened to that message, and there are no references to a trade or information gotten illegally."

"That is not the only thing. It was a series of things that Ethan said and did."

"Can you tell me all the things that led you to report him please?"

Maryl rolled her eyes, dreading the long conversation ahead. She told Mr. Renner about Simon's attempt to tell Ethan about Toxix after the Penn State game, the phone message from Caleb to Ethan that sounded like a warning, and the mail message to Caleb referencing a Buy order. "And I'm sure you can fill in the blanks from your end, right? I mean the SEC can verify the trades and the dates, right?"

"Thank you for your time, Miss Marks."

And that was that. Maryl sat at her desk, tapping her pen on the blue mouse pad with some black logo that had rubbed off long ago. She had sweated through her blouse and wanted badly to go home.

That evening, she sat on her rented loveseat with a bowl of last night's pasta and dialed her father.

"Hey, Dad."

"Is your mouth full?" he asked.

"Oh, sorry. Just grabbing some dinner."

"Well, call me back when your mouth isn't full."

"No, Dad. I'll put it down. I wanted to ask your advice on something."

"What is it?" He sounded tired, but he always sounded tired these days. Life sucked for him right now.

"Oh, if this isn't a good time..."

"Maryl. What is it?"

She told him about her discovery of Ethan's insider info, her call to the SEC, and today's call with the FBI.

Her father sighed. A long sigh. One that made her picture his shoulders dropping an inch or so, and his head wagging in disappointment. "You really know how to cause trouble."

"Dad."

"What I'm hearing is that you are putting Ethan in front of a firing squad. Is that what you want?"

She was going to tell him about the twin but didn't. She felt bad in a way.

"What?" Maryl frowned. "You always taught me to fight my own battles, to be strong, and to counterpunch when they least see it coming."

She heard another sigh. Not a lot of fight left in him these days. It wasn't that she wanted an argument. She just didn't like seeing him so deflated, so resigned, so flat.

"Okay, Maryl. What is your goal? Do you want his job? Do you want to just prove a point that he hurt you? Do you want him in jail?"

"With all his powerful buddies, he'll just get humiliated, but never really go to jail. And it will cost him. For lawyers. And maybe for some fines."

"But insider trading, if that's what he did, is a serious crime. They might want to use this against D&B to make a point."

Crap. Dad was right. This will blow back against my company – the people who employ me. They will not be happy with me.

"Yeah. I see what you're saying, Dad. Thanks. I think I'll make a call to corporate in the morning and tell them what's going on. Just in case."

"Just in case they want to fire you first?"

"Well, yeah."

"Be careful what you wish for, Maryl."

The next morning Frank was silent on the phone.

"Are you still there?" Maryl asked after she had regurgitated a complete dump of the situation to the VP, including the call with Mr. Renner yesterday.

Clearly, she had opened a can of worms.

"Let me tell you what's going on at this end, Maryl. Both New York and Connecticut are "employment-at-will" states so we can fire Ethan with no cause. However, he is under a pretty tight Employment Contract, which he insisted on when D&B took us over. So, we have been working on a list of "for cause" reasons including willful misconduct and gross negligence in the performance of his duties."

"Well, if both are 'at will' states, can't you just fire him for no cause?"

"We could, but he would lawyer up and it would be a newsworthy spectacle. For months. His contract would give him a huge severance amount equal to one year's salary, plus healthcare benefits for the next 20 years, and a bonus of half a million dollars, plus the beamer he's driving, plus a glowing letter of reference. I'm literally reading out of his contract."

"So, he wouldn't suffer a bit if he was fired."

"That was the point of his contract."

Maryl listened as Frank told her there had been several internal complaints to HR concerning Ethan and his management style, even one from another VP whom Ethan had called an idiot. However, Ethan was no fool and had gathered accolades and lengthy letters from external customers expressing their respect and gratitude to him. And then there were the employees who adored him and remained loyal.

"Of course, we believe that Ethan probably authored those letters and had some sort of trades with customers such as company box seats. Nonetheless, as I mentioned, Ethan could easily lawyer up with these in his arsenal, and he knows the press alone would damage us," Frank continued.

"I agree that he probably wrote those himself," said Maryl. "But why is this a bad thing? Now that we are D&B, we could out-lawyer him, right?"

"Yes, and we would eventually win, but that's a moot point now. Innocently or not, you've managed to throw a wrench in our plans. The issue now is that you've drastically shortened the timeline for us to do this. We won't have time to fire him for cause, wade through a court battle, and move players around to cover our customer commitments."

"Oh jeez," Maryl sat down. "How do I fix this? I mean, can I?"

"No. There's nothing you can do right now. In light of what you've put in motion, there is now a factor of urgency. We'll need to get out ahead of this."

"What exactly do you mean by getting out ahead of this?"

"We need to distance ourselves from Ethan before it hits the news. Right now, his name is our name. We'll get smeared in the press for employing an insider trader. But if we fire him quickly, it takes a few months for the FBI to verify the information you've given them, so our PR machine will have time to sanitize us, so to speak."

"I see." Maryl was nauseous with embarrassment. "I really did it this time, didn't I, Frank. I'm so sorry."

"Live and learn, Maryl. Just keep your head down and we will handle it from here. Don't talk to anyone about this... except Ray."

"Why Ray?"

"Because Ray came to us a week ago about Ethan trying to present your new product idea as his own. He gave us a date-stamped copy and all the messages between you to prove it's your product idea and mockup. While we appreciate that, it just means we need to let Ray in on this, so he doesn't push that up the flagpole yet. We can use it later in the lawsuit that we're certain Ethan will bring."

Maryl hung up. *It won't be hard to keep it to myself. Everyone I could talk to has been fired or has fled. And Dad will just say I told you so.*

But she could talk to Ray. She went home at noon and dialed him.

"Hey, Miss Philly," he said.

"Hey, Raymond Sir. A little bird told me you gave corporate my presentation."

"Why yes, I did. You're welcome."

"I just called to say thank you. What do you think they'll do with it?"

"No telling," said Ray.

"Well, I just wanted to say thanks again."

"Seriously? That's all you called for?"

"Not really. Shit is about to hit the fan, and it's all my fault."

"No, it's not. Ethan has it coming. That product is yours. He had nothing to do with it."

"Oh, Ray. I'm not talking about that. Do you have some time to chat right now?"

"I can make time."

"And if you get a call from corporate while we're talking, you should hang up with me and talk to them."

"I would do that anyway, Mel. What's going on?"

"I turned Ethan in to the SEC for possible insider trading."

"You what?"

"Yes."

"Why? I mean, do you have proof?"

"Why? Because he's an ass, and because it's illegal, and because he tried to steal my product idea, and because I almost had his child, and because he didn't tell me he had a twin and..."

Maryl broke down and sobbed, adding to her embarrassment.

"Maryl. I'm going to hang up and call Frank. Then I'll call you back."

That night, Maryl sat in the bath for an hour, staring at nothing, stirring small whirlpools with her toes, refilling the hot water, and staring some more. She didn't regret calling the SEC. She regretted not telling Ray or Frank before she did it. She should have let corporate handle it. Now, it just looked like a lover's revenge, and she might even be fired for it.

When would she learn to simply dance in place while her opponent exhausted himself by punching the air?

Ray had called her back to say that Frank would put Ethan on a 'special project' at corporate for a few days so that they could keep an eye on him. Maryl was relieved that he wouldn't be in the Philly office, but she walked through the days on autopilot, wondering what was happening behind the scenes.

Two weeks later, a message came down from corporate:

Dear Team,

I am writing to inform you of an important decision that will impact our Philadelphia branch. After careful consideration and analysis of our current business needs and long-term strategy, we have made the difficult decision to close our Philadelphia office.

We understand that this news may come as a surprise and may cause concern for many of you. Please know that this decision was not made lightly, and we have explored all possible alternatives before coming to this conclusion. Our primary goal is to ensure the continued success and growth of our company while supporting our valued employees during this transition.

To that end, we are committed to providing each of you with options moving forward. All Philadelphia-based employees will be given the opportunity to either relocate to our corporate headquarters or join our New York City office. For those who choose to relocate, we will provide assistance with moving expenses and help you navigate the transition to your new location.

Alternatively, for those who are unable or choose not to relocate, we will offer a comprehensive exit package. This will include a severance payment based on your tenure with the company, as well as outplacement services to help you find new employment opportunities.

In the coming weeks, our HR team will be reaching out to each of you individually to discuss your options in more detail and answer any questions you may have. We will also be holding a series of informational meetings to provide further guidance and support throughout this process.

Please know that we deeply value the contributions each of you has made to our company, and we are committed to supporting you through this transition. Your hard work, dedication, and expertise have been instrumental in our success, and we want to ensure that you have the resources and support you need during this time.

If you have any immediate concerns or questions, please don't hesitate to reach out to your manager, HR representative, or myself directly. We are here to support you.

Frank Ward, VP

THIRTY-NINE

—◦—

Maryl read it three times. *What? That was the big plan to get rid of Ethan?*

What remained of the team—Patty, Tony, and two other techies—were already in the conference room.

"What's going on? That's not fair. What are we going to do now? This is bullshit." The small group was furious. Frightened and furious.

As soon as Maryl entered the room, they turned to her.

"Did you know about this?" asked Patty.

"No," said Maryl. "I can't believe it either."

"It doesn't say when our last day is."

"I'm sure there will be a follow-up to that message. Look for something from HR next."

"You seem awfully calm, Maryl."

"No, I'm just in shock. And I'm furious along with you. But it may have been the only way they could get rid of Ethan." Maryl stood up. "Does anyone here have an inside connection with HR? Or with someone at corporate who might know more about this?" Maryl offered. "I think I'll call Tom."

"Call him from in here so we can all hear."

She dialed from the large black box on the conference room table. Tom answered.

"What's the word, nerd?" Maryl greeted him in their usual way. "Hey, I have the whole team here in Philly or what's left of it. We just got the mail message. What can you tell us about that? Anything?"

"What mail message?"

"About closing this office. And I have you on speakerphone by the way."

"I haven't seen that message, but the rumor is that Ethan just got fired, so maybe that's it."

The room was silent.

"Really?" asked Maryl. "On what grounds?"

"Don't know. Don't care. I, for one, am not sad to see him go."

"Okay, well, thanks, Tom. We need to digest this. I'll talk to you later."

The team, now sitting around the table, was quiet.

"But what about Daniels?" Patty was thinking out loud. "I heard he was almost recovered. Why not just bring him back to run this office?"

"No idea, Patty," Maryl answered. "I'm just wondering what they're going to do with our clients. Just don't say anything to any clients until corporate tells us what to say, okay?"

"But some of them will be mad. Maybe we should give them a heads up."

"No. No. Bad idea. That will just start a cascade of bad juju between us and our customers. Just wait. This isn't their first rodeo." Maryl tried to calm them, but she had questions of her own.

Was she losing her job because she caused trouble? Was she the bad guy? Were her office mates losing their jobs because of what she did? Was Ethan going to know she was at the root of this? Would he retaliate? Should she call Frank, or just let it unfold according to his plan?

In fact, Frank called her at home that evening.

"I'm sure that mail message got your blood pumping," he began.

"Hell, yeah," she said. "What's the rest of the story?"

"Well, first of all, how did the team take it?"

"They are freaked out of course. You know. *When will this happen? Why did it happen? What about our customers*? And then *my* favorite one, 'Is Ethan coming for me?'"

"I think you're safe. Our HR Director met him at the New York office today under the guise of clearing out his things. We've put a restraining order on him so he can't come within a hundred feet of either office. I thought you would want to know."

"Oh. Wow," Maryl said. "Thanks."

"Yes. And thanks to your call to me, we were able to alert our PR folks for the spin. That's why we had to fire him for cause, in order to distance him from D&B before this news came out about his arrest, which will happen soon, I'm sure. Do you have any more info on that from your end?"

"No. Apparently, I'm out of the picture now that I told them everything. They said they wouldn't be giving me any updates. I've been scouring the papers daily. I'm sure you've been as well."

Maryl was gripping the phone as if it were the safety bar on a roller coaster. "But it will be in the news, right? Won't that be bad press?"

"Yes and no. First, they will have to find him somewhere else such as his home. So, our office won't be shown on the news. Second, we put out a news release yesterday that he has been fired and that we have a no-tolerance policy for any kind of criminal activity, including but not limited to drug trafficking, insider trading, harassment, et cetera."

"Shit, Frank. Now I'm wondering if I should have started this. I guess I could have settled for him losing his job."

"Maryl, is there something else behind this? Did something happen between you two?"

"Oh Frank, it's a long story and not a good one."

"Well, Miss Welterweight, you've got some pretty good punches. Just be careful who you knock out cold." Frank sounded like her father.

"I'm a fighter. You know that."

"I'm just saying that sometimes you can watch them self-destruct on their own."

"Yeah. Patience was never my thing."

"Noted."

"So, now. What do we say to clients?"

"Don't worry about that. A letter went out today to all clients in the New York and Philly territories. Daniels is taking over the New York office now. He will be calling them all to smooth things over and set up the transitions. He's good at that."

"Transitions to what?"

"Well, as the message said, some clients will be supported out of the New York office and others out of corporate. We don't see it as a big problem for our clients."

"And what do you see for me?" Maryl asked.

"I was wondering when you would ask. Well, we like your idea of the new product so much, that you will be offered one of two jobs: A desk and a team in the New York office to flesh out and sell the product, or a desk here at corporate to do the same."

Maryl breathed in a long breath.

"Before embarking on important undertakings sit quietly, calm your senses and thoughts, and meditate deeply." Paramahansa Yogananda.

"New York City," she said. She would meditate later.

The news channel showed the FBI taking Ethan out of a restaurant. He was not handcuffed. It wasn't the movies. But he was flanked by two men who looked like the Blues Brothers. Something about the suspicion of insider trading, and then "in other news" and it was gone.

Sixty seconds and his life was ruined.

Even if his lawyers got him off on some technicality, which was doubtful, he was still fired from D&B and humiliated in front of his friends and family.

Maryl had wielded that sword. She had cut him down. She had used her power.

James called her. "When are we celebrating?"

"Oh, man. Did you see it? I wish I would have taped it."

"I can do that for you. I'm sure they'll show it ten times on the news in the next few days. And even more in the next weeks and maybe months. You know, Maryl, this is not over by a long shot. They have filed criminal charges and arrested him, but now comes all the discovery stuff and motions and hearings."

"I get that. Which will be even more humiliation for him."

"Even if it takes months, he is getting what he deserves."

"And I doubt anyone will hire him soon," Maryl said. "Thanks for supporting me in all this. I know I made you take sides."

"No. No. I was always on your side. It was the right thing to do. And thanks, from all of us who hate that guy."

"Hate the sin, love the sinner."

"What?" James said.

"Something Ghandi said. It keeps rolling around in my head."

"Well, technically, you *did* love the sinner, so I think you did your part." James laughed. Maryl didn't. "Too soon? Hey, take the victory lap. You earned it."

Maryl jumped every time the phone rang. This time it was Barbara.

"Maryl, it's Barbara. I saw Ethan on the news tonight. They also arrested Caleb, and Sarah is out of her mind. She is running around looking for Caleb's pistol to go kill Ethan. She's crazy. I'm trying to calm her down with some Valium. Do you know what's going on?"

"Hi, Barbara. Well, I know enough to tell you that it's complicated. And up until this evening, it's been an internal company matter. I don't even know most of the story." She told a white lie. "They have just shuttered the Philadelphia office. I think we'll all just have to wait and see."

"But Maryl. They took Caleb! What is this all about? Sarah and Chloe are over here now, and she can't stop bawling and screaming."

"Sarah doesn't have any knowledge of the situation?"

"What situation, Maryl?" Barbara's voice was getting louder and lower.

"All I can say is that Sarah needs to get Caleb a really good lawyer. Quickly. And that Caleb should tell the entire truth to the lawyer before Ethan can spin things in his favor."

"Dammit, Maryl. I know you know something. What is it?"

"Barbara. Please. I've already said too much."

Caleb was sitting in his attorney's office. He was out on bail.

"Mr. Stein. Before we discuss anything, I need to remind you that everything you say to me is confidential, but it's crucial you're completely honest with me."

"I understand. I'm just... I can't believe this is happening."

"Take a deep breath. Now, tell me exactly what transpired when they arrested you."

"They showed up at my office this morning. FBI agents. They read me my rights and took me into custody. It was humiliating. My colleagues saw everything."

"Did they present a warrant?"

"Yes, they had papers. I didn't read them closely."

"Alright. Did you say anything to them?"

"No, I asked for a lawyer immediately. That's what you're always supposed to do, right?"

"Exactly right. Good job. Now, what do you think prompted this arrest?"

"I... I may have helped my client make some trades based on information that wasn't... entirely public."

"I see. Can you be more specific about the nature of this information and how you obtained it?"

"It was about a takeover. My college buddy's dad works for the company being acquired. He let something slip on the way home from the Nittany Lions game. We all heard it. I didn't think it was a big deal, but then Ethan insisted that I put in a BUY order for him."

"Ethan Krahlman? That's precisely the kind of information that can lead to insider trading charges. How much did you profit from these trades?"

Caleb winced, "About $200,000. That was my commission."

"I see. And did anyone else know about this information or your trades? Besides Mr. Krahlman? "

"My wife knew I was nervous about something I did. And I may have hinted to a couple of close friends that it was a good time to buy that stock."

"This complicates things. If your friends acted on that information, they could be implicated as well. What communication methods did you use to arrange all this?"

"Just phone and mail messages."

"Those messages can potentially be recovered. Now, have you ever been involved in anything like this before?"

"No, never. This was a one-time thing. I swear. I got greedy. God, I've ruined everything, haven't I?"

"Let's not jump to conclusions. The prosecution will need to prove that you willfully engaged in insider trading. There might be some defense strategies we can employ."

"Like what?"

"We could potentially argue that you didn't believe the information was material or non-public. Or that you didn't act with the intent to deceive or defraud."

"But I did know. I'm a broker for god's sake. I knew exactly what I was doing."

"Mr. Stein, I appreciate your honesty with me. However, I must advise you not to make such explicit admissions to anyone else. Our job now is to build the best possible defense."

"What am I looking at here? Jail time?"

"It's a possibility. Insider trading can carry a sentence of up to 20 years, but that's the maximum. Realistically, if convicted, you might be looking at 3-5 years, plus fines."

Caleb put his head in his hands. "This can't be happening. My career is over. I'm sure I'm fired. My wife will leave me…"

"I understand this is overwhelming but try to stay calm. We'll tackle this step by step. For now, don't discuss this case with anyone. Not your wife, not your friends, no one. Don't go golfing or go to parties where you might slip up."

"Okay. What's our next move?"

"I'm going to review the charges and evidence against you. Then we'll discuss plea bargain possibilities versus going to trial. Remember, the prosecution needs to prove their case beyond a reasonable doubt."

"And if they do?"

"Then we focus on minimizing the consequences. But let's not get ahead of ourselves. For now, go home, be with your family, and try to maintain normalcy. I'll be in touch soon with our next steps."

"Thank you. I… I never thought I'd be in this position."

"Many of my clients say the same thing. We'll get through this, Mr. Stein. One day at a time."

Two weeks later Frank called Maryl.

"Look," he said when she answered. "Thanks for agreeing to stay on there in Philly and help transition your clients. I know you want to head up to Manhattan as soon as possible. And then there's the possibility of legal proceedings and whether or not you'll need to be involved in those. Also, I know you are worried about retaliation from Ethan, but remember. He can't come within a hundred yards of the office."

"But does he know that I'm the one who..."

"I don't think so, but based on his previous behavior, we just don't know, so watch your back. Next, the news is that Ethan is talking about a plea bargain. He doesn't want this to be a long-drawn-out process."

"Hmmm. That probably means he's going to throw Caleb under the bus."

"Who is Caleb?"

"His broker. And his best friend."

"Sounds likely. Not our problem now. Just wanted you to know that you won't have to live under this cloud for much longer. We all want this to go away sooner than later."

Forty

"So, congratulations," Maryl's father said. "A plea bargain is admitting guilt. You got him."

"Yeah. It was that counterpunch you taught me, Dad."

"I raised a girl who is tougher than both my boys."

"Thanks, Dad. That is high praise. But it's not a done deal yet. No one knows exactly what's going to happen next, so I'm still really nervous."

"Well, just tuck in your chin, Mel."

They didn't talk much about her mother on the phone these days, since Regina was neither in remission nor getting worse. The cancer was just there. In her body and in her mind. And George was leaning on his buddies heavily. And drinking heavily. The two went hand-in-hand at this point. His friends didn't know what to say to comfort him, so they just drank together and called it a communication of sorts.

"Well, I gotta go. The boys are coming over." George was done talking. She could hear the ice cubes tinkle in his glass as he replaced the receiver.

She hung up and called Rosalyn, the neighbor.

"Hey, Rosalyn. It's Maryl Marks. I just got off the phone with Dad and wanted to check in with you about how he's doing. It seems he might be drinking a little more than usual?"

"Oh, honey, I think that's just what men do to cope. Their sorrow just gets swallowed with the scotch. But tomorrow I'll take him a cake so I can see how he's doing, okay? A cake can solve a lot of problems."

"Thanks, Rosalyn. He loves cake. His mother used to own a bakery."

"Oh, is that right?"

"Yeah. Thanks, Rosalyn. I have to go."

Next, she called Helen.

"You know when I told you I would come back in a month or so when everyone else had gone back to their lives? Well, that time is now."

"What? Oh, Maryl, that would be lovely. Yes, people have stopped coming by. I know it's just awkward for them," Helen said with manufactured strength. "But can you afford the time off? And the trip out here?"

"Well, my dad doesn't sound so great, so I thought I'd come out and see about him, and you know, check on my mom, and then come spend some time with you."

"You're a good friend, Mel."

"And a lousy daughter, but what the heck."

A week later, they were sitting in Helen's living room, sipping chardonnay.

"This is exactly what I needed," Maryl told her friend, after a frustrating visit with George and Regina, both in their own downward spiral.

"Me too," said Helen. "So how did it go with your father and his cronies?"

"Dad made sure at least one of his buddies was there at all times—almost as if he knew I would get on his case about his drinking and want to talk about what his life will look like after mom goes."

"I guess that's to be expected," Helen said. "And what about the other dysfunctional man in your life?"

She told Helen all the details of the Ethan saga. When Maryl paused, Helen said, "Oh Mel. This is terrible."

"What do you mean? This is great. I'm beating him at his own game." Maryl stopped herself as soon as the words tumbled out.

Helen was nodding. "Yes, the game of cruelty."

"Well, you heard all the horrible things he has done over the past two years. He deserves it."

"Who's to say?" Helen looked at her friend.

"Well, everyone in my office thanked me. No one can stand him. He's such an ass."

"Let he who is without sin cast the first stone." Helen quoted her lord and savior.

"Oh, for Christ's sake, Hel. I mean, Oh for god's sake."

Helen smiled. "I still love you."

"Well, you are making me feel like shit for standing up for myself. I drew my sword. I stood up to evil. My pawn took out his knight."

"If you say so, Mel. Let's have more wine. So, speaking of wine, you said your father was drinking quite a bit?" Helen poured more wine.

"Yes. He just doesn't know how to cope. He's in this period between being married and being a widower, and he's used to being the CEO of everything in his life...in control...always knowing what to do."

"Like someone else I know?" Helen smiled sweetly.

"And these grown-ass men, his buddies, don't know how to support him. So, they just come over to the house and drink and play cards and don't even talk about it. What the hell?"

"Well, we enlightened women need to give them a break," Helen said. "They are all used to being under intense pressure at work and focused on results, so they are powerless when their future is ambiguous, and they have no control over what's happening."

"In other words, they're flaccid." Maryl was feeling worse about her father, but better about being there for her best friend. *Or was it the other way around?* She looked back at Helen and continued, "Yeah, they've been trained to excel at emotional detachment, just like in the military. You remember that George was a boxer in college and later joined the Air Force, so vulnerability was never in his vocabulary."

"No, but cruelty was."

Maryl frowned. "What are you saying?"

"I'm saying that you were raised between Steven and Billy. Your biggest lessons were bravery, deniability, revenge, strength, and may the best man win. But what your father meant was that the one who was the best at *those traits* was the winner."

"What's the matter with that?" Maryl asked defiantly, putting her glass down hard on the coffee table.

"Maryl," Helen said. "When was the last time you cried?"

"Hel, you know I don't cry. It's a waste of time and energy."

"Exactly. And who taught you that? Certainly not your mother. She cries all the time. And mostly for you."

"What?"

"You know it's true. She never knew what to do with you ever since you popped out. She tried to make you the girly girl, she tried strictness, she tried prayer. She cried that she had lost the fight for your soul at an early age, and I think she blamed it on your father when it wasn't your father's fault either. You just popped out strong. Different from her. She didn't understand."

"And you're telling me this to try to get me to cry *now*? Is that the plan?" Maryl stood and walked to the window.

Helen stayed seated. "Mel, you are my dearest friend. I love you for the woman you are. Strong. Independent. Brave. And your heart is so big, but you don't see it. You hate injustice. You hate unfairness. You hate infidelity. And you don't believe in a Catholic God anymore because He allows these things to happen."

Maryl turned back from the window. "And?"

"And you're vulnerable."

"Fuck, no."

"Yes, my friend."

"Just stop."

"I won't." Helen was calm. "I won't because you need to hear it. You need to acknowledge that the beating heart inside you is full of goodness, and grace and vulnerability, and compassion. And I know those are touchy-feely words for you, but they are true ones, and you are all about Truth. Right now, your mother needs your compassion, and your father needs your empathy. You are the only one who can give these things to them."

Helen paused. "And the stakes couldn't be higher, Mel."

"What do you mean?"

"I mean that if your mother and father don't get forgiveness from you for all they have done in this life, they may spend eternity in purgatory. And you as well."

"Oh Jesus, Hel. You're seriously going to use the Catholic shit on me? There's no such place as purgatory."

"Okay. I was just going for a goal there. But I'll back up to the thirty-yard line for another attempt."

They drank more wine and talked about gardens and her children and her artwork and fell asleep grateful for their unbreakable friendship. But Maryl pondered everything Helen had said.

When she returned to her parents' house that night, Regina was in the living room, propped up with pillows, staring out the window. Joey was in her lap.

"Hi, Mom. How are you feeling?"

"Come sit down, Maryl." She patted the couch space next to her.

For once, Maryl obeyed her mother.

"I've been thinking a lot about my life, of course, and there are things I want to say to you before I'm not able."

Joey sensed a subtle change in Regina's blood pressure and looked up at her. She smoothed his ears and said, "It's okay," and continued.

"I know you've wondered all these years why I stayed with your father, and I know I wasn't a very good role model for you. All those men you went through trying to find a good one… I'm sorry about that. But you have to understand, Maryl. It was a different time back then. I had five children, and no job. What was I supposed to do? The church would have banned me if we divorced, and I couldn't bear that. Your father wouldn't have raised you kids—he didn't know the first thing about it—and Joyce definitely wouldn't have wanted you jumping around her lovely home."

She reached for Maryl's hand and held it with her bony fingers, looking deep into Maryl's eyes. "I know that's why you never had respect for me. I didn't stand up to him like you do. I didn't fight. But I did it for you kids as much as anything. And George might have lost his job over the scandal. And then what would we do? We would have had to move to a different town out of shame. Church shame. Neighbor shame. And my folks just loved George. In their eyes, he could do no wrong."

"I'm sorry, Mom. I'm sorry you had to go through that for all those years. I just didn't understand. I thought you were weak. I watched him be a jerk to you so often and you just swallowed it. I didn't realize it was your inner strength that stood up to that. And thank you for keeping the family together. Our lives would have been so different."

Regina's eyes were brimming with tears as she nodded slowly and looked away.

"But why did dad stay? Why didn't he leave you if he loved her more than you? I remember in third grade; he didn't come home for a week, and you just sat in a chair and cried for days."

"You remember that? Yes, Father Caffrey helped us. I had to ask *someone* for advice, and it couldn't be my folks or friends. He reminded your father of his vows and his commitment to his children. I think George also knew he would be banned in the eyes of his Catholic clients. So, he made a promise that he would stay and not see her again—a promise he broke as you know."

"I would hope that he came back because of us, too?"

"Of course. He loved you kids. And you the most. I'm sure you know that. I was always a little jealous of that love you two had. Even when you fought so much, that bond was still there. You need to take care of your father when I'm gone. He will need you. And I've already given him permission to marry Joyce if he wants."

Maryl felt years of anger start to melt—just a bit. All the deep disappointments. All the heartache this woman had caused her. All the cruel things she had said and done. It was hard to forgive, but in that moment, she reached for her mom and hugged her for a long time.

James picked Maryl up at the airport in Philadelphia and filled her in on the status of things.

She snarled at most of the news. "God, I'm glad I'm moving to New York," she told him.

"You are?"

"Well, yes. Corporate offered me a job fleshing out that product I've been working on with Mark and Dan."

"You mean the one on the butcher paper I found under Ethan's bed?"

"Yes, the one he tried to claim as his own idea."

"He did?"

"Keep up, James."

"Snarling again, girl."

"So, I can either have an office at the NYC location or up at corporate in Connecticut."

"Hands-down New York, right?"

"Right."

"That's a long way from Pleasantville, New Jersey."

"What do you mean?"

"Well, since I have a full-time job there, I found an apartment down there. I'll be moving there next week."

"Ugh. That is a long way. You know, I have an idea. Would you like me to bring you back on board as my techie in New York for this project?"

"Hmmm. Sounds tempting, but you know I'm not a big city boy. I prefer the country."

"Right. Out by the hazardous waste dumps."

"I need to stop telling you these bits of information, don't I?"

"Hey. Words can be weapons you know."

A few days later, Maryl got a startling phone call.

FORTY-ONE

She found herself at yet another funeral, surrounded by people who said the word sorry too many times. Maryl shouldn't have been shocked that it had happened, but she was. No one was ready for it.

As she stood in the small gathering of somber faces, she felt strangely hollow. The sanctuary was hushed. Sunlight filtered through stained glass. The mahogany casket gleamed under the soft lights, its polished surface reflecting the tears of those around her. Hushed whispers of such a tragedy and muffled sobs filled the air, a symphony of grief that seemed oddly disconnected from her own emotions. Maryl's eyes fixed on the framed photograph atop the casket, the same image she had once mistaken for a memorial, now a chilling reality.

She was disconnected from the turmoil in her heart at that moment and fidgeted in the pew. Closing her eyes, she retrieved the version of death that Paramahansa Yogananda had gifted her. *"Passing from this world does not erase our BEING or offer a permanent refuge from life's challenges. Nor does it automatically grant everlasting existence."*

Sometimes we must come back around to do it all again. Maryl completed the thought in her mind. *Hopefully to do it better the next time.*

As the officiant, an old man with a dark beard, droned on about a life well-lived and a soul at peace, she couldn't help but reflect on the complexities of that theory. Her gaze fixed on the floral arrangements, their sweet scent a poor mask for the awful truth of the situation.

Pills, Sarah had said.

Maryl felt strangely numb.

The congregation of mourners moved outside to the cemetery, shuffling through dead leaves. As they assembled, she noticed the thinness of the crowd. Perhaps it was the weather. She saw some older relatives, some businessmen, children each holding a small stone, and the requisite staff members and cemetery workers standing by.

The Star of David was draped over the casket. As the haunting melody of El Malei Rachamim filled the air, she closed her eyes, letting the ancient prayer wash over her. At other funerals, the first bars of Ave Maria had the congregation in tears. She noticed this was much the same.

Barbara walked stiffly around the circle and stood beside Maryl at the outskirts of the crowd, hissing in a loud whisper, "I know you had something to do with this. He was only thirty years old. What will Sarah do now? She's totally strung out on Valium and it's your fault. How dare you show your face here." And then she rejoined Sarah's parents who were crying quietly.

"Now would be a good time for a graceful exit, Mel." James stood next to Maryl. He took her arm. "Come on. Let's get you to a happier place," he said as he led her to the parking lot where soggy brown and yellow leaves stuck to the bottom of her shoes. The season was turning. The lot was practically empty.

Gawd, I hope more people come to see me off. How depressing.

The only reason James came to the funeral was to be there for Maryl. She had debated coming herself, but she wanted to see if Ethan would show up and pretend that Caleb's death was not his fault.

He didn't.

Suddenly, she stopped and threw her arm out to stop James, too. Ethan *was* there and was walking toward her.

"Well, well. If it isn't Miss Whistleblower and her sidekick."

"This is not the forum, Ethan. This is a funeral. Leave me alone."

"Leave you alone? That's rich coming from you. If you would have kept your nose out of my business, there wouldn't be a damn funeral."

"Your business? You mean your criminal activity?"

"Be careful, Mel. The fat lady hasn't sung. I will get out from under this and come after you *and* your career."

"Let's go, Mel." James opened the car door and motioned to her.

Maryl stepped toward Ethan, leading with her chin. "So, you're threatening me now?"

"Why not? I've got nothing to lose. You took everything from me. And you killed my best friend."

"You did that yourself, Ethan. Don't try to pin that on me. You did the plea bargain trick and threw Caleb under the bus. You betrayed him."

"No. You betrayed me. Both of us."

"Betrayed you? You betrayed everything we stood for! We were the power couple. That power went to your head. You betrayed *me* and everyone in the company."

"You mean by running a successful business? Being the biggest biller in the country? Taking advantage of opportunities that present themselves? Making us rich? Oh, the horror!"

"Yes, the horror. The fraud, the lies, the people you hurt."

"People get hurt in business all the time. It's not personal, it's just numbers. May the best man win, Mel. I thought you knew that."

"You think you're so untouchable. Well, 'midah k'neged midah' Ethan. Measure for measure."

"Don't you dare throw Judaism in my face."

"It's always been in your face. You just ignore it when it suits you."

"Damn you, Mel. I will drag you into this. Count on it. When this is over, I'll be back on top. And you'll be nothing."

"Goodbye, Ethan." She stretched one long leg into the passenger side. "Maybe someday you'll understand what you've done."

Ethan snorted mockingly, turned his back, aimed his middle finger up to the sky, and walked away.

It was as if he pulled a lever. One that started a truck engine—an engine in a Ford F150 that suddenly lurched and roared through the parking lot. It hit him straight on, causing his body to crash into the hood, and then bounce off the windshield and back down to the gravel. He lay motionless in a scattered pile of rocks and dead leaves.

James leapt out of his car scrambling to dial 911 as he rushed over to see if Ethan was still breathing.

The driver's door of the big truck swung open and Sarah stepped daintily out onto the running board.

"Oh, my goodness. This damn gear shift," she exclaimed, her tone oddly detached. Unstrapping Chloe from her car seat in the back, Sarah scooped up her frightened daughter and approached Maryl with steady composure.

Sarah tilted her head slightly, fixing her Valium gaze on Maryl who was staring at the little girl's similarity to Ethan.

"Striking, isn't it?" Touching her daughter's cheek, she faced Maryl. "Chloe, this is Maryl. Maryl, meet Chloe."

EPILOGUE

She closed the last box and taped it shut. Finally, she could escape to Manhattan and begin a new life.

In the quiet of her half-empty apartment, with its muted green walls that used to stand for money and verdant forests, Maryl could only see the fading green of the cemetery lawns, which now hid boxes of dead bodies.

The Jewish community had stretched their arms around the affected families and quietly absorbed the blow.

James's sources beyond their inner circle had revealed Sarah's own toxic history with pharmaceuticals. In hindsight, her earlier quip about poisoning Ethan's dessert carried a darker edge now – she'd battled addiction long enough to need rehabilitation. Chloe had entered the world born from an angry power move by Ethan, fighting her own withdrawal battle, with Muriel stepping in as surrogate mother while Sarah recovered. The bitter irony? It had all started with Sarah, Caleb, and Ethan sharing Valium back in college, playing at being grown-ups before they understood the stakes.

Maryl reached for her necklace. Bravery was not what she was feeling.

I landed the last punch, though, didn't I, Daddy?

Thank you so much for reading COUNTERPUNCH – *Maryl Morgan Marks: Book 1*

If you enjoyed this story, feel free to leave a review filled with lovely stars on my Amazon Author Page. I only ask that you please don't leave spoilers that will ruin it for others. This is the first book in a four-part series.

Coming soon: Maryl Morgan Marks: Book 2

As the dust settled on the tumultuous events that had reshaped Maryl Morgan Marks' life, she stood at the threshold of a new beginning. Scars still fresh, a spark of determination glimmered in her eyes as she gazed out over the Manhattan skyline.

Little did Maryl know that her journey was far from over. In the coming months, life would throw her a series of uppercuts that would test her resilience like never before.

An old boss and a new career opportunity would beckon, promising the excitement of cutting-edge technology that would forever change the world of library science. But with new triumphs would come new trials—a betrayal of the heart, an unexpected twist of fate that would change her life forever, and a reckoning with the corporate power structure once again.

From the bustling streets of New York to Boston and D.C., Maryl's path would scale the heights of success, only to face a devastating fall that would strip her of everything she had worked for. But, with the unlikely support of her grief-stricken father, she would begin the arduous climb back to self-discovery and professional redemption.

Hey there.

Because you are such an awesome reader, I'd like to give you a little something.

I have a free short story that you might like to read while you wait for my next book.

Just email me, Taylor Zane, at taylor@canterwoodpress.com and I'll send it to you! And of course, if you'd like to know more about this series, use this link.

http://www.canterwoodpress.com

SIGN UP TO BE A SUBSCRIBER and you'll receive the Taylor Zane newsletter about this book and all upcoming books in the series.

Did you know that the best way indie authors like me get noticed is through Amazon reviews? I would love it if you would post a short review on Amazon for me! Thanks so much for reading my book!

Use this link to leave a review:

https://bit.ly/COUNTERPUNCHReviews

Acknowledgments

Many thanks to the incredible team that got me through this first novel. First a hat tip to Brenda Hart who encouraged me to put pen to paper NOW. Major thanks to my coaches, Ramy Vance and Joe Gilbert, and my editor, Margaret McKay. I am so grateful to my first beta readers, Mary Luethe, Barbara Lidikay, Barb Clark, Janice Marvin, Claudia Pettis, Lori B., Ellen Metsker, Chuck Pettis, Jim Morgan, Maralyn Renner, Lisa Shawe, and the dozen other readers and writers who trudged through this process with me as I exhausted their opinions about every little detail—especially my BFF Daniele Costello who carried her cell phone on her tractor in case I called. Your input made this a better book.

Thanks to my Writing Room Zoom tribe at SelfPublishing School who were steadfast in their support and offered insider tips that saved me hours of research time. A big shout-out to Chad Dulac, Chris Duffy, and Levi Drop for reworking my cover mockups (and reworking and reworking) and introducing me to online programs I would not have found. Huge hugs to Anna Hester for designing the cover background in one sitting after sharing much champagne on my birthday.

About the Author, Taylor Zane

F reshly retired from the 'gray suit in a gray box' world where she *lived* most of her stories, Taylor is now a full-time author of a series of Women's Fiction books. Drawing from a rich life of personal and professional adventures, her goal is to give strong (or soon-to-be strong) women a bit of escape from their own lives for a minute and offer a kindred spirit in this rat race of relationships with, and working for...well, humans. Women from their early twenties to late seventies will smile and nod through Maryl Morgan Marks' setbacks and triumphs as she works her way *into* and *out of* situations we've all faced.

Taylor Zane

Questions for Discussion

1. How does the author explore the intersection of professional and personal relationships in the workplace (not just between Maryl and Ethan)?

2. What role does religion play in the family dynamics between Maryl and her parents? How do their conflicts reflect larger societal debates?

3. What early warning signs of Ethan's narcissistic behavior were present?

4. Discuss the symbolism of "The Club" in Florida - what does it represent about corporate culture and success?

5. Discuss the moral implications of Maryl's decision to report Ethan to the SEC. Was it justice or revenge?

6. What role do wealth and social status play in the characters' relationships and decisions? Their worldviews and values?

7. What does the novel say about the challenges that are still facing women in male-dominated corporate environments?

8. Maryl's co-workers, James and Tom, were brave enough to rescue her from Ethan. They risked their own financial security by opposing a powerful executive. Do you think this would happen in today's workplace (men standing up for a woman)?

9. How did the author create conflict and tension in the book? What was the main conflict or problem in the story and how was it resolved?